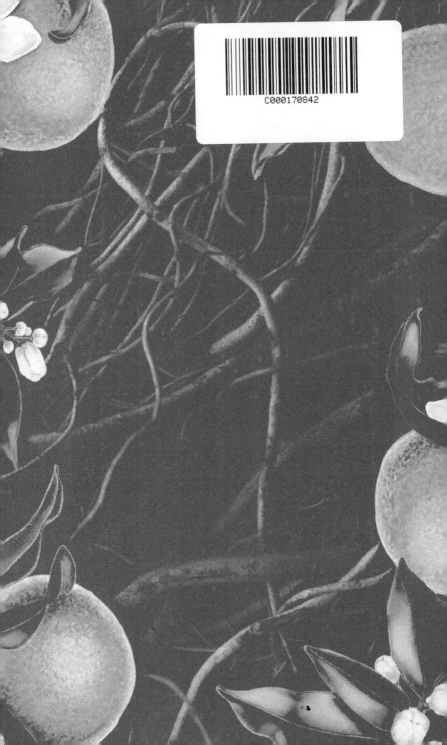

FERTILE GROUND

SALLY GREY

The Book Guild Ltd

First published in Great Britain in 2024 by
The Book Guild Ltd
Unit E2 Airfield Business Park,
Harrison Road, Market Harborough,
Leicestershire. LE16 7UL
Tel: 0116 2792299
www.bookguild.co.uk
Email: info@bookguild.co.uk
Twitter: @bookguild

Typeset in 11pt Minion Pro

Printed and bound by CPI Group (UK) Ltd, Croydon, CR0 4YY

ISBN 978 1915853 950

British Library Cataloguing in Publication Data.
A catalogue record for this book is available from the British Library.

For Mam and Dad.
Thank you, for everything.
And for being absolutely nothing like Clem's parents.

Also for Jen – my strong sister x

The dead body in my back garden is starting to smell. I knew we should have buried some lavender down there with it. Or maybe some of those bath bomb things – you know the ones, pink chalk filled with glitter, make your eyes water.

Life advice: never unbury a body. Granted, better advice might be *don't murder,* but I guess technically I never did that. So, I stand by my original statement.

It'll take me hours to get all this soil out from under my nails, wash the gunk from my hair. But it's worth it, Mother. So worth it.

The night is cold, the breeze raw against my skin. The moon is back, thin tonight, hiding its face behind the clouds. My torch casts a yellow puddle around the grave, makes the frosted grass look grey and my skin look paler than ever. I check the windows around me again – all still black. Good. Someone seeing me out here, re-digging this already badly-dug grave, dragging apart the earth, plant roots and dead twigs scratching my hands, is the last thing I need. The last thing *we* need. If they find out what I'm doing before I can explain, they'll never trust me. And trust is the only thing still binding us together – it's a fraying, over-stretched string already, but it is still there. For now.

Here they are, right by the head. Of course they are. Their sharp edges flash at me, the metal still bright through the mud. Dead eyes stare at me, the white bits are brown with earth, one is completely bloodshot. I could've sworn we closed the eyes… probably best not to think about that detail. I use gloves to pull the dirt-encrusted blades out of the grave, place them inside the plastic bag. Relief floods my bones – I did it. Stage one: complete.

A crow lands beside my foot, peers down into the grave. Its little pearl-like eyes glare at me, accusing, its sleek body gleaming in the torchlight. Don't judge me, crow. We had to – we didn't have a choice. If you were human, you would understand – it's a species barrier. Now move your little feathered wings, I need to re-bury this body. You wouldn't want to be down in that grave too, would you?

PART ONE

Some Time Earlier

Death is strange. It wears different faces: peaceful, tearful, sudden, drawn out, young, old, painful, painless, devastating, merciful, accidental, deliberate, violent, diseased.

This particular death is best described as inconvenient. It smells like old, grey meat. The sun has melted what was left of the tiny, mangled body, essentially leaving me with a curdled pool of goo on my doorstep. It's going to leave a stain, blood invariably does. Bet it was a cat that did it. Fluffy little monsters.

I hunt around in the grass, find a stick and use the end to lift the leaking rat carcass up. At least I think it's a rat, looks too big to be a mouse. Anyway, the mice are all snug and warm inside my walls, not hanging around outside getting mauled by rogue cats. *Flick.* Whatever it is, it's not my problem anymore. Next-door's garden needed a little something anyway. A point of interest. It's very bland.

Inside, I'm greeted by the now familiar scent of damp. Brown and cloying. Ahhh… yep, we definitely have mould somewhere. Or, *I* have mould, I guess. It's odd, being here alone. If I stand at the end of the hallway and say, "Hey, Clem!", my echo answers me. It never used to do that before. Or maybe it did, and I just never listened.

Tracked the damp smell down. It's the sink. Blocked. Great. I shut off the water, move through into the little room off the kitchen. The 'utility room', Mother insisted on calling it. Made our home sound like something from a World War One army barracks: *gather the utilities, boys, we forge on!*

Everything is covered in a fine layer of dust. The old washing machine is standing open, a yellowing note taped over its buttons, Dad's handwriting: *hose-y connector bust will fix monday x.* I push the door shut. Something to worry about later. Hose-y connector. Sounds like a character from a bad spy movie. *Hose-y Connector: spy extraordinaire, ready to carry out her most daring mission yet. Her cover? Plumber.* I would watch that film.

Dad's old toolbox is hiding on one of the high shelves, tucked away at the back. It's padlocked, of course. *All potentially dangerous items should be locked away.* It was right there in the pamphlets, e.g., DIY tools/equipment. I search for the key, trying to think like Dad. *Where would she check? Where could she reach?* The key is sticky with spider's webs when I take it down from the top of the doorframe. I wipe my hands on my jeans, apologise to the spider.

It takes an age to untwist the sink's innards, rummage around inside. I find the blockage though: a large clump of blackened hair. I don't think about where it came from. The strands are all matted together, so it looks like a little creature. A mouse, maybe. Which reminds me, they're the next job.

Putting the sink back together is a lot easier than taking it apart. I wash my hands in cool, clear water and watch it spiral down the plughole. Pride pricks at my stomach. I am good for something. I may not be able to hold onto a job, or a flat, or a fiancé, but I can bloody well fix a sink. Not many people can say that. I bet Nia can't fix sinks. What are they going to do when that bump of hers ripens and their perfect little fruit goes around blocking sinks? That's what I'd like to know.

Dad's kettle is one of those old-fashioned ones that whistles when it's ready. Well, I say whistle, sounds more like the screech of a dying cat to me, but it means I can make coffee, so no complaints here. The milk smells a bit iffy, but it should be fine for one cup. I check the fridge, add to my list:

Fix sink
Get rid of mice
Clear garden
Bathroom
Find key to basement
Buy anti-bac spray
Buy milk
Buy eggs
Ring Billy

I think for a second, sniff my t-shirt. *Yep.*

Fix washing machine

I drink my coffee outside on Dad's old bench. The wood on the armrests has a lattice of little scratches, where he would sit and pick at them. The number of times I had to pull splinters from under his ragged fingernails as a kid, dried blood and sun warmed skin. I wonder who pulled his splinters when I left? I can't imagine Billy doing it, he gets squeamish with a bloody paper cut. Ha, bloody, that's funny. Or maybe it isn't.

The crows drift down onto the patio, batting at the overgrown weeds with their wings. They're big. Bigger than I thought crows could get. But I've been away from the country too long, I'm probably remembering them wrong. They're roosting in the trees that border the garden.

Crows always seemed like the boring, ugly option when I was little, not as pretty as the blue tits, the little robins. Dad always used to say I didn't give them enough credit, that if I thought they weren't beautiful, I was looking at them wrong. *Pigeons*, he would say, *they're the real villains of the piece, Clemmie. Scavengers, the lot of them.* There are no pigeons in the garden.

I go back inside, grab the crusts from my half-eaten morning toast. Dad must have fed the crows, too. They're docile, gentle. For a second, I see him, sitting here next to me. With his smile. Wearing his old, blue jumper and his gardening boots, dropping scraps of fluffy bread into the waiting crowd of wings. He reaches out, tucks one of my dark curls behind my ear, strokes my cheek, his skin rough. I wrap my fingers around his, but they're cold, damp. His eyes are sad. I stare at him until my eyes burn and I'm forced to blink.

When I look again, Dad has been replaced by the crows. A couple have landed on the seat next to me, their eyes fixed on the crusts still in my hand. If I wanted to, I could reach out and pet their glossy feathers. But I don't. Want to, that is. They're wild things, free. I don't want to infect them with my inability to fly. It feels like if I touched their wings with my skin, they would break, like glass, bound to the earth forever more. I just feed them my crusts. The biggest one is the bravest, he eats crumbs right out of my hand. But I make sure to let only his beak touch my palm, never to accidentally brush his feathers. His wide eyes watch me. We have an understanding.

***

I decide to take advantage of the brief winter sun and tackle the garden. Its state is another reminder of my mother, her mind. The left side, the side the crows favour, is a crush of weeds and wild flowers, most of them dead, choked by ice. A patchwork, messy tendrils, yellowish grass. The right side, though, is meticulous. The soil is soft, crumbles apart like cake. Slim rows of plants stand in lines, leaves of bright green, their fruit growing plump. From left to right, my mother has left me with:

Tomatoes
Green beans
Sugar snap peas
Lettuce (the purple kind – exciting)
Radishes
Cucumber (did NOT realise these grew as hanging

fruit – always imagined them growing below ground. Currently look like weird mini pickles)
Strawberries
Blueberries
Raspberries (apparently Mother liked berries…)
Potatoes
Carrots
Apples (currently tiny stumps in pots – need to find somewhere to plant them)

All this despite the weather, the icy chill blowing across the garden, and despite the rest of the garden lying dead around us.

How did you do it, Mother? Nurture these little plants to beauty, so they can blossom even in the depths of winter. Give them such life, such strength, when you couldn't even look at me without criticism finding its way onto your tongue. Without saying, *Oh, Clementine*, in that tone reserved only for me.

A pheasant stalks across the grass. He pops up every morning, spends about ten minutes inspecting the garden, following his little route. I didn't know they came out in winter. Strange birds, pheasants. They look almost regal, the males, with their deep blue-green heads, jewelled red patches around their sharp, yellow eyes. My pheasant is watchful of his subjects – the crows flutter their wings in his presence, as though applauding his arrival, and their conversation drops, only small caws when he's around. I move to the edge of the garden, out of respect.

This whole dance we do around one another feels like an *Emperor's New Clothes* sort of arrangement. None of us have the courage to tell Emperor Pheasant he looks faintly ridiculous, decked out in his regal colours, with his long, brown tail waving behind him, his head bobbing along to some unheard tune. He always stops at the far end of the garden and looks around, as though waiting for someone to tell him what to do next. He needs a royal adviser.

I do a search for what pheasants like to eat: seeds mainly, berries, and insects. He doesn't seem interested in my mother's plants. I add *buy seeds for Emperor Pheasant* to my list, show it to him. He seems to nod. I have done well. His Highness is pleased.

***

A full morning of digging leaves me with a shooting pain in both wrists and a garden which looks much the same as before. Rain will help loosen the frozen soil. I'll try again then.

Some of the tomatoes are ripe, bright red, heavy with juice. I take them inside, rinse them in the sink. My list stares at me accusingly from the table. Two words are printed smaller than the others, my handwriting cramped, as if even writing his name is a chore. Which it is. Everything about Billy is a chore. That's why he's on my list of chores.

Funny word. C h o r e. Or maybe it isn't. I say it out loud, but that doesn't help. The crows can't tell me.

I'll start with the mice. They're easier to talk to than my brother. Most of them are dead. Some of them are missing body parts: legs, little ears, heads. There's a dusty tail behind one of the skirting boards in the kitchen.

Droppings under the fridge. I can hear the live ones, scuttling about inside the walls. Tiny paws against pipes.

Dad refused to have poison in the house. We pretended it wasn't because of Mother. Pushed away the image of her pouring something into her tea. Drinking down big gulps, throat bobbing.

I hate hospitals. Whitewashed walls, hard plastic chairs. The smell always crawled deep inside my lungs, settled inside my skin. Showering didn't help. Still now, I can't use bleach. It'll have to be traps, then. Catch and release. Do it the old-fashioned way, hey Dad? *Treat animals like you treat people, Clemmie. With respect.*

The metal of the tiny door is rusted, the plastic scratched, thin ridges rough under my fingertips. I need cheese. I'll have to add it to the list.

I really need to head into the village. The shop has essentials. I wonder if Greta still runs things there? She might have moved on; she never was the same after Liam died. The death of a child, the worst thing to happen to a parent. Dad would say that whenever anyone mentioned Greta: *God, to lose a child, just the worst thing, the worst.* I'm sure everyone thought he was trying to be supportive, to say the things people say when words are no longer enough. But I saw the way he looked at Mother, eyes pleading for her to agree, to say, *Yes, a dead child would be worse.* It didn't work.

Even at that age, I knew better than to tell him what Mother said to poor, grieving Greta. You can know too much about your spouse. It was a sweaty day, hair in my plait sticky against my neck, tiny Billy screaming in the heat, his face beetroot red. I had opened the mini freezer,

8

dangled my arms down into the cool chill, feet brushing the floor tiles. Reaching towards a pink lolly, nails scratching the packet. I could have picked Billy up, held his kicking legs over the edge, cooled his skin. I didn't.

I listened to Mother murmuring, trying to keep the grey spread of Greta's grief away from her airways. Greta felt hollowed out inside, still listened for his voice in the night, set his place for breakfast every morning. She didn't know what to do with her time anymore.

At least you get some time to yourself now though, a bit of peace. Mother craved peace, hoarded it, kept it all to herself. We left soon after that. She paid in silence, Greta never meeting her eyes. Her hands shook as she handed Mother her change.

I walked the whole way home with one hand on Billy's blue pram, one hand held out in front of me, imaginary lolly stick in my hand, imaginary ice melting over my skin. Imaginary chocolate-strawberry taste on my tongue. Mother never held my hand when we crossed the road.

***

It is still Greta. She's older, thinner, red curls now straight and grey, but it's her. She doesn't recognise me. I know because her eyes follow me about the shop. Suspicion of the outsider. I could be a mad axe murderer for all she knows. Or a thief. Or worse, one of those city types searching for artisanal cheeses and vegan oat milk. Her gaze skewers the back of my neck as I search the cheese section. Cheddar should do it. Check the eggs are whole, no cracked shells. Fresh milk, better get two bottles, I get through enough of it. A small, plastic bag of mixed seeds. Spray bottle of something called *general cleaner*, floral scent, good.

Next to the cleaning products, a fridge, *Entirely Natural* printed in large, green letters along the side. God, they've even invaded the shops here. Rows of green drinks, like liquefied moss. No gaps in the stock. Makes a change – I once saw three women physically fighting over one of those smoothies. The victor got her drink, but she also got a nasty-looking black eye. Insanity.

Large pairs of garden shears hang on the back wall, just within reach. I wonder how Greta got them up there; she's even shorter than me. The blades look like they could do some damage to my garden. I select a pair, put them under my arm. Really should have got a basket.

The mini freezer still stands next to the door, its low hum identical, the same stickers of ice lollies decorating the sides. I remember Billy's sticky fingers against the skin of my cheeks, melted blue ice in my hair, all over his face, down his top. Dad's indulgent smile, his wink. *Shhhh, don't tell your mother.* My chocolate covered lolly clogging up my throat. I'd wanted it for so long and when I got it, the sweetness turned my stomach. I wanted an ice pop. I wanted Billy's choice. My tears were salty, my tantrum came from deep within my chest.

I don't blame Dad. He didn't know what else to do. He never was good with tears. Mother's smack left a red mark against my legs. Billy got ice cream as a well done for not copying his big sister. He ate it too fast, and Dad had to clean blue sick off the kitchen floor.

Greta clears her throat.

"Just these, please," I tell her, spilling my selection onto the counter. I pull the garden shears from under my arm, place them down, blades towards me.

She starts to tap at the till, check labels.

A stack of newspapers teeters next to the till, another protest dominates the front page: *OVERPOPULATION CRISIS WORSENS: ANTI-BIRTH BOYCOTT INSPIRES RIOT.* Manchester this time. A peaceful protest outside an IVF clinic turned ugly. The police were involved. A pregnant woman was caught in the crossfire. I scan the article for a name, an age, anything, but there's nothing to identify her. No pictures. It won't be. Why would she have been in Manchester? Why would she have been at an IVF clinic? Tony clearly didn't need any help there. No, he wouldn't have let her get hurt, it can't have been Nia, there's no—

"£20.75." Greta's voice pulls me out of my thoughts.

"Sorry?"

"£20.75." She gestures to my shopping. "You need a bag?"

I nod, search my purse for the coins. It's a long time since I've spent actual, physical money, gotten so used to contactless. The pennies feel strange and cold in my hands.

Greta puts everything into a brown paper bag for me, lips pursed. She meets my eye for the first time as I hand over the money.

"You moved into that new build then?"

"Oh, no—"

"Just I've never seen you around before."

"I inherited my parents' old cottage. It's Clem? Clementine? Marilyn and John's daughter?"

Greta is silent. Her smile stays in place, frozen. "Oh… oh, Clemmie, of course. You're all grown up!" Nervous laugh. "How… how are you?"

"I'm alright."

"I'm so sorry we didn't make it to the funeral. Things have just been so busy, you know how it is…"

I look around at the completely empty, fully stocked shop.

"Don't worry about it."

There is a pause.

"Oh! Actually… I hope this isn't insensitive, my love, but your father asked me to order this. It's all paid for, don't worry. It just seems silly for me to keep it now."

She starts rummaging around behind the desk, pulls out a small package, sets it on the countertop. She smiles. Pushes it towards me. She looks like a proud parent on Christmas morning, so I open it. Inside is a lump of white plastic, three interlocking nozzles, in the shape of a capital Y. I laugh. *Hose-y connector.*

Greta looks concerned as I smile inanely at a spare part for a washing machine.

"Thanks, Greta."

I place Hose-y carefully inside my shopping bag. The last thing Dad ever ordered. He didn't even order it on the computer – of course he didn't. He came in here, asked for it with his voice, his words. Paid for it in advance. I turn and leave before Greta can say anything else, before the tears come.

The car has been parked in the surprise winter sun, so it's actually quite warm inside.

I update my list before I drive back:

Fix sink
Get rid of mice
Clear garden
Bathroom
Find key to basement
Buy anti-bac spray
Buy milk
Buy eggs
Ring Billy
Fix washing machine (use Hose-y!)
Buy seeds for Emperor Pheasant

I'm doing well, if I do say so myself. Distraction techniques, hey Dad? Make a list. Keep a focus. Don't dwell on things. Keep going. Just keep going.

My phone rings: *Billy.* I put it on the dashboard, let it ring out. Then I pull away. Drive home. Time to put some cheese in some traps.

***

Tuesday today. T u e s d a y... normal day. Yet another normal day. Just ticking off things on my to-do list. You'd be proud of me, Dad. Getting things done. *That's it, Clem. We're getting there.* I never did know where 'there' was. I'm starting to think you didn't either – starting to think no one does.

I pull at the little plastic catch and shake the mouse out onto the grass. She immediately shoots off into the long grasses of the field at the end of the garden. I think of her as a she. She's big, might be pregnant. I'm glad I caught her; don't need little baby mice running riot. Then again, maybe it's just all the cheese. They'll *definitely* come back: free food. Roll up, roll up: cheese without the risk of having your head severed, just sit in a little see-through box for a bit, chill, then back into the outside world. And they've seen the stuff I leave out for the birds, for Emperor Pheasant, they're not stupid. Smart creatures, mice. Smarter than rats at any rate. But then that's not particularly hard, is it?

I head back inside to be greeted by the innards of the washing machine laid out on the kitchen table. I've arranged the pieces by size, with Hose-y in the middle. Originally, they were arranged by colour, but since I washed them I've realised they're actually all the same colour. An off-white-grey mix. I sanitised the table after that. Did it with my new anti-bac spray. As suspected, the claim of 'refreshing floral scent' is yet another marketing trick. Had to keep the windows open all night to get rid of the smell of bleach. Bloody freezing. Ah, that reminds me. I add *fix boiler* to my list.

The metallic buzz of my phone against the worktop: *Billy*. Again. Christ, he's twenty years old, a grown man. I swear I didn't call home this often when I was his age. Granted, our parents hadn't just swerved off the road into oncoming traffic causing a sixteen-car pile-up and been so mangled that a cremation was the only option... but come on. Twenty-seven missed calls? Really?

He's barely spoken to me in two years and now there's twenty-seven missed calls on my phone. God knows how many texts.

Seriously, not even a closed casket. It was a cremation or nothing.

Billy's texts all say the same thing, some variation of: *Please call back it's important!!!!!!!* Seven exclamation marks on that last one. Seven. I turn my phone to silent.

Right, fixing the washing machine. F i x i n g the w a sh ing ma ch i n e. Yes. A new experience. Fixing a sink? I'm your girl. Getting rid of mice? Absolute master. Changing a tyre? I'm practically a feminist icon. This… not so much. But I've taken it apart now, so there's only two options. One: get a man in. Two: fix it myself and then mark the occasion by throwing my still ringing phone out that window. It may be set to silent, but I can still see the little screen lighting up out of the corner of my eye, the little icons flicker-flashing… could they make these things any more annoying?

I hate the way we say, 'get a man in'. Such a sexist phrase. The handyma— handy*person* could easily be a woman. Although, the one in the village isn't, he's six foot three and called Gus, so…

Right, come on, Hose-y, we can do this! I know I definitely need you because Dad bought you. So… come on, you're not being very helpful. I know you're an inanimate object, but you could at least try.

I turn my phone face down on the table. Then pick it back up. Genius. I open my search app, type in, *how to fix a washing machine.*

***

I've only gone and bloody done it, Dad. Gus's services were not needed. A spin cycle has never been so mesmerising. Went to hurl my phone into the newly mouse-infested

15

field in celebration but noticed Tony's name on the screen amongst all the Billys.

Did you get settled alright?

It's been nearly a full week, a whole four nights… okay, I've been here three days, but still, he sends me that?

Did you get settled alright?

What kind of question is that? Maybe I should send back: *Did Nia?* Ha, yes, that's hilarious. She's in my bed, I know she is. Pink yoga loungewear over those sticks she calls legs. I didn't think anyone actually wore that stuff outside of the gym. Her belly will be properly round by now, ripe. Like a fruit. I wonder if her belly-button is sticking out yet? That's an unattractive thing, right? That's perfect, slim woman becoming whale/elephant territory in the pregnancy stakes. She probably makes it look hot, though. Some kind of earth-mother, beautiful life-giver, baby-on-board trickery. Baby weight in all the right places. She's going to be wearing heels and tight dresses a week after the birth, isn't she?

Bitch.

I bet she couldn't fix a washing machine. No, all that glossy, long, perfectly straight absolutely-no-curls-visible hair would get in the way. I spend a few happy minutes imagining Nia trapped inside a giant washing machine, hair pulled out at the root by the quick wash. Her fat bump the only thing stopping her entire body from being sucked into oblivion.

I won't reply straight away. Two hours, that's enough time, right? Make sure he knows I'm not just sitting over my phone, waiting for him to message. Which I'm not. Obviously. I just fixed a washing machine for Christ's sake. I de-moused the house. De-miced?

Okay, I'll message back at 15:42. Two hours. Better make it 15:48, not exactly two hours, that might look suspicious. I could send him a picture of the washing machine. Or is that weird? Well, it's better than a rotting mouse carcass – currently my only other option.

***

I've hidden my ring in her old jewellery box. The one she kept her gold brooch in. God, I wanted that brooch as a kid, wanted to pin it to the front of my top like an oversized gold star. It's not in here now. I wonder if Dad moved it? I suppose you could have drawn blood with the pin.

My theory was that the complicated, little latch on the front would stop me from opening it all the time, from looking in. My theory has been disproved. Conclusively. I look at my ring all the time, lift it out, place it on my finger. Not the correct finger, I put it on my right hand instead. That's meant to be bad luck, Mother told me that. If you put a ring on your left ring finger before you have been proposed to, you doom yourself to spinsterhood. She was full of nice little life rules like that. I don't know why she would tell me these things. Probably her way of trying to keep me innocent, pure. If I was scared of wearing a ring on the wrong finger, then I sure as hell wasn't going to be underage drinking or kissing boys.

I always looked young in comparison to the other girls at school. I wasn't allowed make-up, jewellery, the right clothes or the right hair. I used to be obsessed with lip gloss; it was contraband, forbidden. My favourite was called *Cherry Girl Gloss – make your lips pop!* The fact it was tinted pink felt so grown up. I used to covet these little tubes of sticky gloss, hoard them in a battered old shoebox under my bed. Dad would smuggle them in for me. Mother found them eventually, of course. I had red welts across my legs for a week afterwards. It was Dad I felt sorry for. He cried.

I remembered the *Cherry Girl Gloss* on the night Tony proposed to me. Clearly a strange thing to be thinking about when the man you love is asking you to spend the rest of your life with him, but the woman sat next to us smelt of the exact same synthetic cherry scent. Heavy, hits you right in the sinuses, kind of like those little pastry things. Must have been her perfume. She looked like the type who would wear excessive amounts of perfume, and gold jewellery, which she was. Cherry Bakewells, that's them. It had been bugging me all night and I realised what it reminded me of right at the same moment Tony decided to get down on bended knee, as they say. Maybe that's why it took me so long to answer him, I had too many things in my head at once, couldn't process them all. Maybe that's why he had to repeat his question, *the* question, why he had to prompt me, "Err... Clem", in front of all those diners in that dimly-lit-on-purpose restaurant.

Maybe that's why it felt like I had cotton wool in my throat when I told him, "Yes, yes, of course, haha."

Or maybe I just squeezed my arms too tight around his neck when I kissed him. He realised he was trapped.

I put the ring back inside my mother's now empty jewellery box. It slides around against the satin lining. White gold – I've always thought that was an oxymoronic name. Surely something is either white or gold, it can't be both. But then I thought someone was either happy in their relationship or not, proposing or getting another woman pregnant, and I've been proved wrong there, haven't I? So, really, what do I know?

***

Finally found the basement key. Under the sink in the bathroom, behind a bottle of hair remover and a packet of baby wipes, unscented. I wonder if Dad put it there, trying out a new hiding place. But surely that would be somewhere she would look? Maybe she put it there. Why, I wouldn't know. *She* might not have known. She often claimed she didn't.

The doctors pressed at first. Asked her questions, asked us questions, then asked questions of the answers to those questions. A question loop. Baby Billy sitting on a plastic hospital chair, a nurse crouching in front of his chubby toddler legs. The backs of his shoes hitting the chair legs. *Kick, kick, kick.*

"Does Mummy ever leave you alone? What about your sister, does she leave her? Does Mummy ever make you feel sad? Do you like spending time with Mummy, Billy?"

Huge, kid eyes, vacant and blue.

Then always Dad's voice: "Hey, what are you saying to my boy?"

I was his girl. But they never asked me. Maybe they thought I had some kind of misplaced female loyalty. I didn't. I don't. Not when it comes to her.

I nearly told a doctor once. He was nice. Kind face. Gave me a sparkly sticker – it had a picture of a panda on it, holding a banner that said: *you've been so brave!* He said he'd never known a child so well-behaved. I didn't even cry when he wrapped the bandages around my feet. He told me he was proud of me. I remember sitting on the clean bedding, making sure I could still wiggle my toes through the new, white gauze.

Mother never did well in hospitals, must have needed some air. Or maybe just a coffee. The doctor came in more than once to check on me – I think, now, they must have been wondering why a child with severe burns to her feet had been left on her own. I remember he smiled at me, told me not to worry, that I might have some funny stripes on my feet, but that they would just make me more interesting. I was unique. And they wouldn't hurt forever. I was excited, quite proud of my new, unique, stripy feet.

Then his voice changed. "You really shouldn't have been trying to use the kettle though, you're a bit too young to make Mummy a cup of tea just yet."

I was confused. What kettle? What cup of tea? And why did his voice make it sound like it was my fault that Mother had filled the bath with boiling water? Only a shallow pool, but she stood me in it, held me there, only pulled me out when my feet and ankles had swirling patterns imprinted on them. I screamed so hard I was sick.

I know now what would have happened if I'd told him. Social services at the very least, possibly police, likely a children's home, maybe even new parents, for a while, or forever. No more Mother. No more Billy. I could have had my own room.

I wouldn't say that I'm *glad* that the words trapped themselves inside my stomach, fluttering butterflies. But the doctor squeezed my shoulder until Mother came back. And I missed my chance. I can't say it was a mistake to keep quiet – who knows, my life might have been worse somewhere else. Maybe what I had was as good as things got. Maybe. I wouldn't have had Dad.

The light in the basement doesn't work. I use the torch on my phone, point it at the steps going down. I forgot to put socks on this morning. The light highlights the shiny patches on what I still think of as my stripy feet.

Using my phone means I'm forced to check my notifications. More from Billy. Nothing from Tony. Although I guess my message didn't really require a response. I wanted to say I hoped everything was still okay with the pregnancy (it's them I hate, not their baby – I'm not a complete monster) but everything I tried sounded passive-aggressive. The recent riots and attacks on pregnant women worried me. Tony better be watching Nia and the bump at all hours of the day. If she got hurt, the baby did, and if there was no baby, then there was no reason for me to give up the flat. And I would just end up looking stupid instead of progressive and selfless. Who attacks pregnant women anyway? God knows, I would love to give Nia's face a nice, solid punch, but her baby didn't do anything. It didn't ask to be the product of adultery.

I gave up trying to phrase a text in the end and just sent: *yes*. I was settled fine, thanks very much Tony. Everything was fine. Good. Great even.

It's freezing down in the basement, especially at this time of year. The chill of the concrete leaches through the soles of my feet, into my bones, rises up to settle deep in my stomach. I shiver. Cold little fingertips up and down my spine.

I shine my torch against the stairwell. I was expecting clutter, *stuff*, the things I used to spend far too much time alongside as a kid. I used to list them to pass the time:

Boxes of odds and ends
Old and cracked tiles from the kitchen renovation
Purple lampshades
Blue sofa cushions – greying innards spilling across the floor
A broken tricycle
A broken laptop
A working fan that made a clicking noise when you plugged it in
A shoebox of baby photos labelled Our Little Billy Bear. *Dad's handwriting.*
A shoebox of baby photos labelled Clementine, *underlined once. Mother's handwriting.*
An old mop
Old books
Old dolls I was told I'd grown out of.

I would play with my dolls secretly. Silver linings, hey Dad? I may have been locked in a basement, but at least I could play with my Polly Pockets again. I remember playing Narnia down here as well, I used the old mop as Aslan, an old wardrobe as the doorway into another world. I prayed to really be taken away, somewhere else, somewhere magical. Dad must have moved the wardrobe, maybe he chopped it up, used the wood for one of his bonfires in the garden. The ones the neighbours always complained about. I can smell the wood smoke in my hair.

The basement was her last resort, for when she really couldn't take it – me – anymore. When she needed peace, needed quiet. My record was six hours and forty-seven minutes – that was the time Dad found me. I don't think she meant for him to find out, she forgot about me, probably. It was after that day that Dad started hiding the key.

But none of those old familiar things are down here now. Looks like it's been cleaned out. Swept down. Repurposed. There's a desk in one corner. A stack of notebooks, red covers, ring-bound, college-ruled. I open the one on the top of the pile – Mother's handwriting, strange strings of letters and numbers. God knows. Must have been some new project – she always had something on the go. Dad's suggestion, a distraction, away from her thoughts. An array of beakers and cups stand stacked inside one another, teetering towers. Alongside them:

Tubes and
Measuring cylinders and
Heat lamps and
Coloured vials of unlabelled liquids and
Thermometers and
Bits of string cut to precise lengths and
Weighing scales and
Stopwatches and
Calculators.
A syringe.

Looks like my parents have raided the local school science lab.

A red velvet curtain hangs from the ceiling, tassels on the bottom brush against dust on the floor. That's new. I shine my phone torch across it, the screen says: *New message: Billy: Clem PLEASE I need you!!??!* I grab the edge of the curtain, pull. It swings back easily, curtain rings clacking. The space behind is dark and cool. A sharp smell releases into the room, a sweetness. Earthy undertones.

Something moves in the breeze from the curtain, something waves. Green. Leaves. Jesus Christ, my parents have started a weed farm in our basement. But no, that's not what they are. The plants sit patiently in lines, snug inside terracotta pots. Tallish trunks, leaves, long and thin, gather into a sphere at the top, round, glowing blobs hanging down. Oranges. No, not oranges. Clementines.

There must be about twenty plants down here. I always thought plants couldn't survive inside, especially without sunlight, but Mother must have known more than me. As per usual. These bright, little, orange orbs are thriving.

***

I line up four of the clementines on the worktop in the kitchen. They're nice to look at, perfect spheres, a pleasing colour. I press down, feel the bright skin split, the soft pith slide under my fingernails. Juice drips over my hands. I line the segments up on a plate, so they're curved into each other, like tiny creatures cuddling. S e g m e n t... satisfying word. I say it in my head, then out loud. My voice sounds small in the empty kitchen.

I place a single *segment* to my mouth. The juice stings against the cracks I've chewed into my lips. The taste is gentle on my tongue. Sweet and golden. The flavour of sunshine. Each piece of clementine has its own veiny film. It sticks to my teeth, dry, tasteless.

Before I really realise it, I've eaten almost all of them. Three clementines, gone. Juice drips down my chin. I put the fourth one in the cupboard, so I'm not tempted.

Knock, knock, knock.

A shadow at the frosted glass of the back door. Large. Male. My first thought is, *Billy*, crying on the doorstep, finally pulling me into whatever drama he's so desperate to tell me about. But no, the shape is too big to be my little brother. It feels older, more solid.

It knocks again. *Knock, knock, knock.*

I smear clementine remnants across my hands, wipe them on my jeans, open the door. A big, bearded face nods at me. Lean, muscled body, a sheepish look in brown eyes. Head ducked.

"Gus. Hello."

"Miss Finch," Gus says.

"Oh, please, just Clem." I'm going for friendly, polite, but I just end up sounding patronising, like I'm offering him some kind of perk. Such a selfless gift to allow the use of my first name. God, sometimes I do just hate myself.

Gus stares at my jeans, which have handprint-shaped clementine juice stains decorating them, at my face, at my un-brushed, in fact, unwashed hair. I smile and his stare switches to my teeth, which clearly have orange fragments caught between them.

"Did you need something?" I ask, again going for polite, again coming across patronising.

"Oh… no," he stammers, takes a breath. "My father said I should check you don't need any help with the house."

A warm blush spreads through my stomach, a warning burning underneath it, memories of Gus's daddy from when we were children. From when we were teens. His beady eyes at the window, watching Gus drive me home at the end of the night, like a true gentleman. Curtains twitching next door at my own house, my mother's own beady eyes watching from her bedroom. The look on Gus's face as he dropped his smile and walked away from me, towards his own front door. The way my own face would mirror his expression. I ignore the memories, push them down. Not now.

"Oh, that's kind, but I think I'm alright actually."

"That's what I said you'd say." He smiles at me from beneath heavy eyebrows.

I try another smile back. He nods, ducks his head again and starts to move backwards, down the path, across the garden. I can see Emperor Pheasant hiding behind the long grass, eyeing up this new invader on his land. His head bobs back and forth.

Gus, his hand on the gate, calls, "You always did do everything yourself, didn't you?" Then he waves shyly, leaves.

It sounded like a compliment. People have always said that about me, in that exact same tone, especially when I was a kid. *She's so independent. A real self-starter.*

Such a reliable girl. I don't think anybody realised then that I didn't exactly have a choice.

***

Exciting evening in the Finch household. Spent hours cleaning the bathroom so it's now in a vaguely useable state. Pleased with my handiwork. I might have a bath. The water runs cold in seconds, so I pop the immersion on. There's a worrying noise for a few minutes, but then it stops.

I decide to be really decadent. I've been multi-tasking today. Not only have I managed to clean the bathroom with all natural bubbles, not a waft of bleach stink, but I've also collected some of the fruit from the garden and made my own home-grown smoothie. Strawberry, blueberry and raspberry. I call it the Berry Bonanza. I bet Nia doesn't make smoothies. Tony still hasn't replied.

I pour the pink, gloopy stuff into a tall glass, add a stripy straw from the pack I found at the back of one of the cupboards. There, just like they serve on the Riviera. Ha ha ha. I feel exotic. I love that word: e x o t i c. Love how it feels on my tongue. Although, on the Riviera they usually have cocktails. Smoothies suddenly seem childish, like something a little girl might make. I need to make it an adult drink. I am indeed an *adult.*

Dad's cupboard will have something. I was never allowed near it as a kid. Me and Billy always assumed it was full of sweeties, or toys – something exciting. The disappointment was bitter when we climbed up a tower of stacked chairs just to find a collection of boring bottles, filled with clear liquid that smelt sharp, like Dad's paint stripper. A childish adventure that backfired when Billy learnt what liquor was and how it could make him feel.

I reach for the already opened vodka and pour it into my glass, fill it the rest of the way, up to the top. Mix it with my straw. Now it's a proper cocktail. I take a sip and wince. Delicious.

The water is running hot now. Okay, it looks a little brownish in colour but that's probably just the lights reflecting off the tiles. I don't know why Mother thought brown was a good colour for a bathroom, or a good colour for anything actually. Who decides to decorate and then thinks, *Hey, you know what colour would look really great in here? BROWN*. I fill the bath right the way to the top. I've added some bath stuff, so frothy bubbles hide the colour of the water. Out of sight, out of mind, hey Dad? Perfect.

The water is just that bit too hot, but I breathe through it. The bubbles feel silky against my skin. My feet do their familiar, little tingle. It was this bath. This is luxury. This is all I need. Peace. Some people search their whole lives, don't they? Well, I guess I found it. It was really easy as well. Super simple. My vodka smoothie tastes weird with my salty tears mixed in.

***

Pain judders along my shoulder and up my neck. Pins and needles fizz along my arms, into my fingers. Each time the spade hits the solid ground I get a hit of, well, not white hot pain, maybe a kind of purple bruise colour. Dull, deep.

Stupid bath. Stupid vodka. Can't believe I fell asleep in there. The cold water has seeped through to my bones. It was very brown without the bubbles. Tasted rusty. Not that I drank it deliberately, it was an accident, went up my nose. Must have been dirt from the garden, from my own skin. I need to wash more often.

I swap my spade for the shears I bought from Greta. They're great for hacking back the long grasses. They make a satisfying noise, *snip, snip, ssssniiip*. Their blades glint at me happily in the sun.

The wind is sharp. I'm glad of Dad's gardening gloves and his old boots. They may be three sizes too big but a couple of pairs of fluffy socks and they're fine. He must have removed the laces because of her. I assume. Maybe he took them out for some other reason, but I can't think of one. I can, however, think of her tying the laces together, looping them around a slender neck. Hers or his or a stranger's, it doesn't matter. I've replaced the missing laces with some bright orange ribbon I found in my half-unpacked suitcase. No idea where it came from. It looks quite festive.

I turn back to the spade, but even looking at it makes my muscles shiver. I head over to Dad's bench instead.

Crunch. Crunch. Crunch.

There's been a frost overnight, the kind that sticks; everything is still covered in white sugar. Well, everything except for the veg patch and the fruit plants, they've managed to escape. Colourful against the bright white. The crows peck at the cold soil. One dips his beak against a fat strawberry, the feathers of his head damp with its juice. He flaps his wings wide.

I take my mug of coffee from the seat of the bench, sip

it. It's still hot. Thought I might have to make another, but I'm lucky for once.

The sky is interesting today. Steely with pink stripes. Clouds like paint strokes. Reminds me of painting with Dad as a kid. Measuring the paint, pouring the water, slowly, carefully. But she killed that too, didn't she? Just like she killed everything else. Said the bright colours I used made her head hurt, turned up the news. To this day, I rarely watch the news, it's just depressing and if anything important happens, I'm sure someone will tell me. If I don't need to know, then I won't. Same reason I rarely use social media. Well, that and the endless images of pregnant Nia, gorgeous Nia, wonderful, successful, got-her-life-in-order Nia cluttering up my timeline. I mean, what would I post anyway? A picture of my coffee, the view of my garden, backlit by that beautiful sky? Would probably only get five likes next to Nia's 500 likes – a picture of her in downward dog pose. #yoga. #lovinglife. #TBT. Had to look that last one up, it means Throwback Thursday – it's an old picture, from before she was pregnant, apparently. It's Wednesday. Idiot.

And if I was active online Billy would see, and he would *know* I'm ignoring him rather than just strongly suspecting it.

Oh, here he comes, Emperor Pheasant. He wanders down his catwalk, feathers ruffled, obviously unsure at this cold, new world. I smile at him, grab some seeds from inside. The minute I set the plate down on the patio he struts over. I watch him eat his fill, keep sipping my coffee.

At least someone's eating. I couldn't stomach breakfast, missed lunch. Must have put more vodka than I realised in that smoothie, I spent an hour this morning with my head in the toilet. That reminds me, I need to add to my list:

~~Fix sink~~
~~Get rid of mice~~
Clear garden
~~Bathroom~~
~~Find key to basement~~
~~Buy anti-bac spray~~
~~Buy milk~~
~~Buy eggs~~
Ring Billy
~~Fix washing machine (use hose-y!)~~
~~Buy seeds for Emperor Pheasant~~
Fix boiler
Buy toilet cleaner

I need to research the different brands again. The one I bought last time smelt way too bleach-y.

There comes a point where I have to start a new list, a fresh scrap of paper. But I keep my original one going as long as possible. I like being able to see my achievements, thick lines through them, every time I add something new. It gives me a boost. I *can* do it. I am good for something. Even if that something is *not* holding my alcohol. My mouth still tastes sour. I make myself finish my coffee.

Emperor Pheasant finishes his seeds and starts to bob over to the veg patch. I should probably discourage the birds from snacking on what is essentially my main source of food, but I don't want them to feel unwelcome in the garden. This is their home as much as mine. They have their little meetings here, their gatherings, their families. A group of crows is called a murder. I don't know what it's called when a self-important pheasant joins in. And I do have enough fruit and veg to go round, I guess.

The pheasant watches the crow still pecking at the strawberries. He flaps his wings wide, jumps from foot to foot. He looks like he's standing on hot coals. Or doing some kind of strange mating ritual. Whatever it is, the crow is disinterested, moves away. Maybe he just wanted to get at the strawberries. But, no, he bobs his head towards them, looks closely with one eye, and the next, then shivers his tail feathers and backs off. Not as tasty as the seeds, clearly.

I watch the crow as he wanders back over to the others, trailing feathers. A lot of feathers, actually. He shakes his head, beak still sticky from the strawberry juice. One of his feathers floats close to the bench. I stretch over, pick it up. It's not the usual glossy black, more a muted grey. He doesn't look particularly old. Do crows go grey? I stroke the feather, up along what I think of as its spine – the usually silky feel is gone, it disintegrates in my palm. The spine cracks and breaks into lots of tiny pieces. Dust. I let the breeze carry it away. Maybe the cold has damaged it, the chill so freezing it breaks apart like ice. I always thought feathers lasted for years. Billy had one he kept in a little box on his nightstand. He used to check on it every night, as if it might somehow have disappeared when he wasn't looking. No idea where it went. It's not there now.

I look over at the murder, just to check, but they all look fine. None of them seem bald. They seem happy enough, pecking at the soft soil of the veg patch – there must be a good few worms in there. I don't pick up any of the other feathers.

Emperor Pheasant marches back to the edge of the patio, stands, stares at me. He looks right at my face, looks at me as if he knows something. What, I haven't the slightest idea. It can't be something very big – his head's too small to hold any big thoughts inside. He probably just wants more seeds. Sorry, Your Royal Highness, I'm all out, you've had the lot.

The chill air bites into my skin. I decide to give up completely, try again tomorrow. There's no time limit on this, I have all the time in the world. No one to get back for, no one else to worry about. No one to suck my time away for themselves. I only have *me* to think about.

It's great.

What with this weather, I decide to make soup for tea. I don't have any tins in, but who says I can't make my own? Again, it used to be one of those things I never had time for, but now... well, now is now. And now I have my very own carrots growing in the back garden.

I start to pull the carrots from the ground. The crows don't seem to mind, but Emperor Pheasant jumps away, disappears behind the hedge. I'm destroying his little kingdom. How dare I? I pull exactly ten carrots, a nice, round number, and place them in a little basket I found in the basement. Then I pull another two, just as back-ups. Twelve is still a good number. Ah, social media catnip, hey Nia? I bet she couldn't make carrot soup without live streaming the whole thing to her followers.

Wash, peel, chop. Only takes me five minutes. Forgot how much I love cooking. I keep the two extra carrots back, put them in the cupboard – I can make something else with them. Maybe put them in a pie, or a salad, ooh, roasted veg would be nice. Proper food. No more ready meals.

I thought the little veins on the carrots would disappear when I washed them, or be shaved off when I peeled them, but they seem to go all the way through. Thin, purple lines. Perfectly straight. They must be that special type, the funny coloured ones you can get in the posh supermarkets. Maybe they're not quite ripe yet. I wonder if they'll taste any different? I guess that's the trouble these days though, isn't it? We're so overly sanitised we can't deal with food that looks like it came out of the ground. Just because something hasn't been grown in a lab, vacuum packed and shipped halfway across the country in a temperature-controlled van, doesn't mean there's something wrong with it. In fact, there's probably more right with these carrots than with the highly processed stuff I've been eating for years. I pop my peeled and chopped carrots into a pot with:

Butter
Garlic
Salt
Pepper
Cream
Parsley I found in the garden
Coriander I found in the cupboard
And finally,
Stock I bought from the shop (those little cube things, magical).

Amazing. Nia definitely couldn't do this. Puréed carrot is such a brilliant thing for babies when they start eating, they love it. What's she going to give their baby, frozen chicken nuggets? Ha. Yeah, the type with chicken feet and chicken bones and chicken eyeballs in, disgusting. No, she'll be a brilliant mum. She's brilliant at everything. Absolute bitch. Anyway, *Entirely Natural* does that range of organic baby foods now, so she doesn't even need to learn to cook.

I wash my hands in front of the newly cleaned bathroom mirror, picking out the orange peelings from under my fingernails. My nails are going to be permanently tinged orange soon, what with all the carrots and the clementines.

My hair has gone brittle since I got here, the usual waves now just tangles. Maybe it's the cold air, with being outdoors all the time. Or maybe it's the fact Dad doesn't have any conditioner. I could just cut it all off. That would solve multiple problems. *Yes, Clem, there's an idea.* I bet Nia would never cut all her perfect hair off. She's far too vain. #selfiequeen is all over her Instagram. Not that I've looked online recently, I've kept to my rule not to look at social media. I'm doing great. I've never understood people who can't leave the online world alone for five minutes, who feel physically sick when they're away from their phones. Have them practically surgically attached to their hands. Well, I'm not one of those people. And I'm not too vain to do this. I know what you're thinking, Mother, but guess what? You're not here anymore. You can't tell me what to do. I won't let you.

The only scissors I can find are my nail scissors, leftover in my suitcase from the days I actually cared about manicures and not scratching delicate male skin.

Got to file those sharp points off, hey Tony? I start by snipping at the ends, the scissors surprisingly effective. They're rubbish at cutting nails but apparently good for hair, as long as I use the very tips of the blades. Takes a while though, too long.

I walk back into the kitchen, my soup now bubbling happily away in the pot, take the knife from the table.

Back in front of the mirror, grabbing handfuls of hair, blade against the strands. Much shorter now. The knife is much quicker. Dark tangles fall into the basin – hairy sink. Looks like I have some kind of super fluffy cat sleeping in there. The blade makes a sharp noise as it slices away the hair. Sounds like *shing, sshhing, ssshhhhhingggg…*

Hmm, what do you call that hairstyle? Choppy bob? Pixie crop? Unique? Yeah, it's pretty unique.

I like it.

Yep.

Good.

Makes my eyes look bigger at any rate. That's a thing, isn't it? Bigger eyes are better.

I take the hair out of the sink in handfuls and plop it in the bin. It's a bit wet now, feels horrible. I suddenly need it gone, out of my sight, and I'm so glad I've cut it all off, away from my skin. It seems contaminated somehow, infected. How was this dead straw ever attached to my head? That's all hair is, isn't it? Dead strands, stuck to your scalp, hanging, limp. Think I'd rather have Medusa's snakes. At least they would be useful. You could train them to do tricks, or to bite people you didn't like.

I need to blend my soup.

***

Just as I'm sitting down to my steaming bowl of blended carrots, looking like something from a posh soup advert, a car pulls up outside. Typical, right? The car is blue, flashy, stupidly low to the ground. Tony. I want to kick my heart when it leaps so high. I don't want to ask what he's doing here. I don't want him here. This is mine, my place. He can't come and take this too.

I can't do this.

Knock, knock… knock. Always annoyed me, that pause between the second and third rap – why can't he just knock like a normal person?

I move over to the door. Trace his outline through the frosted glass with my finger. I haven't missed him. I have *not* missed this. I am my own person, I am an adult woman, I am single. This is fine.

I open the door.

Those eyes.

I feel like I've been punched in the chest. Like I can't breathe. Why did he have to come here? I've been fine without you, Tony. I was getting there. Why did you have to ruin it? Why did you ruin everything?

"Clemmie, thank God."

The relief on his face. Why? He can't have changed his mind. He wouldn't. *I* wouldn't, if I were him.

I realise I haven't moved. He's just staring at me. I'm staring at him. Hahaha. A staring contest. We haven't stared into each other's eyes like this for ages. It's funny. Or maybe it isn't. Tony isn't laughing.

"What happened to your hair?"

My hand drifts to my head. "Cut it."

"Right." He's still staring. He doesn't like it. "Can I come in then?"

No.

I stand back from the door. Tony stalks straight into the kitchen. Where do you get that confidence from? Probably the same place you get the arrogance, and the ability to propose to one woman and impregnate the next. Bastard. Christ, I've missed you.

"Why are you here?"

"*Why are you here?*" He mimics my voice. Just like he used to.

He peers around my kitchen. It feels like he's looking at me naked. But not like before. Now, it feels like a judgement.

He sniffs the air, looks at my soup bowl. "What is that?"

"Soup."

"It smells... interesting?"

"Yeah, well, it's homemade. I bet Nia doesn't make you homemade soup."

He starts going through my cupboards. "Come on, Clemmie, we're not doing this now."

True, *we're* not doing anything, you made quite sure of that, Tony.

He pushes against my shoulder, trying to open more drawers, searching through cutlery and riffling through plates.

"What in the hell are these?" He takes hold of my spare carrots, still in their little basket.

I snatch them off him, stroke their skins.

"Did you use those to make that soup?"

I look at him.

"Well, no wonder it stinks, they're clearly off. Still my silly little birdbrain, hey?"

The pet name makes me smile. *He hasn't forgotten.*

Then he pours the soup down the sink.

"Tony!" I watch the orange gloop glop down the drain. Well, that's going to block everything back up. Brilliant.

"Come on, I'll make you something else."

"That took me ages." I know I'm pouting.

"How about pasta? Have you got any sauce?" He starts rummaging in the fridge.

"I wanted soup." I sound like a child.

Tony sighs, puts his hands on his hips. I try to smother my smile. His teacher stance. He commands no respect in the classroom, the kids all love him too much.

"Clemmie, seriously. Where did you even get these carrots from? They're all… manky."

"For God's sake, that's the problem nowadays, everyone's so overly sanitised you can't deal with food that looks like it came out the ground."

Oh, that's good, Clem, that's very good, you've got him there.

"I'm fine with food that came out the ground, but I do prefer it to be the ground of *our* planet. You know, Earth carrots, not whatever these things are."

I dip my finger into the sink-soup remnants, bring it to my lips.

He grabs my hand, pulls, pushes. I stick my tongue out, try to reach the soup, end up licking his arm. Grinning, he switches his grip, touches my waist, my hips. His other hand drifts to my neck and my stomach fizzes. His skin against mine still makes my head swirl. I can smell his aftershave. Sharp lemon. Knock-off designer, a birthday present, from me. He still wears it. Our faces are close, his eyes on my mouth. Then his lips twitch and he ruffles my shorn hair. I feel the laugh before I hear it, it starts deep within my stomach, and I flick the soup into his face. He yelps, shakes his head, like a puppy.

"God, if you can't cope with a bit of soup, you're really going to struggle when the baby throws up on you." I feel the air contract. *You had to spoil it all, didn't you, silly, little birdbrain.*

Tony clears his throat, drops my hand. He looks at our feet, close together, mine bare, his in new, blue loafers.

"You really should wear socks, you know. These flagstone floors get cold."

"Yeah, you're right, it is cold. You know what would have warmed me up? Soup." I know I'm being petty, annoying. I don't care. *He's* the one who just turned up. He doesn't have the right. Not anymore. Your girlfriend is the person you randomly drop in on. Not your ex, not the jealous one, not the person whose life you just ripped apart. Or maybe your nan, you could drop in on her unannounced. Oh God, am I the nan figure now? Have I become *that* woman, the one people bring tea and biscuits to and wrap warm blankets around and feel sorry for?

"Seriously, Clem, you're alright here, aren't you? There's hot water and stuff? A proper bed, proper food?"

"Yes, Tony, it's my parents' old cottage, not a crack den." He doesn't need to know about the mice. They've gone now anyway.

Tony nods. "Okay then. Good."

He looks at me with those eyes.

My breath sticks.

Silence.

I watch my hands against the table. They don't move.

"Listen, about the funeral. You know I would have been there if I could."

"It's fine." People thought I was crying about my dead parents anyway.

"Clemmie, I am sorry, really." He takes my hand in his, threads our fingers together.

I snort, toss my head. Like a horse. *Super attractive, Clem, well done.* But I don't want to seem attractive, do I? Not to the father of another woman's baby, that would make me as bad as them. Nia may be better than me in many ways, but at least I'm not a cheat. I have that going for me. A loyal horse. Who can fix a washing machine and make a mean carrot soup.

"You took your ring off."

I look at him.

He strokes my bare ring finger. Then turns our entwined hands over. He's still wearing his. He insisted on getting one, even though it's not tradition. I think he just wanted something else expensive to wear.

My stomach rolls. It takes a lot of effort to keep my face blank.

"I was going to," he says, "then I didn't... I was worried it would get lost, what with all your boxes leaving and all Nia's stuff arriving."

I just keep looking, not at him anymore, at the space above his left shoulder. I untangle my hands from his. Concentrating. Blank face. The air has turned the consistency of my carrot soup. My mouth fills with a rush of sour-tasting water. I swallow, try to blot out his face, ignore the words spilling from between his lips.

"You know I never meant for it to happen, the…" He gestures at his stomach. "I didn't just want *a* baby, I wanted *our* baby."

I throw up in the sink. It's mainly that watery-gunge stuff you get when your stomach's pretty empty. But mixed with the congealing soup, it looks like proper vomit. I can feel him behind me, caring murmurs, soft hands. My head spins and he tries to lift me. He always did have weak arms – noodle arms I used to call them. And then he'd laugh and cuddle me with them. He can't hold my weight, so we sort of stagger as one, over to the sofa. I never did understand why Dad put a sofa in the corner of the kitchen. This is the first time in my life it's been useful.

Tony wraps me in a blanket, gets a bucket, strokes my hair. All the things you're supposed to do. He asks me what I've been eating, disappears outside, comes back in angry. Something about the veg patch, about the soil, about the birds. I tell him, the birds are my happiness, about how they eat seeds straight from my palm. Then his face is too close to mine, fingers pulling at my eyes, feeling my forehead, brushing against my lips.

"Clem, are you listening? You can get really nasty diseases from birds; you shouldn't be feeding them like that. And you'll encourage rats!"

I giggle. Not rats. Mice.

"I don't want you eating anything from that garden, do you hear me? It shouldn't be *alive* like that. Clem? Hey!"

He grabs my face, hand under chin. Harsh. It hurts. That's new. He's never been physical before. Must be a new side of him Nia's brought out. He was never like this with me.

"Was it like that when you got here, huh? Was it?"

I don't like this new Tony. I don't like his rough hands, his hard voice. I don't like the fact he's still wearing his ring. How am I meant to hate him when he's still wearing his ring? When he regrets what he did. When he wants my baby, not hers.

"Right, you're coming back with me. Come on, let's get you to the car."

I shake my head. He's pulling my arm.

"Clem, you can't stay here, you clearly can't look after yourself. Look at you!"

Well, that's rude.

"I was only sick because of *you*, saying all these things about babies and *our* baby and wearing rings. It's not my fault you knocked up another woman. It's not my fault I couldn't get pregnant."

I'm shouting, loud in the small kitchen. He looks stunned. I never shout. Well, almost never. I'm calm Clem, unflappable. I didn't shout the first time he told me what he'd done, what they'd done. I didn't shout when Billy told us why he'd been fired. I didn't shout when they told me my parents were dead. I shout inside my head, instead. Ha, that rhymes. I must smile because Tony moves away from me. I realise I'm standing up, the blanket draped across my shoulders like a cape.

"Get out."

"Clemmie?"

"I said go, get out, leave, adios, au revoir and farewell."

He stares at me like I've lost my mind.

"Why are you even here, Tony?"

Tears blur his eyes. "I wanted to make sure you were alright, to see you, for myself… I missed you."

No. No. No, he doesn't get sympathy, he isn't allowed to cry about this, that's my bit, I'm the one who had to leave, I'm the one who was cheated on, I'm the one who found out I can't have a baby, I'm the one whose parents have just died. I'm the one who didn't have a proper mother and who will never *be* a proper mother.

He starts to cry properly, actual sobs, tears track down his beautiful face. And I hate him. He's pathetic. He doesn't know what real hurt is.

The knife I used to chop the carrots is still on the table. An urge runs through my body. Sharp and cool. I could do it. Easily. Even picking up the knife would change our relationship forever, introduce Tony to a bit of fear, let me feel that power. Sticking the knife in him would change everything. I could draw blood, give him a permanent scar. I could chop a particular part of him off. I could watch him bleed out on the kitchen floor.

"Clemmie, please."

I pick up the knife, walk around him, place it back into the drawer. Close it tight.

His face is covered in snot, and he paws at my sleeve. I make the mistake of looking at those eyes. And now I feel sick again, sorry for him, sorry for me, for us.

And then we're kissing. And then I'm pulling him into the bedroom. And then his hands are unbuttoning my jeans. And then I'm taking off his shirt. And then we're naked, on top of one another, mouth on mouth on skin. And then his breath is quick in my ear. And seconds ago,

I was fantasising about stabbing this man to death in my kitchen. And now I'm as bad as them.

And now I really do have nothing going for me. I'm not even a loyal horse.

It wasn't even good.

Not like I remember.

I suppose I had just been sick.

I think about her, alone – well, not technically alone, she has the bump, so again she has more than me. I wonder if she's asleep, or if she's stayed up, expecting him home tonight. I don't think Tony knows how to belong to just one woman. He doesn't have the capacity.

I go outside, into the garden. It's dusky now, one of those winter nights where the darkness settles itself in early. I look at the veg patch, at the fruit plants, still growing happily, bright and green amongst the frosted grass. The soil soft and springy. I don't know what Tony was talking about. There's nothing wrong with it, is there, Dad?

He leaves in the early morning. An awkward hug. A cheek kiss. A 'you're not going to tell – no I won't say anything' exchange. And I'm back where I started. Minus some carrot soup.

***

I've been a busy host lately. First Gus and our inevitably awkward doorstep meeting, then Tony, and now, someone else at the door. I thought I came here to get away from all the people. And to put the house in order, obviously. The knocking is quieter this time, smaller. Bird-like. The shadow looks like a woman, a small one. But there I go

45

again with the gender stereotypes. It could just be a really tiny man.

The problem with stereotypes is that they're often, annoyingly, proved right. A petite woman with a flood of silver hair stands on my doorstep. She looks at home in my chaotic garden. Why does everyone in this village knock at the back door?

The woman stares at me. She has pretty eyes, the kind that sparkle with the knowledge of something. She's very old, at least eighties, although I'm not known to be the best at guessing ages. I thought Tony's mum was sixty-seven. It was no great loss, she never liked me all that much anyway.

The woman on my doorstep doesn't say anything. Just stares. I try my smile again, safe in the knowledge that this time I've picked out all the clementine from between my teeth. She smiles back. Her entire face creases, the skin dotted with sunspots and tough looking, like leather. She's missing an eye tooth. She is one of the most beautiful women I have ever seen.

She reaches her hands out and closes her fingers around my wrists. Her skin is cool to the touch, her nails painted a sharp, electric blue. She peers down at my sockless feet, their stripes pink and raw in the sun. She nods. Then she says: "Hello, Clemmie."

Her voice is younger than her body, clear, musical. It warms me and for the first time since the funeral, I feel my heartbeat slow and my shoulders lower. It takes me a moment to recognise the feeling, unfamiliar as it is. Safety.

She unclasps my hands, walks in, settles herself at the table. She nudges the chair next to her with a foot, nods her head, as if telling me to sit. As if it's her house, not mine.

I feel a strong, burning anger. How dare this woman invite herself in here, into my house, saying my name and making me feel calm when I have no right to be? I have no right to be feeling good things. She has no right to make me feel like this.

I sit down. Not in the chair next to her, in the one across from her. See, old woman, I make my own choices. I am an adult.

She smiles at me again. Those teeth, chipped and pointed.

Who the hell are you? I want to scream in her face, but I don't, and then the anger cools, dulls down. Replaced by that safe warmth again. This is exactly what I didn't want, what I've been trying to avoid, too much emotion, *feeling*, feeling everything all at once. Not now. It's too soon, too much. I can't.

My phone flashes desperately on the table. *Billy. Billy. Billy.*

The woman looks at it, her smile broadening further. I turn it face down.

"Sorry, hello." My voice is defensive. "Who – who are you?" *Who, who,* I sound like a bloody owl.

The woman's smile drops. I don't know why, but I feel guilty.

"Oh, I didn't know. I hoped, but I didn't know."

What is she blathering about? Maybe she has dementia, maybe she thinks I'm her daughter, her mother, her nurse. But she knows my name. A coincidence? A fluke? She looks so desperately sad.

"I'd hoped you would remember me, my darling. I even brought you this." She giggles like a naughty schoolgirl, the

47

sound peeling years away from her face. "Your favourite. Once. I don't know if it still is, but I thought, why the heck not?"

She pulls at her huge coat and produces a wrapped package. A cling-filmed brick? Oh, no, wait, something edible? A cake. A coffee cake. Even before the rich, roasted smell hits me, I know. Coffee cake. Just looking at it, I can taste it on my tongue. Comfort, golden brown. Deep sweetness. Sticky.

Maybe *I* have dementia? Can you get dementia at twenty-five? I think you can, I remember reading something about it. Or was that arthritis?

"It's me, darling."

It all comes in a rush: chocolate scented hugs and bright afternoons laid in piles of soft grass and warm cups of milk and daisy chains looped through my hair, curved around Billy's baby wrists, twined around her neck and sleeping cosy under soft blankets and baking coffee cakes and eating the cake batter off wooden spoons and Dorrie. Dorrie. It's Dorrie. Before she says it, I come round the table and bury myself in her arms. She laughs into my hair.

"Dorrie. Of course I didn't forget, I didn't forget, I didn't." I say it like an incantation, a spell, as if I can make it true.

"It's alright, my darling. It's alright."

I think it's those words that break it, that dam I've built inside me. I can't find my distractions. And I cry. Heavy, heaving sobs. Snotty, unattractive crying. Real tears. Proper tears, not the kind that run gently down your face. The type that hurt, the type that pour.

"I'm sorry, my darling girl. I'm so endlessly sorry."

I'm a child, collapsed on her lap, tears stinging tired eyes.

***

Dorrie held me until I stopped crying. Then she showed me some old photos and I cried some more. Billy with a smile and clear eyes. Before. She held me again.

I complain about my childhood. Not to other people, just to myself, inside my head. The only person I've ever actually told about Mother, about who she really was, is Tony. And look where that got me. But I complain all the time to myself, about how I didn't have a proper mother, the kind who cooks you tea and tucks you in at night, the kind who scares the monsters away and cheers you on no matter how bad you are at whatever pointless thing you're doing. The kind who never tells you she has a favourite child, even if she does. The kind who loves you.

But I did. I had Dorrie. I *have* Dorrie.

I'm going next door tomorrow, to bake coffee cake with her, just like old times. She said I can help her finish off her strawberry tart for the village coffee morning. I said I could bring her some of my strawberries. She just looked at me, cocked her head to one side. I've picked a basket full for her.

I feel about seven again, too giddy to sleep, my stomach swooping with excitement. It's strange, sleeping on the ground floor, after so long spent in Tony's high-rise flat. But I haven't started on mine and Billy's old room yet, so the master bedroom it is. At least it's closer to the bathroom.

Rrrrrrrr... I forgot how quiet it is in the country, how you can hear every little thing. Like the car that's currently idling outside. The headlights catch my curtains and I put my head under the pillow. Go away.

BANG.

My body jolts upright. Christ, who slams a car door like that? They'll wake the entire village. Absolutely no respect. Young kids, no doubt. Ah, yes, it seems I have completed my transition to Easily Annoyed Country Bumpkin Spinster. Kudos to me. I'll be attending Neighbourhood Watch meetings next, waving placards with *Drown Out Noise Pollution!* spray-painted on them.

Another *BANG.* If that's my wheelie bin falling over, I'm going to be furious. There's old soup from inside the sink in there. I am *not* scraping that off the pavement.

Thud, thud, thud. The front door. Interesting knocking technique. Sounds like they're using their whole body. Jesus Christ, if I've moved away from the crime-rife city only to get slaughtered in my bed by some sort of moors murderer, I'm going to be more than furious. I *will* haunt him from beyond the grave. Or her, Clem, women can be murderers too, come on.

I sit up in bed. *Tap, tap.* Christ, they're at my window.

"Clemmieeeee, Clemmmm."

Bleeding hell, it's like Cathy and Heathcliff.

"Come on, Clemmie, it's freezing out here."

I know that voice. Oh no. Please, God no. Please, I'll do anything, anything.

I run into the kitchen, grab my phone from the side. It's nearly out of charge but the notifications still clutter the screen. I should never have put it on silent.

A new flood of messages from Billy:

Clem I'm serious we need to talk

I need you please can't you be my sister for once ??!?!

You are such a seLFISH BITCH

I will come down there

Please Clemmie xxxx

CLEMENTINE ANSWER YOUR BLOODY PHONE

Why do you hateme???

I never asked for anyof this x

hateyou hateyou hateyouhateyouhateyou bitch

Im comn

Conf

E-Coli

Jesus stupid predicative text

coming

No. Why? No.

"Clemmie! Come on, I need to pee really bad."

Go away, go away, go away.

"I have to tell you something." The letterbox judders and my little brother's wide, blue eyes appear in the gap. "Clem!"

I sink down onto the floor of the kitchen. Close my eyes.

Great. Now he's singing. My brother may be many things, but a singer, he is not. Dad's favourite Christmas song, that one. About being drunk at Christmastime. Ironic, really.

"Clemmie." He's whispering now. God knows why. "It's really important. I heard them at work. I wasn't meant to be there, but I was... they said it's in the food, Clemmie. I don't want you to be here. You're my sister... I love you, Clemmie. I miss you." There's tears in his voice now, crowding in against his words.

I wonder what it is this time. Cocaine? Pills? There was one called speed. All three? Definitely vodka. God, I don't care. A headache creeps its way through my skull.

"They said it's in the food!" And he's shouting again. Perfect. "It's in the food and the drinks. They're putting it everywhere, Clemmie, EVERYWHERE."

I open my eyes. Billy's lanky figure is visible through the glass, backlit by the neighbour's lights. He's going to wake everyone. I make myself stand, walk forward, open the door. Billy is spinning in circles on the grass.

"Everywhere! They're going to wipe out the human race, they're going to *kill us all* and they knew Clem… *They knew*."

I grab hold of him the way Dad showed me. Pull him towards the house. It's hard, with his ridiculous height.

Neighbourly faces appear at windows, plump men in dressing gowns out on the street. "Everything alright, love?"

"Hello!" Billy shouts, waving madly. "Did you all know too? Did you?"

I slap my hand across his mouth, "Yes, all fine. Sorry, he's just had a few too many. You know how it is, boys will be binge drinkers, hahaha."

The concerned dressing gown men nod, turn towards their houses, mumbling about the good old days down the pub, getting into states just like that one, what times, hey, lads, etc, etc.

I bundle Billy towards the cottage, glancing at Dorrie's windows as we pass. They're pitch black. Billy bites down hard on my hand, freeing his mouth.

He keeps singing, even louder this time.

"Come on, everyone! Sing it with me!"

He seems to be cycling through the entire back catalogue of the greatest Christmas hits.

I smack him in the mouth, shove him into the cottage. He looks at me, holding his jaw, eyes dark. Then he smiles wide, too wide.

"Hey, sis."

He tries to hug me, but I shove him off, push him into the wall.

"No, Billy. We're not doing that, we aren't *that*. I don't care what you've taken, and I don't care why you're here. This is what's going to happen: for one night *only*, you may sleep on the sofa. Then, in the morning, you will leave, and you won't come back. Got it?"

He stares at me for a second. "For one night onlyyyy in a village near you! The wonderful… the magnificent… Clemmie!" He tries to make me dance with him.

Dear God.

I shake him off again, grab the sheets to make up the sofa. He follows me into the kitchen.

"Anything to eat?" He starts opening the cupboards, forgetting to close them, tosses his jacket towards a chair. It immediately falls on the floor. I do my best to ignore him.

Then he stops, he goes very still, he starts to make a kind of whimpering noise. Then he screams. Long and loud. Surprisingly high-pitched for a man.

"What's the matter?" I grab his shoulder and he drops what he's holding.

It hits the floor with a *squelch*, seeping greyish liquid. Billy scuttles away from it. I bend down. It's my

53

clementine. The one I saved for later. Except it doesn't look like a clementine anymore. Its skin has split, the plump segments have turned to mush, their vibrant orange now a purply-grey. It smells vile. Like mould and gone off fish. Billy leans over and throws up on the floor. And then on himself. And then on me.

I say nothing. I step out of my ruined pyjama bottoms, glad of my dressing gown, and throw them straight in the bin. I scrape the sick off my feet and put that in the bin. I scrape the clementine off the floor with some kitchen roll and put that in the bin. I pull Billy's jumper off, a stupid Christmas thing with a picture of a reindeer on it, then his shirt, and put both of them in the bin. I use kitchen roll to clean his face.

Billy clutches at me. "Yes, Clem. Yes, you genius." He grabs my face, kisses both cheeks. He's extremely sweaty, his breath sick-sour. "Yes, we hide it all and then they can't find it—"

"Okay, yes, great idea," I say, directing him towards the sofa.

Talk to him like you would a child, just agree and nod until you get him where you want to go. Alright, Dad, you watching? I'm doing it just like you said. See? I can be a good sister. I can.

I sit Billy down on the sofa. His eyes are huge, rolling around inside his skull, his pupils a deep, deep black. I sigh, push his hair back off his face.

Sometimes I could kill you, Mother used to say. I think I know what she meant.

"I knew you'd know what to do, Clemmie. I just got scared, you know?"

54

I nod, stroke his forehead, lie him down.

"I just got really freaked out and when… they said about Dad because I don't think they… I don't think they know he's dead…"

Wait. "Billy, what? Who said what about Dad?"

"You changed your hair." He touches my head, smiles, slurs, "I like it." His eyes close.

"Billy, you talked about Dad at work?"

"We had… a Christmas… party." And he's asleep.

If he's been badmouthing Dad at his new work, I'm going to kill him. I pull a blanket round him, pick up his jacket from where he dropped it. A slim rectangle falls out of the pocket. *Entirely Natural: Staff Pass: William Finch.* Jesus Christ, *great* ID picture. Hahahahaha. Something else in the inside pocket. A baggie of white power. I drop it. Breathe. Pick it up. Go into the bathroom. Flush it down the toilet.

Billy is snoring in the kitchen. Better go back in to check he's sleeping on his side. Don't want him choking on his own vomit. I sit down on the cold floor beside the sofa. I watch him sleep. I cry.

***

I'm woken early by the sound of footsteps. My first thought is, *Billy.* But no, he's still passed out on the sofa. Guess I fell asleep in the kitchen. They say sleeping on the floor is good for your back. They're wrong. No idea who *they* are anyway. The footsteps must have been the postman. I've been dreading this moment. Opening letters addressed to my parents from people who think they're still alive.

Dealing with bills. Having to cancel Dad's magazine subscriptions.

There's nothing on the mat. I open the door. Emperor Pheasant is on my doorstep. Well, that's not strictly true. His body is on my doorstep. His head sits a small distance away, upright on the ground. Facing me. *Placed.* His little eyes blank. The shears I bought from Greta stick out of the grass, blades buried into the earth, handles sticking up, saluting the morning. The soil around them is sticky and I don't have to touch them to know the blades are coated in hot, dark blood. It looks like the ground is haemorrhaging, the dull grass stained with crimson. It's fresh. That thick, meaty smell hangs in the air.

I peer out at the street. Empty. I place one bare foot onto the doorstep, careful not to touch the tiny body lying there. My heart is loud in my ears.

No one.

No car pulling away. No front door slamming. Just footprints.

There's a cool breeze, frost on the grass. A pair of small, fresh footprints head towards my door and away again. I shiver, curl my arms around myself. The image of my front garden blurs, tears catching in my eyelashes. Snot drips from my nose. I wipe it on my dressing gown sleeve.

Emperor Pheasant's wings are twisted at an angle, his lacy feathers clotted with gunk. His stomach has been slit, a mess of tiny organs spilling out.

My body feels cold.

I reach a hand out, as though to touch him, but I can't. I can't. I chew my nails and taste clementines.

I'm on my hands and knees scrubbing congealed blood off the front step when Billy wakes up. His socked feet appear in my eye line.

"Clemmie?" He's wearing that familiar hangdog expression – his morning-after-the-night-before mask. But there's fear there as well, a sharpness amongst the usual dulled blue of his eyes.

I nudge the pheasant-filled bin bag behind me with my bare foot, try to hide the mess of red with my blood-stained sponge. There's a slick of pink-tinged liquid on my hands.

"Nothing. It's nothing. Just a cat leaving me doorstep gifts, I think."

Billy's face scrunches, his mouth curling in disgust. "Fluffy little monsters."

Then he puts a hand to his forehead, turns, goes back inside. It's a whole six minutes twenty-seven seconds (yes, I counted) before the vomiting starts – think that's a new record. Kudos to him.

I lug the full bin bag round to the wheelie bin, which I have to right after Billy's assault on it last night. My one piece of luck: none of the other bags have split. I pour the bucket of blood-tinged water onto next-door's grass, chuck my sponge away, wave faux-cheerfully to a man walking his small, fluffy dog – neither of them looks like a pheasant murderer. But then again, I guess you never know, do you? I don't think I look like a barren orphan, but here we are.

Back in the kitchen, I dig Dad's old radio out of the drawer. Haven't been able to bring myself to turn it on since the funeral, but anything to cover up the sound of Billy vomiting. He's so dramatic. No one needs to retch that loud. The plug hangs at a strange angle, the wire fraying at the end. It'll be fine. Probably.

"*—Always great to hear from our listeners, thanks for that one, Ben. Now, next up we have the legend that is Whitney, with 'I Wanna Dance with Somebody'.*"

See, fine.

Dad hated this song with a passion. He once made such a fuss in the local pub that they still don't play any Whitney to this day. I don't know what his problem with it was, I think it's good. Okay, it's not as great as everyone makes out, but it doesn't make your ears bleed. I'll happily listen to it.

I turn the radio off. Sorry, Dad. I can't believe I feel disloyal to a ghost.

The retching has been replaced by moaning. I won't rise to it. He did this to himself; he can deal with it himself.

I put the kettle on to boil. Throw a teabag in a cup. Billy's favourite mug is in the far back of the cupboard, I'll have to stand on a chair to reach it. *Sccccrape.* The chair shudders to the left. Jesus, just nearly broke my neck making tea.

I wonder how long it would take for someone to find me if I did die in here. If I slipped and broke a limb, put out my own eye, snapped my spine. How long would I have to lie here, on the cold kitchen floor? Slowly spreading blood, staining the grout. Mother would go absolutely mental, she was always proud of the cleanly tiled floor. Well, now it smells of old sick, Mother, and it has a long, dark scrape left by the chair leg. Markers of her children's near-death experiences.

The kettle screams at me, so I pour the water into the mug, add too much sugar.

Billy is laid on the floor of the bathroom, curled into a tight ball. I place the tea in front of him. My hands go to my hips before I realise I'm standing like she used to. I will not turn into my mother. But I will not give him sympathy – Dad was too soft. I need my own stance. I settle for one hip cocked and what I imagine is a stern expression, but my little brother just smiles up at me. I must be doing it wrong.

"Thanks, Clemmie." His voice is hoarse, ragged.

"I want you gone by this afternoon."

I walk back into the kitchen. Make a cup of coffee for myself, take the bread outside to feed the birds. They'll be hungry, wondering where I am. Shoving my feet into Dad's old slippers, I step out onto the patio. None of them come to greet me, but they don't fly away either. They're indifferent to me. Maybe they're too tame, maybe I'm killing them, training them out of their scavenging instincts. It's too easy to just come and get bread from the small woman in the small house. Especially now there's no pheasant guarding her garden.

That's what would happen if I died. I see it now. If I died, my body would wait inside the house, neck broken on the kitchen floor and skinny, dead birds would litter my garden, little skeletons still waiting for their bread.

There's a buzzing noise coming from inside the kitchen. Music, voices: "*Well, Claire, it sure is a problem, thanks for phoning in. I'm sure we can all agree, these riots have to stop. If you feel threatened in your area, please go online and head to our website. There's a link there to our*

59

petition to end violence against pregnant women – come on,
guys, let's get those signatures, let's be heard!"

I'm sure I turned that radio off. Stupid thing, probably
faulty. Something else you never got around to fixing, hey
Dad? I flip the switch, then unplug it at the wall, just to be
sure.

"Clemmie?" A pause. "Clem, I puked on the floor."

I put my coffee mug back on the side, replace the
bread, grab the mop and a bucket instead. You're killing
the birds, Billy.

***

I'm crying over a bloody pheasant. Never thought that
sentence would cross my mind. Tears drip off the end of
my nose into the sink. Why do tears taste like salt? There
must be a reason, some biological evolution thing.

I put a saucer of seeds on the patio before I realised.
Went to get them back and the starving crows were already
huddled round, beaks full to the brim of the forbidden
royal seeds. No doubt they'll be meeting officially
sometime soon, to elect the new Emperor. They need to do
it quickly: those birds need leadership, otherwise things in
the garden will descend into anarchy.

Just Googled it: apparently tears are full of things
called electrolytes that create electricity in our bodies
and brains and happen to contain salt. So obviously that's
terrifying and I wish I'd never read it. Electricity in my
brain? Wait, if I'm tasting my tears, swallowing them,
what if I'm taking in too many electrolytes, too much
electricity? What happens then? I might explode. Might

have stumbled across a Spiderman situation – if I drink a pint of my own tears every day, maybe I'll get electric-based superpowers. Maybe I could electrocute Billy with my eyes. Always a silver lining. Better start collecting my tears – I'll have to get a special jar, label it *orphan tears, tears from a barren woman*. The childless weirdo is always cast as the witch, right? Maybe that could be a life goal for me – a new path to take. I already live in a crumbling cottage, the outlier in the community, no one would struggle to believe it. I would definitely have been hanged by a witch hunter back in the day. Why not just take the easy road, fulfil the stereotype? I have always wanted a black cat. I would name her Cosmo. As in the cosmos, the stars and universe and stuff, not the cocktail. Even though everyone would think it was after the cocktail. Maybe I would call her Galaxy instead. But then everyone would just think of chocolate.

Crash.

Billy's definitely knocked over something expensive. We don't even own anything expensive, but he'll have found some kind of antique upstairs and smashed it into a million pieces.

I peer at myself in the bathroom mirror. My eyes are bright red – probably the salt from the tears eroding my eyeballs. I'll go blind soon if I keep going like this. Or at the very least need glasses. The strong type, the ones that make people's eyes look huge and creepy, swivelling about inside their heads. I suppose it would add to the unstable witch ensemble. I should get a long black dress. And a hat.

If Billy asks why my eyes look like they're bleeding, I'll tell him I've taken up pot – he won't believe me obviously, but it'll stop him asking any more questions. Hopefully.

Crash.

That's two antiques gone. We could have gone on *Antiques Roadshow*. He's ruined our chances now. Idiot.

***

Spiralised carrot looks much better in photos. My offerings look kind of like weird, orange witch toenails. I don't have an actual spiralizer, obviously, so had to use the apple peeler. But I'm not making excuses – I've never been very good at cooking. Billy knows that and I can't blame him for not touching the salad. It's limp – looks like I feel.

Billy moves the grey leaves around his plate. He's *very* hungover. The scrape of the fork against the china is making my teeth grind. The inside of my mouth tastes like soil. I push my own plate away.

My brother looks up, his eyes meet mine. Tears hover at his lash-line, threaten to spill. It's funny, isn't it, how often grown men show you the little boys they once were?

"Clemmie—"

I shake my head, stand up quickly. I know what he's going to ask me, and I won't hear it, I can't – because I know if I do, I'll let him stay.

"Clem, please, I don't know what will happen if I go back there."

I brace my hands either side of the sink, try to breathe in through my nose, out through my mouth. In through the nose and out through the mouth. God, what is that smell? The bin? Don't tell me it's the sink again. The salad? I take Billy's plate away from him. He's still talking. How did you block it out, Mother? The whining. How were you able to ignore it, to ignore us?

***

I used to lie in bed at night as a little girl and scream into my pillow. I became quite the expert at it. It's all about the angle, you see. Too low against the mattress and it gets hard to breathe, too high and you end up almost sitting up straight and hurting your neck. You have to rock back on your knees, balance just in the middle, place your nose just at the edge of the pillow – that way you can breathe in deep and scream out, long and sharp, whilst the fabric absorbs it all. See, I bet not many people know that. These are the kind of important life skills my childhood taught me. Billy clearly never learnt the same technique; I can hear him sobbing from here. I'll have to teach him one of these days. The way his life is going, he's going to need it.

I pull the pillow away from my face, sigh, swing my legs out of bed. The door creaks as I open it, the kitchen tiles cold under my feet. Billy's tears hot against my skin as I wrap him in my arms, rock him back and forth. How did we get here, Dad? Whose fault was it? Mine, or hers?

PART TWO

Greta has Christmas decorations strewn around the shop. Cheap, gold tinsel, handmade paper garlands, a tiny wilting tree with a single red bauble hanging from the very top. Mustn't have been able to find an angel. Or a star. She probably threw all that stuff out after Liam – I remember him running around clutching a shiny, silver star when we were young. Billy snatched it off him once. Liam didn't cry, he just nodded, let Billy chew on one of the star's points. He went and got a pretty, smiling angel and put her at the top of the little tree instead. She had curly, golden hair and a golden dress, with a tiny golden wand and little golden shoes. I asked Mother for one just like it for our tree. I waited and waited – we never got one. We had to make do with the angry, squashed looking fairy with the bent wings and the wonky neck. She must have been sat on one year, or dropped down the stairs or something. She used to frighten me. I would lie in bed, terrified she was going to shake those broken wings loose, crack her broken neck and scamper into my bedroom. I was convinced she was going to try and steal my teeth – rip them from my gums like a twisted version of the tooth fairy. Blood everywhere.

Dad told me Liam's lovely golden angel was one of a kind, special, and that's why we couldn't buy one, because the only one ever made belonged to Liam. I must have been about fifteen when I first saw the rows and rows of special, one of a kind golden angels waiting patiently in their mass-produced boxes at the supermarket in town, smiling down at me benevolently. I never told Dad I saw them. He'd tried, I understood that much.

I look around the shop for Greta, but she's not at the desk. My list has crumpled itself up inside my bag, so I smooth is out against the counter. Billy managed to throw out my old list – of course he did – so I had to start a new one. The boy's never cleaned anything, never thrown any actual rubbish away in his life, and he manages to bin the one thing in the kitchen I actually need. I wasn't as angry as I could have been – I couldn't have carried that piece of paper round with me anyway, not with the words *Emperor Pheasant* printed so carefully, so happily. *Stop it, Clem, you can't smell blood, not really. It's all in your head. Just all in your head.* Which reminds me, Billy's request for painkillers. He's 'not sure' why he's getting such bad headaches at the minute. I didn't point out the obvious.

So, my new list looks like this:

Paracetamol
Ibuprofen

Milk
Coffee
Bread
Eggs
Chicken

Billy has added the word, *Chocolate*, in shy, cramped handwriting at the bottom. Annoyingly, I feel myself smile. I tried to remember what was on my old list. There was more than one thing, I know, but the only one I could think of was: *Fix boiler*. Mainly because the house is now so cold that I've lost feeling in my fingers and toes and Billy has a hot water bottle permanently attached to his body.

I also need to: *Check water tank*. Or Dad's approximation of a water tank – it's outside and mainly collects rainwater. He hooked it up to the house one summer with metal pipes and a hammer from the shed. There's definitely something wrong when the water coming out of the taps is so brown even Billy won't drink it.

I don't know what Greta's been doing in here, but there's barely anything left on the shelves. Feel like I've walked into some weird, Black-Friday-style panic-buy atmosphere. Do other people know something we don't? Has there been some kind of dystopian, end-of-the-world announcement that I missed whilst I was cleaning Billy's sick off the floor? Because I wouldn't be surprised.

"Hello?"

No response. No movement. A light flickers above the cheese section. Greta must be re-stocking, she's probably somewhere in the back. There's no milk left, no coffee, no chocolate. No paracetamol, no ibuprofen, no medicine apart from a tub of Vicks VapoRub. Reminds me of colds when I was little, Dad sleeping on the floor beside my bed in case I woke in the middle of the night. Kind man. No eggs, no chicken, some bread but it looks kind of stale. I take the plastic wrapped packet anyway, wipe a layer of dust from its surface, head to the desk.

Wait.

Pop my head into the little room at the back. No one in there. Nothing much at all in there. Just a chair and half a packet of cheese and onion crisps, their smell hanging in the air. God, I'm hungry.

I walk back through to the counter.

Wait.

Open the bread and stuff a piece into my mouth. Reseal the packet.

Wait.

The bread is sticky and heavy against my tongue. I swallow hard. A layer of phlegm rises, coats the back of my throat.

Wait.

I put a fifty pence piece on the counter. Leave.

***

Gus's bulk is leaning against the bonnet of my car when I make it outside. I ignore the flutter in the base of my stomach as he turns, looks at me. He waves. I wave my loaf of bread back at him.

"Clem." His shy eyes blink at me. "How's everything going?"

I panic for a second, think he must know something, must have seen Billy arrive. God, I can just see his daddy's face now, rictus at the sound of my brother's terrible, *terrible* singing. He must have sent Gus out to find me, his little spy. But no, we're not seventeen anymore. Gus is a grown man, I'm a grown woman, his father doesn't run his life anymore. Surely. If Dad's last email was anything to go by, the old man's bedridden nowadays anyway. At least we didn't have to do that, did we Dad? At least this way you kept your dignity.

I realise Gus is still staring at me.

"Oh, yeah, all good. Thanks," I say.

"Getting some supplies?" He points at my loaf of bread. The packet has grown hot in my hand, sweaty. I open the car door, toss it on to the front seat, swipe my damp palm against my jeans. Smile.

Gus braces one large hand against my car. His nails have a fine layer of dirt underneath, gritty and black. He places his other palm against his neck, takes a breath. Clears his throat. I look at my feet. I'd forgotten quite how shy he is, how different he is to the men I've grown used to. God, this is painful. I move to follow my bread into the car.

"Greta re-stocked yet?" Gus nods his head back at the tiny shop.

"Oh, I don't... no, everything's pretty empty."

Gus shows his uneven teeth, sharp against the curls of his beard. "Yeah, bet you've forgotten what it's like here, huh? City girl."

His eyes roam over my face, my body, my exposed neck. One of his eyes flickers – an attempt at a wink? Why? Christ, is he trying to flirt? Horrifically, I feel myself begin to blush. He must see the pink flush, grins again, brown-eyed gaze heavy on my skin. What he could be looking at, I have no idea. I'm wearing an old pair of baggy jeans, big boots and Dad's old windbreaker, for God's sake. Who's ever flirted with someone wearing a windbreaker? The red from my cheeks has deepened, is starting to work its way across my chest.

"So, do you know when she'll be done then?" I ask. Distract, distract, distract. Don't let this happen, Clem. I ignore the tug of memory in the base of my stomach as he drops that smile, ducks his head in that familiar way.

"Well, it varies, depends how big her delivery was. Why, you need anything particular?"

He mangles the word, par-tik-lur. Reminds me of Dad.

Right, I'll have to do it – bring out the surefire way to wrest the conversational power back from any man, especially a large, shy, bear-like one: "I got my period this morning."

Fantastic, blush successfully transferred, back in control, good.

"So, have you got any painkillers?"

It's not really a lie, Mother, giving pills to Billy will numb the pain in my own head because it will stop him whining. See my logic? It's a great plan.

Gus mumbles, blushes brighter, mumbles again. Clears his throat. "Ah, I have some cold medicine back at the house? Would that do?"

Or then again, maybe not.

***

It's cold on the front step. Gus invited me in. Of course he did – *Well trained that one*, Mother would say. May have been well trained, but he still wasn't good enough, was he Mother? For the daughter you didn't even like. Didn't have his own car, no expensive suits, no flashy penthouse flat. Didn't have the right job, didn't bring the right bottle of wine to the house. As if we're a family who know about things like the right wine. Tony had all of those things, Mother, and look where that got me. It should have been an alarm bell straight away that she liked him. An extremely large, extremely loud alarm bell, painted in bright warning colours. Right in front of my face.

I didn't want to wait inside, didn't want to risk seeing the old man's sick room. Risk being pinned underneath his sharp gaze, a piece of me trapped forever in this house, caught under glass like one of those pinned butterflies in those insect collections people have. I will never trust anybody who collects insects – I don't even like pressing flowers. Odd, to keep dead things in a book.

Gus has left the front door open a crack. Mother would never allow such a thing – to let the heat out in such a fashion is akin to a mortal sin. I'm surprised Gus doesn't know this. Maybe he just doesn't care now his daddy can't see into the hall anymore. He may be a nasty old man, but he can't be as formidable as Mother. She could tell if a door had been left open, something had been spilt, something was out of its approved place, even if she wasn't in the house. Even if she was asleep. Even dead, I can still feel her watching me, in her house, ruining the precise order of things. It's just fortunate her hands can't slap my skin from that side of the veil.

That smell drifts out of the hall – the smell of a sick house, the smell that tells you someone is slowly dying in here, enter at your own risk. There's a clean, white box stood on a small table by the door, looks out of place in amongst the mess. Green lettering on its side: *Entirely Natural – All Natural Holistic Medicines.* Wouldn't have thought that was Gus's daddy's style. Then again, if you're in that much pain you probably don't care about your principles anymore, you do anything, take whatever they tell you. I ate three egg yolks a day after my diagnosis because someone told me it helped improve fertility. I hate eggs.

"Here you go. Sorry it's not anything more, but it does say it contains paracetamol."

Gus holds a bottle of cold medicine out to me, the *Entirely Natural* logo bright on the label – an outline of a tree, yellow-gold branches stretching out, out, out. I think it's supposed to symbolise the Tree of Life from the Bible. There's two shadow figures either side, one with long hair sprouting from her head. I presume they're meant to be Adam and Eve. Their marketing team must have forgotten that the fruit the two took from the tree was actually forbidden. Now it's used as a marker of health, nutrition, the 'right' choice. I didn't know they'd expanded into the non-holistic side of things. The bottle feels cold as I clasp it in my hand.

"Thanks."

"Sorry it's already half gone, I had a bit of a head cold earlier this month."

I want to tell him he doesn't have to explain himself to me, but my mouth stays shut. I glance at the white box on the table again and Gus sees me looking.

"Oh, that's – it's my father's medicine. It's not proper painkiller, it's that all-natural stuff it—"

"I was going to ask how he is. Your daddy."

Gus is breathing hard, like he's been running. "Fine, he's... well, no, he's dying really. Can't get out the bed no more."

"I'm sorry."

"Ah, it's alright, he doesn't need to be able to walk to keep doing his favourite hobby."

A sad smile. A code from when we were kids, his daddy's favourite hobby, complaining *about* his only son *to* his only son. His tongue still works then; the tumours mustn't have spread there yet. Worse luck.

"I've been meaning to give you these." Gus reaches behind him, produces a wilting bunch of flowers. They don't have plastic or paper round them, just a dirty looking piece of string tied in a rough bow – he must have picked them himself. Daisies. My favourite.

"I'm so sorry, Clemmie. Really."

The lonely boy with the horrible, dying father feels sorry for me. Great. Before I can reply a thin, reedy noise floats down the hallway. It takes me a second to realise that's now his daddy's voice. He sounds like an old woman.

"Gus? Gus, is that door open?"

I was wrong, he does have some of Mother's powers. They clearly attended the same 'how to torture your children' seminar.

Gus will tell me he'd better go now, close the door in my face.

"I'd better go."

Yep.

I nod, clutch my cold medicine and dying daisies, smile. The door closes with a *thunk* and I can hear Gus's

72

low rumble, reassuring his daddy, yes the door is closed now, no, all the heat hasn't escaped from the house, no, it wasn't anyone important at the door. I turn to see Billy standing at the edge of our garden, in full view of the neighbours and in the full blast of the freezing wind, in just his boxer shorts. I'd better put the kettle on.

***

Blood stains my knickers again. It smells thick, animal, alive. Unexplained infertility – no babies, but don't worry, you'll still get the familiar searing pain each month and bleed unnecessarily all over everything. Especially anything you own which happens to be white.

The doctors don't even try to find an explanation anymore. You can see the relief in their eyes when they give the diagnosis – *at least that's one that won't come back in with a swollen belly, hope in her eyes*. I would put money on the doctor we saw finding a cure and keeping it to himself – he was an obvious anti-birther. He even had a pamphlet on the benefits of abortion on display in his office. There was always a smell in his consultation room, stale, like old dust and expelled breath.

Childless women are still spurned. Of course we are, always have been, always will be. No matter that we're in the midst of an overpopulation crisis, we're still weird. They've just found a way to attack the mothers now, too. Mothers are selfish, desperately so, putting everyone else at risk by pushing another human into our already over-crowded world. Us childless women are hailed as martyrs by the anti-birth crowd, whether we like it or not. We have sacrificed everything, our future happiness, our chance to be unconditionally loved until our deaths by our devoted offspring, to save others. But of course, we must be deeply sad inside, smiling through our pain. God, I feel the anger of those women who are childless by choice, their *own* choice, who would be childless whether we had a crisis or not, but who are still endlessly pitied, told they're saving lives with their selfless choice.

I once saw a group of pro-birthers throw a can of paint at a young woman, scream at her for supporting propaganda, for backing the government's plea to really *consider* the number of children we have – whatever that means. I'd seen plenty of pregnant women harassed before but never the other way round. How did they know she didn't have children? They could have been at home, waiting for their mother. But she didn't have kids – I know because she screamed back at them, told them she was supporting nothing but her own desires, that she'd never wanted children, regardless of the government tax breaks, the perks, the promises of secure jobs and housing for childless couples. They didn't believe her, obviously. Just gave her the finger and left her dripping paint all over the pavement. I didn't do anything.

I wasn't thinking of others, or the global economy, or the government incentives – inside I *am* crying. I'm one of the ones smiling through her pain. God, I hate clichés.

I don't know how women who know they don't want to be mothers stand having to bleed each month. Seriously, what is the point?

There's a website that counts the deaths around the world. In real time. That's as they happen. No, really. Billy showed me it. It just goes up and up and up. Forever. Dad's in there somewhere. So is Mother. I wonder if their numbers are next to each other or if they've been separated by some dead stranger. There's a birth one, too, but Billy doesn't watch that one. Just the deaths. He doesn't cry, doesn't react, barely blinks. He simply stares, sits and stares at it.

Sits.

Stares.

God, I worry about that boy. Apparently, he was standing in the garden half-naked because he thought it would make the house seem warmer when he came back inside. I genuinely have no words.

Those flickering numbers are hypnotising. I've been watching them for an hour now. I should be asleep. The light from Billy's laptop screen is hurting my eyes. I confiscated it, along with his phone, so he couldn't contact any of his friends. He can do what he wants with them, but I'll not have drugs in this house.

I sip my glass of wine.

He has the death website saved in his favourites bar.

I should really have the big light on, but I don't. Just the little bedside one, giving out a muted red glow – gives the room the same atmosphere as those houses on horror films where they never turn the real lights on and go down into creepy basements by themselves, never lock their doors. Sounds familiar – maybe I'm really just a character in some film, there for others' entertainment. It would be quite reassuring really, to know none of this actually matters. Less pressure on me anyway.

The radio blurts out bright noise, breaking the night. Christ, what have I said? Do. Not. Use. The. Radio. *If I've said it once, I've said it a thousand times*, as Dad would say. I never understood that saying – if you've said it once, then you've just said it once, that's why you say, I've said it once.

The radio is singing 'Jingle Bell Rock' to itself in the kitchen.

"Billy!"

Nothing. Of course.

I sigh, shove my feet into Dad's slippers. Out in the hall, I can see Billy's blankets screwed into sweaty bundles on the sofa, an open copy of F. Scott Fitzgerald's *The Great Gatsby* face down on the chair's arm, keeping his place halfway through. It's the copy I bought him for his birthday a few years ago. I'm amazed he hasn't lost it, frankly, or sold it or something. Dad used to read it to us on a night. It was only when I read it for myself as an adult that I realised he'd changed the ending. Gatsby and Daisy don't end up together and there's considerably more death and crying than I remember. It's a slim novel, but tracing the spine with my thumb I can feel the tell-tale creases of a well-read book. The pages at the beginning look dog-eared, but the later ones look practically brand-new. Looks like Billy prefers Dad's ending too.

The toilet flushes and I replace the book.

The happy Christmassy-ness on the radio is giving me a headache. I flick the switches, unplug the radio and put it back in the drawer.

"Clem?"

Whiny – it sets my teeth on edge. That's if they were ever off edge since my brother arrived.

"I told you not to use this, the plug is fraying. I need to fix it."

"Clemmie, there's something wrong with the sink."

What now? He points at the door to the bathroom, like a child who wants you to deal with the monster under the bed.

I walk into the bathroom, up to the sink. Nothing wrong with it. Billy comes up behind me, his breath hot and sour near my cheek.

"Watch."

He turns the tap on. The water is still that strange, brownish colour. No longer just a tinge, it's dark, smells odd, bad. It flows down the plughole, then it stops, starts to come back up. Billy lets it climb halfway up the sink then he twists the tap again. The plughole gurgles, like it's retching, waits a moment, then swallows the water back down. It lets out another rumble, like a satisfied burp. We listen to the sound of the water moving through the pipes.

"What did you put down there?"

"Nothing, it just started doing that. I was only washing my hands."

"Right."

His eyes darken, the baby blue irises look navy in the dim light of the bathroom. "Why do you never believe me?"

"Oh gosh, that's a hard one." I tap my chin, faux ponderous. "Maybe it's the years and years of lies, the stealing, the deceit, the partying—"

His hand grasps my arm, hard. "You know that's not my fault."

"Of course, yes, nothing's ever your fault, is it?"

"You shut up. You don't know anything, you stupid bitch."

Spittle hits my cheek. This is new. There are three people inside my little brother. Baby Billy: the apologetic, whining child desperate to earn your love back, to hear those three magic little words, 'I forgive you'. Party-Boy, Good-Time Billy: maybe on something, definitely drunk, usually singing. And In-Between-Jobs Billy: unemployed, whiny, spent what's left of his money on pointless stuff, furtive, secretive, time to keep your purse close and your possessions nailed down. But this is a fourth guy – I don't know this man. His voice is low and dangerous, his grip strong, his body a lot bigger than it was before. His shadow stretches well above mine on the wall. The edge of the sink digs into my hip.

"You don't know anything, anything, anything."

His nails dig further into my skin. He shakes me, and I notice the muscles working in his arms. When did he get those?

"You never listen to me, ever. Too bothered about your own life, your own petty problems. So you can't have a baby, so what? Get over it, Clemmie. Maybe nature knows something you don't, maybe there's a reason you're not meant to be a mother—"

I slap him hard across his face, feel the sting in my own palm, mirrored in the red mark on my brother's face.

We stare at each other.

Then my little brother sniffs and fat tears begin to roll down his cheeks, baby blue eyes cloudy again. He looks tragic, standing there, the imprint of my hand harsh on his cheek. Guilt settles in the pit of my stomach. This is Baby Billy's superpower – doesn't matter what my brother does, everyone forgives him eventually. Or at least I do.

The sink gurgles in apparent sympathy, then makes a spitting sound. I turn round and feel my stomach clench, sweat prickle my skin. Matted hair floats in the bottom of the sink, it swirls and sticks to the side of the porcelain. A smell fills the small room, black decay. More hair vomits up from the plughole, dark, wet clumps.

I feel Billy come to stand behind me. He makes a noise in the back of his throat. Then I hear his vomit hit the toilet bowl.

Toilet cleaner, that's what I missed off my list.

***

I've just got Billy to settle down to sleep when the back door rattles with a loud *knock, knock, knock*. This must be how new mothers feel when someone wakes their baby. Well, probably with considerably more love towards the baby itself. A shadow waits behind the door, only small. I press a finger to my lips, tell Billy to get out of sight with a flick of my hands. His eyes tell me, *no, I'm not a dirty secret*, but he still gets up off the sofa, wanders away down the hall. That's the best word to describe the way Billy walks, he w a n d e r s.

I straighten my top, spread the throw over the patches of sweat Billy's left behind on the sofa. Don't know why I feel nervous. Like I've forgotten something, something important.

Oh.

That's because I have.

Dorrie stands on my back doorstep. Her eyes are still kind, still smiling, but there's a question behind them now. And that's worse than hurt. Curiosity killed the cat, and I don't want to have to scrape any more dead animals off my front path.

Stay silent, I beg my brother, *stay hidden*. But we never have been the kind of siblings who can communicate telepathically. Dorrie's head quirks as something bangs somewhere in the house. He'd better not be in my room. Dorrie looks past my legs to the pair of blue men's socks laid on the floor, the copy of *The Great Gatsby*, splayed forgotten, still on the arm of the sofa.

She smiles.

"So that's why you never showed."

The twist of guilt in the base of my stomach knots itself tighter.

"Don't worry, darling. I made some myself. Thought I'd bring it round for you both. I assumed that was him back the other night."

"It's my boyfriend… fiancé. He's – we made up – he's staying over for a while."

"You always were a terrible liar, Clemmie." Dorrie grins, revealing her missing teeth. "You going to let me in, then? Been a long time since I've seen little Billy."

She steps up and into the kitchen, pushing a cling film wrapped oblong of cake into my hands as she passes. *Nothing gets past old Dorrie*, Dad always said. I used to tell him off – *you shouldn't call a lady 'old', Dad, it's not polite*. And she would howl laughing, a laugh too big for her body, swirling, like music. Dad would laugh too, more than he ever would with Mother around. Well, he never laughed with Mother around. I suppose he must have done at one point, but it was before I could remember. Before me, probably. Likely my fault – most things were, are.

"Not so little anymore, though, are you?" Dorrie says. I turn to see Billy standing in the doorway, his shoulders hunched, sheepish. He doesn't say anything, just stares at our old babysitter with something approaching wonder. She somehow envelops his long limbs with her tiny frame.

I hear her whisper to him, "What have you been doing to yourself, now, my love? What have you been doing?"

Then he's crying again, but softly this time, not the hysterical sobbing I have to deal with. She always did calm him. I have to turn away, their reunion strangely private. A horrible loneliness curdles in my chest. Why am I like this? He needs her more than me. He's a wreck, a grieving mess of a man-child. I'm a functioning grown woman who can fix up a crumbling old cottage and process the death of both her parents, all in the same week.

She's putting his socks on, cuddling his feet with her skinny, old fingers. He smiles.

I've never known why jealousy is known as the green-eyed monster; it always feels pale yellow to me, jaundiced, stale. Leaves you cold like some kind of terrible sickness. Leaves you outside looking in. Nobody likes to play with the jealous kid, they suck the life out of everything. *You can be annoyed Clemmie, be sad if you need to be. Christ, even get angry if you have to. But don't be jealous, sweetheart, jealousy solves nothing and complicates everything. It's a nasty emotion, twists up your insides. It's no good.* Failed again, Dad. I'm sorry.

"Mugs still in the top cupboard, darling? I think we need some tea."

Dorrie starts to bustle around the kitchen, seeking teabags, spoons, milk. If w a n d e r brings to mind Billy, then bustle is the word for Dorrie. I move to help her reach the mugs, but she's nimble up and down on the chair. No chance of *her* slipping and falling – Dorrie's no fool.

Billy watches her, a childlike vacancy on his face. For the first time since he arrived, there's no tension in his body, no worry in his eyes. She's smoothed out the creases on my brother's forehead just by being here.

"Dorrie, does anyone else know?"

She turns to me, cocks her head again. Bird-like.

"That he's here – does anyone else know?"

She smiles. "No, darling. I doubt it. Anyway, things have changed since you were last here. People tend to keep to themselves now, aren't so nosy anymore."

I think of Gus leaning against my car (was that only just this morning?) asking all those questions. Yes, Clem, because the boy was misguidedly trying to flirt. Is that a word, misguidedly? Probably not.

"I'm just her dirty little secret, aren't I, Clemmie?" Billy grins, but his eyes show worry. He knows what it would mean for people to find out he was back, what would happen. If they knew he was here right now, what they might do to him. And what that would do to me. I can't lose anybody else.

Dorrie opens the fridge. "Have you two been eating these?" She holds up a basket, full with some of the veg from the garden, the carrots and some tomatoes I picked this morning. The skins of the tomatoes already look wrinkled, shrunken – maybe the fridge is turned up too high, too cold for them. I make a mental note to add *adjust fridge temp* to my list, wherever I've left it. I'm sure I brought it in here after I got back from next door, but I can't see it anywhere.

"Yeah, they're rank."

"Oh, charming. I won't go to the trouble of making

you anything tonight then, shall I? Enjoy the hunger."

"Better than the constant puking. They've got to be off, right Dorrie?"

Of course it's my fault he keeps throwing up, of course it is.

"There's nothing wrong with the food." I grab the veg back off Dorrie, guard the basket with my hands. "If there were, I'd be sick too." And I'm not.

"You know, just because I've got my eyes closed, doesn't mean I'm always asleep, Clem." Billy gives me a long look. "And closing the bathroom door doesn't make the room soundproof."

Shut up, Billy. Don't listen to him, Dad, he doesn't know what he's talking about. I'm completely fine. And this food is completely fine.

Dorrie's eyes go big and round as she stares at my hands. A thick, rotten smell drifts up towards my face and something damp tickles my palm. I look down to see the pile of tomatoes moving. Billy shrieks as a stream of maggots work their way out of the lattice at the base of the basket, flow over my hands and land in a messy pool on the floor. They writhe there, meld with the colour of the tiles.

Billy holds my hair back in the bathroom. His hands are gentle, his murmurs kind, and for a moment he reminds me so strongly of Dad I can't breathe properly. And now I'm crying, snot trailing down from my nose. I wipe it, stringy, against the back of my hand. I feel Dorrie drape us both in a blanket and I sit with my brother in a huddle on the floor, not watching her as she begins to clean the kitchen. I press my palms together and try to block out the soft wriggle I can still feel against my skin.

***

I'm starting to think my parents may have been secret hoarders. I mean, who keeps old corks from the tops of champagne bottles in a plastic bag? Well, probably from prosecco bottles considering our family finances, but still.

Apparently, once your children move out their old bedroom becomes a dumping ground for any random rubbish you manage to gather together. I know couples who kept their kids' rooms exactly the same when they left home, like strange little shrines to people who haven't died yet. I don't know which is worse. At least they didn't get rid of all our stuff, just packed their own stuff on top of it. My old pink bear peers out at me with glass eyes from behind an art deco lamp with a ripped shade. Without picking it up, I already know it doesn't work. Never will. I'm glad Billy's not staying long because there's no way I'll be able to get this room cleaned anytime soon.

"Clemmie?" *Think of the devil.*

I look at the pile of boxes stacked in front of me. They're high – almost to the ceiling. I could just duck down behind them, hide, no one would ever find me. I could live inside my little cardboard world for ever, sleep on cardboard pillows, eat from cardboard plates, talk to the cardboard birds.

"Clem?"

I open the door, look at my little brother. He's shivering so intensely his whole body is shaking, his jaw clenching, the muscles on his neck standing out. His hot water bottle hangs forlornly from his hand. It's now so cold in the house I've taken to wearing Dad's puffer over my own coat. He holds the hot water bottle out to me, its blue fabric cover marred with bobbles.

"I can't get the top off," he says in a small voice. He looks as though he could start crying.

I take the bottle off him and find I can't either. It's stuck.

"We'll have to use the bottle opener." Found out early on living here that the opener Dad usually used for beer bottles also works on hot water bottles.

Billy follows me back down the stairs like a little lost dog and stands hugging himself in the kitchen whilst I re-boil the kettle. Dad's radio sits on the side, its frayed wire plugged in.

"Do you have a problem with your memory?" I glare at him. Don't think I've ever glared at anyone before, but that's the only way to describe what my eyes are doing right now, they are g l a r i n g. If this boy electrocutes himself, I swear, I'm going to kill him.

He looks at me with his confused, puppy dog eyes.

"Stop. Plugging. This. In. It's broken! I keep, keep, keep on telling you. God, you really don't listen, do you? Never listen to anything anyone tells you. How you managed to land this job of yours I will never know. I'm surprised you could coherently answer the bloody questions in the bloody interview."

I slam the radio back into the drawer, shove it closed.

"I – I didn't, Clemmie. It wasn't me."

"Of course it wasn't."

I fill the water bottle up with boiling hot water, thrust it back at him without its cover on. He gasps at the burn of the rubber against his bare arm.

"Put a coat on if you're cold."

He follows me back up the stairs, dogging my steps, protesting it wasn't him, he didn't do anything. Can't bear for anything to be his fault, even though the majority of problems in my life link back to him, especially now. Especially my current headache. I really need to find that cold medicine Gus gave me, anything would be better than nothing right now.

"Well, then who the hell was it, Billy? Huh? There's no one here but us. What, you expect me to believe the ghost of our dead Dad drags himself up from his eternal slumber to come plug a radio in every now and again?"

Billy blanches. We've never actually said it, addressed the fact they're… that our parents… that we're orphaned. That we're alone. Yeah, we have each other, but really, we're alone now, aren't we, Dad? Alone together. Billy just stares at me, breathing hard. He looks like I've punched him in the face.

"—*And we're just coming up to 11:30am this Sunday morning. Now, let's get an update on the roads out there.*"

I stare at my brother, standing there in front of me, and then at the noise floating up the stairway. A man's voice, familiar, chatty. Billy follows my gaze.

We walk down the stairs together, slow, slow, to see Dad's radio back on the kitchen counter, plugged in, blaring the Radio One traffic update. Apparently, there are queues on the M1.

I turn it off.

I feel a cold prickle down the back of my neck, along my arms. Billy makes a small noise, a whimper. I stare around the empty kitchen, feel my own hands begin to shake. Someone's been in the house. It's the only explanation.

Someone has been in here, touching our things, walking through our kitchen, breathing in our air.

I head to the door, jiggle the handle. Locked. From the inside. Just how I left it. I feel a sense of relief – who goes around breaking and entering people's houses just to plug old radios in anyway? And it's not like we have anything valuable to steal. The old kitchen appliances still stand calmly on the kitchen counters. Billy's makeshift bed is undisturbed, his copy of *Gatsby*, probably the only thing worth any cash, still nestled within the blankets.

I can hear my own breathing, loud in the space. Or maybe it's Billy's laboured breaths I can hear. His eyes are wide and swivelling in his head.

Wait. Locked from the inside.

I try the door again. Locked from the *inside*. I rush to the front door, try it, same thing. Whoever came in here, whoever turned that radio on, they're still inside the house. I fly back into the kitchen and grab a large knife from the drawer.

"Stay here," I tell Billy.

I half expect him to protest, "Oh no, Clem, let me. I'm the big man, the strong male, I'll protect you." But that's more Tony's style. My brother just nods fast, curls into the foetal position on the sofa, hides his body under the blanket.

The point of the knife shakes as I check the rooms. There's only five rooms, but it seems to take forever to go through them all. Each door swung open creates a prickle in my chest, fear has lodged itself in my belly. I check behind the clutter, under the beds, behind the mould-spotted shower curtain in the bathroom. Nothing and no one. The house is empty. We are alone.

Breathe in, out, in. Out. Come on, Clem, where's that logical mind of yours? I can hear Dad laughing at me, standing in my childhood bedroom, brandishing a knife at Billy's old brown teddy. Mr Snugs he was called. He's missing one eye now. It gives him a forlorn look and, ridiculously, I feel ashamed, as though he's a real bear, really suffering. Like those animals on the daytime adverts – please help our donkeys.

Billy screams. I run in a blur down the stairs, half fall at the bottom, nearly impale myself on my own weapon.

"It's okay, I'm okay." Billy stands at the back door, hands raised in apology. He knows he just almost gave me a heart attack. "It just gave me a shock, that's all."

He points to the frosted glass set into the door. A dark smudge mars its surface, dead centre, looks like paint.

"I think it might be dead, Clem. It hit hard."

His words make perfect sense before I open the door. It's happened before, birds flying into windows, broken wings, beaks, necks. I've seen a fair few over the years. Dad would assess them, and we'd help those we could. We nursed a robin back to health one Christmas, healed its broken twig-like leg. Dad called it a miracle; Mother called it a disease waiting to happen. I called it Bobbin, Bobbin the Robin. I cried when he got better and flew away. He never even looked back.

But this bird is no Bobbin. This crow didn't fly into this window, it can't have flown anywhere in long time. This crow has been dead days, maybe weeks. Its rotting body has left a bloodied stain against the glass and the smell of its leaking entrails makes us both lean back, cough. It's a hodgepodge of moulting feathers, their sheen dulled, delicate bone and blackened blood. Flies gather on the body, joining the maggots already feasting on the mess of what was once a stomach. Billy pushes past me, into the back garden, crouches down. I continue to stare at the carcass on our back step. I'm going to need another bin bag.

"Clemmie." He points at the ground. Footprints. In the frost covering the grass. I feel a wave of déjà vu, push the image of Emperor Pheasant to the back of my mind. Those shears better be where I left them, down in the basement.

The frosted footsteps don't lead all the way to the step this time, but stop halfway across the garden. I turn back to the door to stare at the blood on the glass. Someone came into our garden and threw a rotting crow carcass at our door. What the hell happened to a good old-fashioned rock?

"Clemmie, we should take up Dorrie's offer."

"No, Billy."

I will not hide behind an old woman. I will not drag her into this. Whatever *this* is.

"But this is weird, right? That's two dead birds left on our doorstep now."

Damn, I didn't think he saw Emperor Pheasant.

"Not *our* doorstep, Billy, *my* doorstep. It's not your problem because this isn't your house. And it's not two birds left. It's one pheasant *left*, and one bird *thrown*."

Billy just looks at me.

"You can throw yourself back into work on Monday, forget all about dead birds."

"I'm not leaving you here alone with the Bird Murderer, Clemmie."

"Let's be honest, it'll stop the minute you leave, won't it?"

It's *a low blow*, as Dad would say, but I don't get to see the expression on Billy's face because I'm trying to drag the mop and bucket out onto the step. They're not heavy, just awkward. He doesn't offer to help.

"Come on, Clem. We could have a family Christmas over at Dorrie's."

"Dorrie isn't family."

"She's as good as!"

"Well, she's better than you, I guess. Although that's not hard, is it?"

He brushes past me, back inside the house. Disappears upstairs somewhere.

Guess I'll clean all this up myself then, shall I?

***

Billy fell asleep on his old bed. Don't have a clue how he managed to clear enough space with all the boxes piled on the mattress, but he did. There's not even a sheet on, no pillow. I suppose it might still be comfier than the sofa. I only noticed today that half the springs have gone. Thought I'd clean the floor whilst I had the mop out, and it caught on the metal spindles sticking out the bottom. He never said anything. Obviously. Well, that's Billy all over, isn't it? Ignore the problem and it'll go away. Or someone else will deal with it.

A bubbling noise comes from my stomach, and I realise we never ate tea, or lunch. Or breakfast. Maybe there's something wrong with my brain, it's not sending me signals that I'm hungry, reminding me to eat. And it's telling me I should let Billy stay another night. Which is clearly insanity.

My head throbs. Where's that cold medicine? I hunt through my bag for it, look around my room, peer around the kitchen. I try to think about where I could have put it. *Retrace your steps*, Mother used to say. Granted, that was mainly so she didn't have to get involved in the hunt – *Well, I don't know where you've already looked, do I?*

I check the cupboards, maybe Dorrie put it somewhere. Perhaps in the bathroom, thinking we keep a medicine cupboard. We don't. Good idea though. Now *she's* dead and buried I can keep things wherever or however I want. Yeah, just you watch me, Mother. Billy must have raided these cupboards because there's only one slice of bread left. Okay, it was a mini loaf, but Christ leave some for the rest of us, boy. By which I mean me. I take the crust out of the bag and shove it into my mouth. Instant regret. It clags and sticks to the roof of my mouth. I reach over to bin the plastic bag and see the bottle of cold medicine lying on a bed of smelly salad leaves. Billy. Right, that's it. I got these things for us to share but, of course, he takes it all for himself. Why I expected anything less, I don't know. Yep, there's definitely something wrong with my brain.

I take the bottle out of the bin. It's still half full, same as when Gus gave it to me. Doesn't look like he's had any. Okay, so that's way more annoying.

"Billy!" I don't care if he's sleeping. I stomp up the stairs, Dad's slippers surprisingly satisfying to march in.

Billy wasn't sleeping like I thought. He's crouched in the corner of the room and when he notices me stood at the door, he tries to disappear under the bed. He's clutching an empty Tupperware in his hand, it's plastic yellowing with age. I've been stupid. So, so thick. I yank the empty tub out of his hand, and I'm greeted by the face of a dead girl. God, she was beautiful. And young. They both were. Billy's smile is huge in the old photograph, his arms loose around her slim neck. She's wearing a sparkly pink badge that says *Sweet Sixteen* on it in bubble letters.

Billy was only small when he started hollowing out a section of his mattress – the perfect place to hide his precious things. At first, these things were harmless: small pebbles and oddly shaped leaves. Then when he got older, pictures cut out of magazines and photographs, then condoms, then little pastel-coloured pills. The kind you hear about on the news. The kind that stupid teens take, trying to impress each other. The kind that kill innocent young girls, ones with their whole lives ahead of them.

"There's no need to shout at me." He pouts. "I was just looking."

I rip the photo into little bits and watch as something shatters inside his eyes.

"You shouldn't have this."

He shrugs and I feel like slamming his head into the metal bed frame. He might want to wallow, and it's not like I'm a stranger to that feeling, but it's not just about him. It never has been. What about me? He doesn't even care, he would just leave me alone. *Alone* alone. Selfish, that's the best word to describe Billy. Just simply selfish.

I put the cold medicine on the floor in front of him. He pulls his knees into his chest and looks up at me with those big bug eyes.

"Why was this in the bin?"

"Don't know," he mumbles.

"Billy." I stare him out.

"I don't want you taking that stuff, Clem. Where did you even get it?"

I start to laugh. How many times have I said the exact same words to him, pleaded with him, begged him to tell me where the hell he got the current God-knows-what he's insisting on taking? Probably from some random man in the pub toilets.

"It's not funny, you shouldn't buy *Entirely Natural*."

"I really don't think you're in a position to tell me what I should or should not *take*."

Billy pulls himself onto all fours and carefully stands, very conspicuously making sure not to touch the bottle.

"Clemmie, no, please listen to me. This is different, it's not safe—"

"Ah yes, because ketamine is so safe, isn't it? You want me to start doing tabs of acid with you whenever I have a headache? Is that it? Just snort a line of cocaine to get rid of my period pains?"

"Clemmie, come on, you know I only do that stuff sometimes. Just on nights out. It's fine."

"Sure, Billy, because that's *so* normal. Are we really pretending that's normal?"

"No! I just..." His voice is too loud in the small room. He's standing up now, too close to me, his eyes sad. He grabs my arms. "I need you to promise me,

93

Clem. You never touch it, understand? You never go near *any* of it."

I shrug out of his grasp.

"I—"

There's a noise from downstairs. Singing.

For a second, I think Billy thinks I've said the words, or sung the words, more accurately. But it's not me, it's Kylie.

Neither of us moves. It can't be. It's not possible. I checked the doors before we went to bed, actually pushed a chair underneath the handle of the back door. There's no way. But Kylie keeps singing. I feel Billy's hand take mine. I squeeze.

We head downstairs. I can't tell if it's my palm that's sweaty, or Billy's.

Kylie is still singing about her Santa baby. Always creeped me out, this song.

I check the front door first, still locked. From the inside. The kitchen is empty. The radio stands on the counter again, Kylie finishing up her song. The back door: still locked, and yes, from the inside. The drawer is open. I let go of Billy's hand.

"It's her," Billy whispers. He's doing his puppy dog routine again.

"What? Look, I don't know what's going on here, but if I find out it's you doing this, I *will* kill you."

"How could it have been me? You *saw* me, we were together upstairs."

"So, you just expect me to believe the radio floated out of the drawer, plugged itself in and tuned in to Capital?"

"No, that's not what I'm saying—"

"Well, what are you saying? And don't you dare mention ghosts to me, or I'll kick you out of this house right now."

"Who else could it be? All the doors are locked, there's no one in the house other than us. It's *her*! She's haunting us."

"Billy, the spirit of our dead Mother is not haunting us. And if she was, she wouldn't be using this radio to do it – she always hated this thing."

I stare at the radio sitting innocently on the counter. *How did you get there, huh?*

Billy sounds like he might be hyperventilating. Christ. I can't take much more of this.

"You know, before you got here, nothing *weird* happened. There were no dead animals on my doorstep, nothing moved mysteriously about the house, and I didn't have hand-shaped bruises on my arms."

I roll up the sleeves of my coat to show him the imprint of his own fingers on my skin, from where he grabbed me yesterday.

He stares in horror. His lips tremble. "Clem, I didn't mean... I didn't know."

"I said you could stay a few nights, a *few*, you've been here at least... well, too long, you've—"

"I lost my job."

I rip the plug of the radio from the wall at the same time as the words leave Billy's mouth, so his announcement is met by a thick silence. Then I hear a sigh, a disappointment exactly like hers, leave my own lips and I see the tears fill his eyes. I feel her irritation burn my stomach.

Billy crouches down on the icy tiles, covers his face

with his fingers and begins to sob. His shoulders shake. I stand there, holding the dead radio in my hands. I don't say anything.

Looks like we'll be having a family Christmas after all.

PART THREE

How's living alone going?

Possibly the most obnoxious text I have ever received – that anyone has ever received. In the history of texting. E v e r.

God, I feel like a hormonal teen. Please, Future Me, I beg of you, never go back to the online dating, the apps, the bright pink websites claiming to already know your soulmate, to already have their name and address on file. Along with their bank details. I can't cope with this banal exchange of little black words on a flickering screen. Each word enshrined in the digital stratosphere forever.

Anyway, I'm not alone, Tony. Not right now. I have the apparent ghost of my dead parents haunting their old home, my unemployed little brother and a bunch of drowned rats.

Oh, yes, there's rats in the water tank.

Yes, the water we've been washing in.

Yes, the water we've been drinking.

I actually found the first one inside the pipes under the bathroom sink. It was sad looking, all slimy and pale. No wonder matted fur kept floating up the plughole. The rest of them were bobbing around inside the tank, little bloated lumps of black slime. Actually, some of them were quite big. Apparently, some rats can grow to the size of small dogs – what kind of small dog, though? There's a lot of variation there. I mean, there's a big difference between a Chihuahua and a Border Terrier. At least we know they can't get as big as a Great Dane.

This plastic seat is unnecessarily uncomfortable. People coming to the doctors are already in discomfort, why would you purposely buy something for them to sit on that's so hard? I've been monitoring myself and Billy for symptoms of Weil's disease. The main effects are fever, headaches, nausea, vomiting and loss of appetite. Four out of five. Probably the highest I've ever scored on a test. *Definitely* the highest Billy's ever scored.

I'm not alone, I'm surrounded by lovely nurses x

I hover my finger over the blue arrow of the send button. Press delete instead. The last thing I need is for Tony to come down here. The only thing that could be worse would be if he didn't come. I won't take that chance.

Who knows how Weil's disease could affect an unborn child? Oh, *Weil's disease and pregnancy*, a top hit on Google: *miscarriage, IUFD* (something called intrauterine fetal death – can't be good, it has the word 'death' in it), *stillbirth, maternal death*. I put my phone away.

"Clemmie!"

Billy is waving a piece of paper at me, a huge smile on his face. Dorrie follows him, her shoulders back, head high. She looks fierce, strong next to Billy's childlike joy. I feel a surge of lightness in my chest. Feel myself smile.

"It's okay, we're fine!"

"I told you." Dorrie's eyes glint. She doesn't smile, just looks over her shoulder as the doctor approaches.

"You and your brother do not have Weil's disease. You can rest assured there's nothing wrong with either of you, apart from perhaps a bit of malnutrition." Dr Robertson – he knows us well, our mother was his best patient. Probably kept him in fancy holidays and fast cars with all her imaginary ailments. Oh yes, we go to a private doctors, have done since I was small. We could never pay for proper heating, couldn't get repairs done on the house, but at least my mother could come to this drab surgery every couple of weeks and pay a man with eyes far too big for his head to poke and prod at her perfectly healthy body, prescribe her *rest and relaxation* and collect his big fat cheque at the end of it.

"Nothing wrong? With either of us?"

I move my eyes across to Billy. The good doctor knows about Billy's party habit, the periodic panic attacks, the complete inability to hold down a job. Still won't diagnose him with PTSD though – although I suppose to get a diagnosis like that, you'd have to discuss the T that caused the D, and Billy can't do that.

Dr Robertson nods. "Well, obviously, Clementine, there are some other issues to address, but nothing pertaining to the collection of rats you tell me you found in your water tank. Although, I wouldn't advise drinking any more of that particular water." He chuckles, that annoying *heh heh* that was the soundtrack to my childhood Sundays, waiting for my mother in this very chair.

I became convinced during my teen years that they were having an affair – my mother and Dr Robertson. I was wrong, of course. That wasn't what my mother wanted from men. She didn't want them to desire her, she wanted them to pity her. To paw at her with soft fingertips, but never go beyond the sterile, the professional. Dr Robertson became her version of Billy's drugs. He became an addiction. One she never let go of. If she hadn't been in that car that day, she would still have been right here, right now. Her obsession.

***

Dorrie is driving us home in silence. Her radio doesn't work. She taps at the steering wheel with her too long fingernails, their tips digging into the foam wheel cover. Maybe she's annoyed with me because I haven't accepted the offer of Christmas at her house yet. Well, she needn't be annoyed much longer. Her house has working heating, a maggot-free fridge, and an actual fireplace to hang your stockings. Our house is freezing and infested with vermin – it's not exactly *Sophie's Choice*, is it? Plus, we have zero decorations – Mother's decision, obviously. What was once a spindly plastic tree with a few baubles and a scary fairy became a bare tree and then a snapped-in-half tree and then a nothing.

"I wish you would come to mine for Christmas, love."

Yep. God, I'm good. I can read people like books.

"Well, I was going to talk to you about that actually—"

"That's Clem-speak for 'thank you, Dorrie, we accept.'"

Billy's smiling head appears between the front seats. I give him a look with just my eyes, but he doesn't notice. Or he doesn't care. He's probably already planning a warm night in front of the fire, decorating the tree, sipping mulled wine.

Dorrie alternates between watching the winding lanes ahead of us and my face.

"Yes, as long as you don't mind," I say, if only just to make her concentrate on the road.

"Mind." She smiles, shakes her head. "Sweet girl."

I focus on the hedges whipping past us at high speed, try to steady my breathing. Dorrie drives fast. In. Out. In. Out. In. Out. Now I'm thinking about my breathing it's actually getting faster. Great. My chest aches. Yet another doctor telling me there's nothing wrong with me, in the face of obvious symptoms. I swear I must have a temperature. I fiddle with the car heater, try to turn it down.

"Oh, that hasn't worked for years, darling."

Why is it when you pray for heat it all arrives at once and suffocates you? Sweat stands on my skin, beads trailing along my forehead. My breathing's definitely getting faster. A rush of saliva floods my mouth.

"Pull over."

"What's that, love?"

"Pull over!"

Dorrie comes to a dead stop in the middle of the lane. I scrabble at the door, practically fall into the ditch at the side of the road. I get vomit on my leggings. Damn, I've only had them a couple of months. Then again, they were a please-forgive-me pity gift from Tony, so really they deserve to be covered in bile. And they're coral pink: Nia's favourite. Make of that what you will.

Billy hovers behind me. "You okay?"

The contents of my stomach lie in the ditch – mainly

rat-flavoured water and a couple of slugs of Gus's cold medicine that I took when Billy wasn't looking. Yes, the same cold medicine I took out of the bin, don't judge me, I had a headache. Correction: I *have* a headache. Thanks so much for your valuable assessment, Dr Robertson. Maybe there *was* stuff wrong with Mother all these years and he's just bad at his job. Then again, maybe not.

Now that I think about it, he doesn't have any certificates hung in his office. Doctors usually do, don't they? Little framed bits of pride. Or is that just in films, so we know which characters legitimately have access to drugs?

"Come on, Clem, let's go home."

Sounds like a line from a film. Billy holds his arm out, as though I don't know the way back to the car, guiding me like I'm eighty. I reach for his hand and walk the five, six steps back to the car. Dorrie cups my chin, gentle, turns my head side to side. Then she nods, gives a little hum, and drives the rest of the way home, silent.

***

Billy's packed a suitcase for us – "Just stuff we might need, you know." We're going next door for a few days, Billy, not Antarctica for six weeks. The suitcase is old, red leather. No wheels, just a pair of handles, a long shoulder strap. Dad's, I think – although I don't know why, I never saw him carry it. Maybe it's Mother's. From another life, before she had kids, before she met Dad, when she went places, *travelled*. When she was another woman.

The amount of stuff Billy's brought, you'd think we were never coming back. Dorrie's going to get a shock when he appears at the door with that. He's gone the back way, across our garden, the field next to it and over the fence into Dorrie's garden, so as not to draw attention. I can see him out the kitchen window, ducking and weaving like some kind of tall, thin spy... a tall, thin, *bad* spy. Billy is not a subtle man. He trips over the suitcase's adjustable strap and topples forward into the fence. *Ouch*. I feel a smile tug at my lips. *Idiot*.

I have a sudden flash of memory. A tiny Billy breaking free of the garden, chubby toddler legs out of control as he hurtled straight across the field and *smack* into that very fence. Shock on his little face. He didn't cry, just picked himself back up, waved at Dorrie through the wooden slats. Mother was hysterical. Obviously.

Funny how history repeats itself. I watch Billy wave sheepishly at the shape of Dorrie through the fence. Then he climbs over it and both he and the suitcase disappear from my eye line. He's asked me to look for his book, *The Great Gatsby*. Says he's lost it. How anyone who lives practically in one room can lose anything is beyond me, but that's Billy – loves to go above and beyond, doesn't he? I shake out the blanket, check under the sofa cushions, down the back – nothing but little balls of dust and hair. No book.

I need one of those handheld hoover things – what're they called? Bet they're expensive though. Maybe I can get a knock-off version. Wonder if Greta stocks that kind of thing?

I check everything in the kitchen is turned off. It would be just our luck to spend a lovely Christmas at Dorrie's and then return to find the cottage burned to the ground or flooded, or both. Although I don't know how both would work – wouldn't the two disasters just cancel each other out? Who knows, some freak of nature situation would probably allow it to happen for me. I can see the headlines now: *desperately unlucky woman leaves rat-infested home, returns to discover it engulfed by new phenomenon – the 'fireflood' – exclusive pictures on page nine.* A journalist's dream, that interview. Great scoop.

No book.

I head down to the basement, watch the rows of ripe clementines through the dim light, green leaves swaying. My feet are bare, the floor so cold it burns. I was going to bake a cake as a Christmas present for Dorrie, a coffee one, to make up for the baking session I missed. I haven't had time, of course. I never do. I don't have anything for Billy either, but that's fine because he definitely hasn't got me anything. He never does.

I pick two round clementines, put them in my coat pocket. Their skins are shiny, warm to the touch. A clementine from Clementine. I can put them in their stockings. A traditional present is better than no present at all. At least it's not coal. Although Billy's probably should be.

I look at the plants a moment longer, their colour so vibrant they almost seem to glow. Pick another of the bright orange orbs for myself, for later. Funny, I'm sure I didn't leave those shears here. They sit on top of an old chest of drawers, left at the bottom of the stairs, their blades turned out. Dangerous. I washed them – obviously, I'm not an animal – but here, in the shadows, I feel like I can still see the blood, slick against the sharp metal. I hear the flutter of wings, see those sharp, bright eyes, the little bobbing head. God, I miss him. I get it now, Dad, why you cared so much. They're special, precious, these birds. It must take a special kind of cruel to harm such a majestic, such a sweet thing. A living, breathing creature. A life. Two lives now: the image of that crow's shrivelled body, its melting bones, won't leave my head. My fault again. Whoever has been doing these things must have been watching the house, must know my routine, know I feed them, watch them, need them. It's not Billy they're angry at. It's not Billy that loves the birds, it's *me*.

No, I definitely didn't leave those shears there. I put them in a box for this very reason, because I didn't want to have to think about what they were used for, what they were covered in. I put them in that box, over there, the one that's been opened. If Billy's been in here moving things about, I'm going to have to yell at him again. It's not good for him to be down here on his own. What if he lost his balance in the dark, hit his head against the stone steps, toppled one of the many piles of stuff down on himself? That door sticks as well, what if he got locked in here and panicked before I could get him out? How long would it even take me to realise he was down here?

No book.

Okay, so I've not checked every box, but frankly, Billy, if you put it in one of the endless boxes down here or up in the bedroom, it's lost forever, and you should just forget about it now. Save yourself the heartache. Should have got him another copy for Christmas. Should have pre-empted the loss. Amazed he kept it long enough to lose, to be honest, thought he would have sold it for the cash a long time ago. It's a limited-edition cover, apparently. Didn't realise until after I bought it – never would have got it for him if I'd known. You should never give a limited edition anything to a serial misplacer. Waste of money.

The door at the top of the stairs creaks – must be a breeze blowing through from somewhere. A shiver tiptoes along my spine. I take a last look at my mother's collection of clementines, my namesakes trapped down here, hidden away, safe, and head back up the stairs. I lock the door to the basement behind me, put the key into my pocket. One way to make sure Billy can't get down there.

I half expect the radio to be on the counter when I come back into the kitchen, blaring some awful pop song. But no, it's still tucked in its drawer, fraying cord wrapped around its body.

I slam the door shut, shake my head. Christmas Eve tomorrow, just enough time to convince Dorrie she should let me at least *help* cook the Christmas dinner. It's the least I can do.

***

I knew we should never have opened that second bottle of wine. No one needs to hear my brother's singing. No one should be subjected to that level of pain. And no one should drink so much wine and eat so much food that they find his terrible rendition of *Holly Jolly Christmas* hilariously beautiful. I can't remember the last time I laughed this much. The last time I smiled like this. The last time I was happy. Probably sometime before Nia arrived in my peripheral vision and after I left home for good. Quite a small window, then.

A stick of toffee covered chocolate sticks out the side of Dorrie's mouth like a cigar – one of the gold ones from the obligatory chocolate tin. She says she can't chew them anymore, her teeth aren't up to it. So she sucks them to death instead. Takes her ages to finish just one.

"Just makes them last longer, darling," she says.

My favourites are the bright pink ones – the sugary fudge coats the roof of my mouth, my teeth.

I lie back on the sofa, watch Billy clumsily adjust his blue paper hat in the mirror, nod proudly at his own reflection. Feel my full stomach, heavy and warm. The lack of headache across my skull, the liquid softness of my limbs. This. This is true luxury.

Nothing else matters but this moment. I read that somewhere when I was little. I think it's supposed to be 'life-affirming', one of those inspirational quotes people like Nia love plastering all over Instagram. But it just made me feel terrified, like my whole life I'd missed loads of important moments by not noticing them, not cherishing their apparent importance. This is the first time I've really understood what it means – it's not talking about random moments, each moment of every day, but moments like this one in front of me. Moments of happiness. Moments we'll remember, years later, when mine and Billy's skin looks like Dorrie's and Dorrie's skin is just a memory. I don't have many of these moments left. But now I have this one. My body feels warm.

It doesn't even matter that my presents to the only two people I actually have left in my life – the only two people I actually like (yes, I am admitting Billy is alright sometimes) – were lumps of rotting mould. Billy shrieked when he pulled his clementine out of the stocking, watched with round eyes as it rolled to the corner of the room, trailing gunk like a snail trail. My clementines were no longer round, bright orange, but grey, misshapen. They stank. Dorrie didn't complain, just told me, *It doesn't matter, darling*, and calmly bagged up the rotten blobs, binned them. She said it was nothing to worry about, they must have just been off, the room was too hot, they sweated inside the stockings. But I saw the dark look she gave the bin bag – I saw her put it in the outside bin. I picked them just the other night and when I slipped them into the stockings on Christmas Eve, they were perfect, juicy, fresh. By the time Billy woke us up at eight on Christmas morning, they were dead. Rotten. That's not normal, is it, Mother? Not normal at all. Maybe it's me, maybe I'm hallucinating. Maybe those plants in the basement are all dead. They should be, according to Google. Citrus plants, just like any other plant, need certain conditions to survive:

Light

Heat

Outside air (or at least non-stagnant air)

Plant food / fertiliser

Water

My clementines are in a freezing cold basement with no windows. I can't imagine Greta would stock anything like plant food at the shop. And they haven't been watered since I got here. At least, I haven't watered them. I told Billy he shouldn't go down to the basement, that there was no point denying it, I knew he'd been down there. He just looked at me strangely, slowly shook his head – "I haven't been down there, Clemmie, you know I don't like it down there." Admittedly, already three glasses of wine deep he might have misremembered, or just straight out lied of course, he's good at that as we all know.

But he's right, he doesn't like it down there. He never has. Didn't spend as much time down there as me, didn't have enough experience with those four damp walls to get used to it. Panicked. The splinters worked their way under my fingernails I banged at the door so much, shook the handle, made enough noise that at least he didn't think he was alone down there. So he knew I was there. Never thought I would try so hard to get *in* to the basement until the day she shut him in there. Until I heard him crying. He was four. Dad tried his best, but she wouldn't tell him where the key was. *What can I do, Clemmie? What can we do without the key?* I always thought he disappeared off that day to get his tools, come up with a way to break down the door, crack the lock. But he was gone too long for that. Now I think he probably just couldn't bear those cries. Needed to get away from the house, until she was ready to give him the key, to let her son out. Now, I wonder if he went to the pub. I remember the smell of beer, strong, earthy. I remember telling myself I was wrong, that I must have got mixed up, that he was out looking for a way to help. I remember lying to myself. Guess it runs in the family, hey Dad?

Nothing else matters but this moment. She posted one of those inspirational quotes yesterday – Nia – a new one to add to her ever-growing selection. Yes, okay, I broke my one rule. I never followed the girl on social media, that would have been beyond weird, but she has absolutely no security on any of her accounts. She's basically asking for a stalker. And I know her username – @NiaYogaGuru – bit big-headed. She's an inner-city yoga teacher with a qualification from the internet, not a Tibetan monk. She posts her entire life on there, all laid out for her 2,876 followers to see. Surely she can't know *all* those people. Who knows that many people? Countless posts – literally. I spent about an hour scrolling through pictures of food, yoga, food, Tony's stupid smiling face, yoga, sunsets, yoga, food, all peppered with motivational quotes and an overly heavy use of the prayer hands emoji. I don't even think she's religious, just #blessed by life. That baby's first word is going to be 'hashtag'.

Big journeys begin with small steps. She's written the words in large cursive script over a picture of black and white squiggles. It has 1,672 likes. Already. She only posted it last night. God, people really will like anything these days. I mean, what does that even mean, really? She hasn't even created anything; she's definitely stolen that quote off the internet. People are essentially liking the fact that she can use Google.

The caption says: *Can't wait to see you take your first small steps with those tiny feet and help you begin your big journey into life. #love #family #perfection #baby #mummytobe #scanpicture #complete #bestChristmaspresentever.* So, I guess she *has* created something. Weird, seeing an announcement post, most people have stopped doing those now. And it's not like she just found out, she's had the bump for months now. I stare at the fuzzy squiggles until they become a tiny, curled body, little head, two tiny feet just about visible, kicking up.

Hundreds of comments:

ClarenceLovesYoga:
You'll be the best mummy @NiaYogaGuru!

zac_efrons_wife:
Oh my god oh my god oh my god I cant breatheeee!!!!!! So excited for you angel xxxxxx

tinamina:
yessssss the best news!!! So happy you've told everyone!! xxxxx

NiaYogaGuru:
@tinamina love youuuuu x

lucys-in-warrior-pose:
does this mean you're taking a break from teaching classes?

Darren_1992:
congrats gorgeous x #yummymummy

its_a_mothers_world:
welcome to the world of sleepless nights and leaky boobs girl can't wait to meet your little one xx

NiaYogaGuru:
@its_a_mothers_world she can't wait to meet you lovely! x

fly-high-yoga:
beautiful news may her spirit glow as bright as yours my love

tonybrown18:
make time move quicker haha

NiaYogaGuru:
@tonybrown18 she'll be here before you know it babe x

I never understand why couples comment on each other's photos and then comment on those comments. They're probably sat together on the sofa, both glued to their phones. Why not just speak to each other? Why post these things so other people have to see them? Like me.

There's a few new comments, posted this morning. Some poor souls clearly didn't get the presents they wanted for Christmas:

TomClaythorpe:
@al_bright this is what I was talking about mate

al_bright:
agreed stupid bitch

suzieshoes:
@katyyyyy isn't this your yoga teacher?? Ewwww find another quick hahaha

Stand_against_overpopulation:
@nomorebabies @stop-the-madness another one – disgusting behaviour @NiaYogaGuru do you not care people are dying and suffering so you can pop a baby out your selfish vagina?????? #stopoverpopulation #antibirth #selfishparents

She really needs to think about upping her privacy settings. This isn't just harmless yoga shots anymore. Why isn't Tony telling her? Should I tell her? No. Again, that would be weird.

Nothing matters but this moment. I look up and the moment has passed. Dorrie nods on the chair next to me, her sticky toffee cigar has dropped from her mouth onto her cardigan. Soft snores come from Billy's throat, his head pillowed on the sofa next to my waist. I reach out, stroke his hair. It's tangled, straw-like – he needs to start using conditioner. The moment is over, and I forgot to live it. Nothing was more important – and I forgot.

***

It's early when we hear the car. We'd all woken when it was still dark so decided to go for a walk across the fields – like fugitives, hiding in the shadows. I can hear the movie-style voiceover now. Long walks in the cold can actually be enjoyable when you know you can head back to a nice, warm house, a fire, a home-cooked meal that doesn't smell like rotting flesh. When you know the water you're drinking hasn't had rats swimming around in it – or at least, not recently.

Boxing Day is always a weird time. All the festivities are over, and no one really knows what to do until the anti-climax of New Year hits. Always a dodgy time of year for Billy – way too much binge drinking and casual drug use at New Year's parties. Particularly the ones he goes to. I'll be keeping him with me this year, just until January rolls around, then he can start looking for a new job. Or maybe I can convince him to beg for his old one back, give him a second chance. I watch him smile at Dorrie through his hangover as she hands us both cups of steaming tea. He found paracetamol under Dorrie's sink this morning, knocked back double the dose, claimed he had a headache. *It's fine, Clemmie. They always build in contingency with these things.* I just looked at him until he said, *I don't have a problem, calm down*, and walked away from me. I didn't argue because I didn't want to be a hypocrite – I wash three of the pills down with my tea. Baby steps. We'll do baby steps.

A Muppet's Christmas Carol is on BBC One. I let the brightly coloured nonsense wash over me, allow Dorrie to bustle around us, handing us biscuits, lightly charred pieces of toast. I've given up trying to help – she won't let anyone else into her kitchen. "Don't you be taking my one skill away from me now, darling. Cooking's all I have left!"

Billy grins at the puppets bouncing around on the screen, folds his legs underneath him, criss-cross. The tea is hot on my tongue, sweet – Dorrie puts sugar in everything. It's good for you apparently. I don't know if it's specifically my sugar intake, but I do feel better. Just in general. Ignore the hangover and I'm pretty sure I wouldn't even have this headache. Just shows what an effect lack of heat has on our bodies. Even Billy's cheeks have colour in them.

"Now, who's that?" Dorrie peers out of the window.

Ah, yes, the car. The movie voiceover sounds inside my head: "I've got a bad feeling about this." I get up, move to stand behind Dorrie. The heat from my mug of tea prickles at the skin of my fingers as I watch the car's headlights flash, locked. It's blue, sleek, low to the ground.

Tony.

Again? Did he not get the message last time? I mean, yes, we slept together. But it wasn't like that. Was it? Did I even want it to be?

Nia's scan picture flashes into my head. The fuzzy squiggles. The long-legged man striding towards the front door of the cottage helped make those squiggles, they're part of him, they *are* him. They are not me. I will never have any squiggles of my own. I will not take Nia's squiggles away from her. He shouldn't be here. He's *needed* now, responsible. Those squiggles will need him far more than I ever did. Far more than Nia ever will. How does he not know that?

I watch as he knocks at the cottage door, imagine the sound, loud inside the hollow rooms. No one in, Tony.

Dorrie looks at me, one eyebrow raised. She cocks her head to one side, that bird-like movement again, sharp eyes dance. "This is the one?"

"Yeah, I never got it either," Billy says, appearing behind us, the Muppets forgotten. His mouth is full of biscuit.

Tony checks his Rolex, looks up, around. Shivers in his three-piece suit. Shiny grey. New.

"A real fancy man, hmm?"

Under their disapproval, Tony's expensive clothes, fast car, designer jewellery no longer seem suave, sophisticated. They make him look like he's playing dress-up. And he is, to some extent. He's just a secondary school teacher, not even a very good one. He earns a normal wage, probably actually below the average. His main aspiration is to become the headmaster. A respectable job, yes, but not

115

one that requires a wardrobe of swanky suits and overly gelled hair. To look at him, you'd think he was some kind of high-flying lawyer. Or a spy. That he spends his days laughing in the face of danger, escaping death by a millimetre, not correcting the spelling of 'necessary', and confiscating chewing gum and vapes.

We continue to watch as he peers through windows, disappears behind the cottage, reappears at the other side of it. He even looks under the plant pots on the doorstep, presumably for a key. He bangs a fist against the door again, his own annoyance setting him off-balance, so he wobbles on the uneven crazy-paved path. It's Billy who starts to laugh first, until we're all giggling helplessly at this smartly dressed man tripping over his own feet, flummoxed by the first door which hasn't simply swung open to him at his command. When he slips on the frosted grass and ends up with mud up his sleeve, I think I might pass out I'm laughing so hard.

"His *face*," Billy gasps.

Dorrie actually slaps her knee, like someone from panto.

"Duck!" I shout as Tony turns our way, starts to march towards the house. We all three crouch down on the floor, our backs against the wall, shushing each other like naughty children. There's a *knock, knock… knock* on the door and we smother our giggles behind hands. Billy's tea sloshes onto the carpet, joining a host of biscuit crumbs. We watch the joy in each other's eyes.

There's a silence, then, *blinggg, blinggg, blinggg*. My phone lights up, buzzes itself off the table to bounce onto the floor in front of us.

"Shh, shhhh, shhhhhh!" I flap my hands, try to squash our laughter. Billy's eyes water with the effort.

I clear my throat. Calm, professional, breathe. "Hello, Clem speaking."

"Clemmie?" His voice is still deep, still familiar, but something about it is different. Lacking. It doesn't make me nervous anymore, doesn't make me shiver and it's only now that I realise maybe that fizz of excitement wasn't excitement. Maybe it wasn't a nice feeling at all. Maybe it was just a constant buzz of worry – worry that I wouldn't measure up, that I would say something wrong, something stupid. That I wasn't good enough. Good enough for a completely normal, average man with a big watch.

"Who is this, sorry?" I wink at Billy; he dissolves into more giggles. Dorrie grins at me – *that's my girl*.

"Clem? Can you hear me? Hello?" The confusion in his voice, the annoyance – he sounds like a child. A whiny one. Hmmm, this trait seems to be a trend with the men in my life. I watch Billy peep over the lip of the windowsill, duck back, peep over.

"Tony?"

The shock, the surprise, wow, Tony, really? Calling little old me? To what do I owe this utter privilege? God, I should have been an actor.

"Yes, what? Who else would it be?"

Of course – because who else would possibly want to call me? My life is entirely empty without you, Tony, obviously. He never did understand sarcasm.

"Listen, where are you?"

"Where am I?"

"Yessss, Clemmm, *where are you?*"

117

Surely a man about to have a baby should be reserving this kind of emotion for the mother of said child. I thought us being broken up meant I wouldn't have to deal with this kind of thing anymore.

"Why?"

"What do you mean *why*? *Where the hell are you*?"

I place my finger against my lips, smile at my brother, go to the front door.

"Look, I know you're not in the cottage, because I'm here, okay? I came round, Clem, because I couldn't bear to think of you all alone at Christmas. Sat amongst your dad's things."

I walk outside, down Dorrie's garden path, my socks soaking up the light frost on the ground. Chill air sweeps across my skin, plays with my hair.

"You need to move on, Clemmie. You can't just wallow for the rest of your life."

"Who says I'm alone?"

"Look, Nia agreed – very graciously I might add – that I should come down here, spend Boxing Day at least with you."

I come to stand directly behind him. If I turn I can see Billy and Dorrie in the window, practically glued to the glass.

"And now I get all the way here and you don't even answer the door. Why is the house in darkness?"

I tap him on the shoulder. He makes a high-pitched *squeak* noise, jumps into the air, whirls around, eyes wild and breath hitching.

"Because I'm not in the house," I say.

"What are you *doing*?"

"Talking on the phone to you." I smile.

Tony just stares at me. He's furious. Amazing. This is an even better reaction than I could have hoped for. What the hell did he think was happening? Maybe this village has a reputation for a mad-axe, shoulder-tapping murderer that I don't know about. I sneak a look at my audience in the window – yep, they're loving this. Almost as much as I am. This is what it must feel like to have the upper hand over Tony Brown. Feels good.

"You should really have called before you drove all the way here, you know. I can't spend time with you right now – I have plans."

His face scrunches up, skin wrinkling. So, *this* is his confused face. Genuinely quite ugly. And I'm not just saying that. Honestly. It's like I can hear a crowd cheering in the background.

He splutters, makes a few unidentifiable noises. Then he looks up, catches sight of the window. His mouth drops open.

"*Billy's here?*"

There's something dark inside his tone. I've always regretted telling him what happened, but now more than ever. The inside of my stomach goes suddenly hollow, like the bottom has dropped out of it. He turns to me. And he smiles. We're back to the usual script – he's back on top. Equilibrium restored.

"Who's the old woman?"

I turn away, start to walk back towards the house.

"Hey, I'm trying to talk to you." He grabs my arm, pulls me back. Great, that's going to bruise. He knows I bruise easily. He's never yanked me like this before. I've never walked away from him before.

"I'm busy. I have to go."

"Do people know he's here? Does *Gus* know?"

I'm surprised he remembers the name, really. It was a long time ago that I told him. A weak moment on a long night after a strong drink. We'd been out for dinner. Somewhere fancy, I don't remember what it was called now. It doesn't matter really. What matters is that I got tipsy – okay, drunk – and I split my heart open and spilt the dark, hidden parts of it all over Tony's crushed velvet sofa. I thought it would be fine, convinced myself it could never come back to haunt me, to haunt any of us. Because why would Tony hurt me? He loved me. Because he would never leave me. Because we would be together forever. What's mine was his and what worried me, hurt me, he would share. He would help me with. He would take as part of himself.

Idiot.

Tony shows me his teeth. He knows they don't know. That no one knows Billy is here. And he knows no one *can* know. And I can see it in his eyes – that he's going to tell them.

"Of course not," he says. He nods, looks around, as though random villagers are going to jump out from behind the bushes like we're in a musical. Don't think I'm really Dorothy material. I don't have a Toto and Gus is way too tall to be a Munchkin. I suppose Mother could have been the Wicked Witch of the West. Crushed under a Honda Civic rather than a house. A modern twist on the tale.

"Everything alright, darling?" Dorrie appears at the door. "Ah, you must be the famous Tony. Why don't you come in for a cuppa, my love?"

Good plan, Dorrie. We poison him – arsenic in the tea. Chop his body up in the bath. Bury him in bits in the fields behind the house. Starting to think Nia and her lump of fuzzy grey cells would be far better off without him. We'd be doing the world a favour really.

"Finally, some hospitality." Tony smirks, stalks into the cottage.

I look across the street, peer at Gus's house in the distance. There's no movement. No curtains twitching. With any luck the old man will have died over Christmas and Gus will be too distracted getting the smell of death out of the bed sheets to notice the Audi in our driveway.

Inside I realise how cold I am. My feet have gone numb, the sudden warmth making my skin prickle and shiver. Dorrie drapes a blanket over my shoulders, ushers me into the front room.

Tony is peering with disdain at everything: the sagging sofa, the old-fashioned TV, the stained tea mugs. Billy. The room looks different with him in it. Less cosy, more… drab? What is wrong with me? Five minutes ago, I couldn't remember why I ever liked him, an overgrown child slipping on ice. But now – now *I* feel like the child. Back into my old role. Now he's invaded my safe space again, we're back to our old ways. A cliché yet again, Clem, finding the arrogant posh boy attractive.

Tony clears his throat, perches on the very edge of the sofa. "So, Billy… you're back for Christmas? That's nice of you, supporting your sister."

He makes it sound anything but nice, he makes it sound ridiculous, pointless, stupid. Billy hides behind his tea mug, just a pair of wary eyes. Guess Tony has the same effect on my brother as he does on me. I mean the shy, worthless feeling, not the attraction buzz. I assume. Then again, the amount of secrets Billy keeps, who knows. Actually, he hasn't had a girlfriend since…

"Here we are!" Dorrie bustles in, a new pot of tea and a selection of biscuits perched on a tray. Tony picks at the offering. He flicks his eyes up at me – *really, babe? A long way from afternoon tea at Harrods, isn't it?* Oh yes, Tony, because taking your adult fiancée to a child's toy department for a birthday treat to eat tiny sandwiches and miniature pink cakes is what every woman dreams of. Worst twenty-fifth birthday present ever. And that's coming from someone whose parents got her a handheld blender and a brother who got her nothing.

"So, to what do we owe this pleasure?" Dorrie sits down directly across from Tony, sharp eye contact.

Tony takes a sip of his tea, makes a facial expression best described as a grimace, and replaces the mug on the tea tray.

"Well, I didn't realise Clemmie had company – she never said anything." He looks up at me, still standing in the doorway, blanket round my shoulders like a cloak, like I should have been updating him about my life. Because everyone checks in with their ex. "Didn't want her all alone at Christmas so thought I'd pop down, you know."

Just a four-and-a-half-hour drive, just *pop* down.

"You can't stay."

Everyone turns to look at me.

"I didn't say I wanted to…" He says it like I'm the one presuming, makes it seem like I want him to stay, like I'm the homewrecker. I feel sick. Everyone keeps looking at me. Silence.

"Oh, I forgot!" He bounces up, marches back out the front door. I see him walk across the street, over to Gus's front door, knock, point, tell him. Billy is here, right there, just across the street. Clemmie is harbouring a fugitive. Gus storms over, takes my brother by the throat, slams his skinny body into the wall, reaches a huge hand out, pulls Billy's guts out and splatters them across the walls. I blink. Tony is back in the room, a large green box in his arms, Gus's door still closed, never opened.

"For you." He hands me the box. It's awkward to hold, heavy. Billy's eyes are glued to it, his breathing sounds loud in the small space. I can smell his sweat.

"Need the toilet." He scrambles up, practically runs out of the room. Tony watches him as he leaves, a look in his eyes, a knowing. No, Tony, that's not where he's going – he was fine before you arrived, this is your fault – no other reason. Besides, there's no drugs in this house. He doesn't have any with him. I know because I checked. Anyway, he doesn't have a problem, Tony. So shut up.

"Here, love." Dorrie moves some cushions, taps the sofa. I place the box down beside her.

"Aren't you going to open it?" Tony asks me.

"No."

"Sorry?"

Ha, that's thrown him.

"No."

He stares. Dorrie is gazing at the tea tray, as though it's the best thing she's ever seen.

"Why would you bring me a present?"

"Well, I don't know if you've noticed, but it is Christmas." He gestures around him, at the decorations, the empty chocolate tin, the christmassy Muppets still bouncing around on the TV screen. "Come on, little birdbrain." He laughs.

"But we're not together anymore." The words sound hollow inside my head. Echoing. Make my stomach twist.

"So, I'm guessing I shouldn't be expecting a gift from you, then?"

Why is he smiling like that? Like his destruction of my life is some big joke? I really, really, really want to slap him across the face. I seriously consider it.

Bang.

All three of us jump.

Billy.

I've never seen Dorrie move so fast. She's only one step behind me.

I burst through the bathroom door. Thank God, he didn't lock it. Billy is on the floor, hands over his ears. His whole body shakes like a scared puppy. Dorrie's bottles of perfume and pots of cream are strewn across the floor, spilled from the shelf over the sink. One of the spray bottles has broken, the extreme smell of rose making my eyes sting.

"Sorry, sorry, sorry." Billy looks like he's going to be sick. Tears trail down his neck. Dorrie doesn't say anything, just sweeps the broken glass carefully to one side and sits down on the floor next to him. She holds his shoulders firm until the tears slow, until his breathing calms. I kneel in front of him. Touch his knee.

"It wasn't on purpose." He gazes up at me, big eyes

round. It's the look he used to give *her*. No. *Please don't give me that look.* Does he think I'm going to scream at him? Tell him off? Does he think of me as *her*?

"We know, sweetheart." Dorrie smiles. "It's just a panic attack."

I nod. I should have been the one to say it. Why am I not saying anything? Why don't I know what to say?

"God, it stinks in here."

Of course he's still here.

"Get out."

"Sorry?" He laughs – he never takes me seriously.

I put my hand in the centre of Tony's chest, push him out of the room, down the corridor, out the still open front door. Of course he left it open, of course he did.

"So, I come all this way, bring you a gift, and you throw me out of your house? Sorry, not even your own house – you throw me out of an old woman's house."

"I didn't ask you here, Tony."

"You didn't have to."

My stomach hurts. Those fizzy squiggles fill my head again.

"Come on, Clem, you can't really be happy here. Back of beyond, hanging out with an old crone and a psycho in there."

God, I want to hit him, slam his face into the wall. I settle for slamming the door instead. But his foot keeps it open.

"Just because he's your brother doesn't mean you have to be so loyal. You're not a dog." He smirks. "I mean, is he really worth all this? If I was you, I'd leave him alone with a stash of paracetamol and a bottle of vodka. Wouldn't take long."

Surprising how much blood one nose can produce.

Especially when it's introduced to the edge of a very solid door. Is he actually crying? Well, it is a shame about his suit, blood *is* notoriously difficult to get out.

"Here's what's going to happen: you're going to get back into your car, drive back to the city, go back to the life you chose when you slept with a twenty-year-old and got her pregnant. You're going to look after her and her baby and you're going to forget you ever came here. You're going to forget you ever saw Billy and you're not going to say anything to anybody. Or I'll tell Nia how you really got that bloody nose."

Because Nia never agreed you could come here, Tony, that much is obvious. The poor girl is sat at home. Waiting. Just like I used to.

"You're insane."

"Sorry, what was that? It's difficult to hear you through all the…" I gesture at the mess that is his face.

"You've broken my nose!"

"Oh, stop being so dramatic, Tony."

"This is assault! You've *assaulted* me!"

"You stay away from my brother."

I slam the door, this time just *near* his face. Wait until I hear his car engine start up, listen to him speed off down the street, check the door for blood, sponge it off with some damp kitchen roll. Can't have him marking Dorrie's lovely paintwork now, can we?

***

Quick check of Instagram. Recently discovered you can sneak a peek at someone's story by sliding the previous person's story along, rather than clicking on their little profile bubble. Not a good discovery. Now I can look at her story without fear of her realising I'm stalking her. Am I stalking her? Probably. Whatever it is I'm doing, it's weird. Alright, I'm not hiding behind the nearest lamppost wearing a trench coat and a baseball cap but it's the digital equivalent really, isn't it? And how would she know CityGirl457 is the woman whose life her womb destroyed? Yes, the username was chosen when I lived my other life. Should probably change that now. CrowGirl59. Already taken? Huh, did not expect that.

An image of her hands cradling her bump – a window and skyline of the city in the background. *Waiting for Daddy to come home...* love heart emoji, baby emoji, family emoji. Knew it.

I log out of the app. Can't remember my password, so maybe that will stop me from looking at it so much. It's a pointless activity – I know full well I can just hit the 'forgot password' button, change my password, log back in.

I lock my phone, put it down on the coffee table, sit on the sofa. It sags under my weight. Billy's still crying somewhere in the background. Dorrie's comforting murmur floats through the air. He'll be okay. He'll be fine. We're safe here, hidden. No one knows. Tony won't say anything. He wouldn't dare. He doesn't know what I'd break next.

I unlock my phone.

BirdsAreBetterThanPeople

New password cannot be the same as old password.

Typical.

***

Tony's gift is in the bin. The outside bin. I didn't put it there. Don't get me wrong, I don't care. Why would I want a pity gift anyway? Always think it's offensive when people buy you perfume, hair products, health products, like they're dropping you a not-too-subtle hint that you smell, need to wash more, need to lose weight. And who in the world would want to drink matcha tea, in a bath of rose petals, surrounded by the scent of sandalwood and peony? Nia, probably. I should have realised really. The box had small white letters printed on the side: *Entirely Natural.* Billy's tears are obvious now. Trust Tony to remind him of the fact he's jobless and, without me, homeless, prospectless.

I knew the moment was too good to last.

"Out like a light." Dorrie closes the kitchen door softly, comes to sit opposite me at the table. The wooden surface has lines scored into it. I remember making them when I was little, digging my nail into the tabletop, *scratch, scratch, scratch.* I look at her face, feel like I should apologise.

"He'll be alright, love. He'll come around to it."

"I don't want him to come around to it, Dor. He can't stay here with me forever."

She cocks her head at me, places another steaming cup of tea in front of me. I've never had so much tea in my life. My teeth are going to be stained as brown as Dorrie's are soon.

"He'll have to find another job. My savings won't stretch to us both living here… *I'm* going to have to get another job."

Dorrie's brows drop in confusion. "They're not paying you enough, darling? Why didn't you say? Just tell them you need more."

I smile. "It doesn't quite work like that. They replaced me with one of those predictive text writer things – they don't need copywriters anymore."

Alright, Mother, you win. My English Literature degree really was pointless. Congratulations.

Dorrie shakes her head. "Replaced?"

"Yeah, the office is going ninety-nine percent digital apparently."

"The office?"

I can hear Dad's voice in my head – "Is there an echo in here?" Please, Dorrie, don't lose your mind yet – I can't cope with Billy without your help. I'm not as good with him as you are, you know that. Don't leave me.

"Yes, my office. In the city? Well, not my office anymore."

"Oh." Dorrie scratches at her neck, swallows. "Well, if you need money, I can give you some."

"No, no, I can't take your money—"

"Oh, please don't do that thing where people get funny about accepting money. I'm not doing anything with it, darling. It's just sitting there. You might as well use it... get Billy some proper help?"

"Dorrie, I'm not using your money to send Billy to yet another digital-detox yoga retreat. It's pointless. It doesn't work. Clearly. He's already been on at least three. That I know of. Look how they turned out."

She sips her tea. I don't know how she drinks it so hot. I have to let mine sit for at least five minutes.

"No, you should spend it on yourself. Spend it on something nice. What have you always wanted to do?"

"I can't use this money for that. It needs to be used for something good, something better."

I've made her upset. Why do I always do this? I can never just have a nice, normal conversation; someone always ends up in tears when I'm around.

Dorrie moves to the cupboard above the sink, rummages around behind the coffee mugs. Takes out a crisp, white envelope. Hands it to me.

"Please, take it. I want you and Billy to have it. You have more entitlement to it than anyone else."

I open the envelope. A slim contactless payment card sits inside, *£10,000* printed in small numbers in the bottom right-hand corner. I open my mouth.

"No, don't say anything. You need money, I have money. Problem solved."

She stands, takes both mugs of tea, pours the liquid down the sink, starts to wash them.

I stare at the card. The envelope feels damp in my hands, sweaty. I listen as Dorrie cleans, dries, puts away the mugs. Boils the kettle. Fetches two new mugs, re-pours the tea. Places one in front of me. Touches my hands, closes my fingers around the envelope. Why the hell does my old babysitter have £10,000 sitting in her cupboard? Do they even have contactless payment in the village?

"That boy needs tea." She picks up the other mug, bustles off with it. I thought he was meant to be asleep.

The envelope feels hot in my hands. I put it down on the table. Stroke its surface with my fingertips. There's a tiny, embossed bump in the bottom right corner, spiralling tendrils. A little tree. Grey lettering, practically invisible against the bright, white paper. Cursive font. *Entirely Natural*. The beginnings of a headache prickle at the edges of my skull. I think of the box in the bin outside, Tony's smile as he presented it to me, the fear on Billy's face, his tears, Dorrie's eyes avoiding mine, the medicine in Gus's hallway – *It's my father's* –, the bottle of cold medicine, thrown away half-full. *I lost my job.* The branded freezer in Greta's shop, rows and rows and rows of unopened drinks, unwanted products. The other shelves bare, empty. *Just tell them you need more.* Dead birds on my doorstep. *It's Dad... I don't think they know he's dead.* The £10,000, too much money, money Dorrie doesn't want to use, on the table in front of me. *You have more entitlement to it than anyone else.* Rats in our water tank.

I feel sick. I put my forehead down on the table, let the wooden edge dig into my skin, press down until it hurts, until my mind stops shouting at me, goes blank. I sit back up, sip my tea. Too hot. My tongue burns. I stare at the envelope, at the curved letters, the tiny, little tree. I pick it up, put it back behind the coffee mugs, in the cupboard over the sink.

***

They say a space does feel different when you've been away for a while. The air unused and foreign, the rooms empty, dull. The memory of last being there far away, only half-accessible. But this is another level. Although, I suppose, most people don't return from their holidays to a host of dead crows on their kitchen counters. The smell alone is enough to make me want to burn the cottage to the ground. There's blood on Mother's tiles, deep in the grouting. If she wasn't already buried, she'd drop down dead. It would be my fault, obviously. Feathers in the fruit bowl. All the fruit has turned rotten, more maggots in the apples. Where do they come from? How do they get in? Surely, they weren't already living in the bird's eyes before they died? Because from the mess in the rest of the house, it looks like the birds were alive when they first came into the cottage. At least that's how I explain the bird mess in my bed to myself. The slick, black feathers stuck to the light fixtures. The muddy imprints of bird feet on the carpets, walls, sofa.

They must have come in through the letterbox. It's the only entrance that wasn't locked. All the windows shut, all the doors locked. I know because I had to go round and unlock them all to get at least some of the smell out.

They must have had a small crow conference before they began to die, one by one, to ensure they laid themselves to rest in smaller and smaller circles. Dad's radio sits at the centre of the death spiral – the fraying cord wrapped closely around the largest crow's neck, making its little marble eyes bulge. I wonder how it managed to do that with its wings. Same way they managed to unlock the basement door, I guess. Because I know I locked that door before I left, just like I locked all the others. I know I kept the key with me. It's been in my coat pocket the whole time. Crafty crows – maybe they plucked each other's feathers, used the end of the quill to pick the lock.

I wish Dorrie would stop looking at me like that. Okay, my explanation isn't the most likely, I'll freely admit that, but at least it's more believable than Billy's insane Ghost Parents theory. I would believe in super-intelligent spy crows before I believe in the angry spirits of our dead parents using their afterlife to terrorise their only children. Although now I think it through, that does sound like something Mother would excel at. But she would never want her kitchen in that state, no payoff would be worth that. Even my tears.

"Clem!"

I've just got the last of the bird mess out of the hall carpet, Billy, please don't tell me you've found more. I've run out of anti-bac spray and no, Dorrie, I'm not using the bleach you brought. I'm not replacing the current horrific smell with another one. What would be the point of that? She's insisted on cleaning the bathroom. She better not have used anything other than soap and water like I showed her. I'll be able to smell it if you've used anything stronger, Dorrie.

"Clem!" Billy's voice echoes up the stairs.

"I've told you not to come down here."

The basement looks like it might be more of a tip than before. But really, who can tell? There's no evidence any of the birds got trapped down here, though. Thank God. At least none of the poor creatures died alone and cold in the darkness. At least they all died together, en masse. At least it was a shared experience. They're very social animals, crows.

Billy is standing as far away from the clementine trees as possible, his body practically moulded to the far wall.

He points at the stack of boxes at the bottom of the stairs. They're not in a stack anymore, their contents are strewn across the floor in a mess of:

Odds

Ends

Things

Bits

Bobs

And various other unidentified pointless items.

The shears still sit on top of the chest of drawers, blades pointing out. Really need to move those. I didn't hear Billy drop these boxes. I look at his face, his eyes. Don't say it, Clem, he's trying to help. He's trying his best.

"What did I say? Don't do anything, don't touch anything. Your only instruction was to sit on the sofa and not move. How hard is that?"

"It wasn't me, Clem."

Of course it wasn't.

"What's going on?" Dorrie's steps are unsteady on the uneven stairs. I see her slip, flail down the stairs, body soft like a ragdoll, head split open like a ripe fruit on the cold flagstones. I blink and she's halfway down the steps, concern on her face.

"Dorrie, no, go back up. Neither of you should be down here, it's not safe."

"Clem, you're not listening."

"I may be old but I'm not an invalid, love."

I try to usher her back up into the hallway, Billy's fingers pulling at my sleeve. A cold breeze blows through the basement, fluttering the leaves of the clementine trees, the orange orbs bobbing. Dorrie shivers. She needs a shawl round her shoulders. How have I ended up looking after an old woman and a small child?

"Clemmie!"

"Gosh, there's a lot of stuff down here, isn't there?"

Yes, thank you, Dorrie, we do all have eyes.

"Are they your mother's clementines? Her research?"

"We really all need to go back upstairs, these stairs are uneven. The boxes are fragile, they could fall."

"Looks like they already have, love."

"That was Billy."

"Clem! Listen!"

A scream builds inside my throat. God, I need them both to leave. I need everyone to leave, even Dad's ghost if it really is down here somewhere.

"What!"

It's not a question. I don't think I've ever actually bared my teeth at anyone before, like a rabid dog. Maybe Tony. Yeah, probably Tony. Billy bares his teeth right back and I get another glimpse of that man I don't know, the one who left bruises on my upper arms. I feel rather than see Dorrie's head cock to one side.

"Look!"

Billy points to the far wall, past the clementines, past the red curtain and the piles of science things, the stacks of notebooks. To the bare stone wall. Only it's not a bare stone wall. Not anymore. I guess it never has been. Did I never see it, as a child? All the hours I spent down here. The hours of boredom. Narnia. There never was a wardrobe, was there, Dad? But I guess she kept it locked then. I don't think it's locked now, though.

A large, wooden door is set into the far wall. Boxes have

been moved aside, creating a walkway, a space large enough for someone to walk through. The door is stiff, but with a bit of a push it swings open. A small space, big enough for someone my height to stand up comfortably, the sloping ceiling brushing the top of Billy's head. Another door. What is this, a bad game show? *What's behind door number two?*

Dorrie's brows are so scrunched together her forehead looks crumpled, puckered. Billy's hands shake – *I don't have a problem, Clemmie.* The door's lock is rusted, old. It's also broken. I reach for the handle. We all three look at each other. I feel like we're on one of those ghost adventure shows, from American telly, like one of us should be filming this.

My breath goes funny, the cold air hurting my lungs.

I turn the handle.

We're outside.

There's a door in the basement that leads to another door that leads to a set of stairs that lead to the garden. Round the back of the water tank. We have to shimmy alongside the tank, move sideways, to get into the garden. It's a tight squeeze, but it is possible. Yes, Billy, even more possible if you're a ghost, more than more possible if you're a spy crow. But more *likely* if you're a live human. Far more likely. And, if you are alive and human, it's much easier to come through the unlocked basement door and plug in an old radio, switch it on, than to spirit yourself through a locked front door, or even a locked back door. I would imagine it's also much easier to catch a few birds and carry them through the basement into the house if you're not a ghost. *Much* easier.

"Billy, was the basement door unlocked?"

"I – I don't remember."

Of course, pointless question. I head back inside, through the first door, the second door, up the stairs. I know I locked this door when I left, I *know* I did. I remember it clearly. But I remember the fact that it was a working lock even more clearly. How could I forget, Mother? Now the handle hangs down, the metal pin inside broken. Whoever heard of a ghost who needed to break locks?

***

NiaYogaGuru:
Luckiest girl in the world. Can't believe I found the sweetest man on the planet and that he wants to be mine!!! #family #couplegoals #love #future #happiness. Red love heart emoji, family emoji, engagement ring emoji.

ClarenceLovesYoga:
amazing news!! Such a cute little family xxxx

Darren_1992:
Worst. News. Ever. Im totally kidding babe thats amazing congrats beautiful no wonder he wants to put a ring on your finger xxx

stop-the-madness:
you are the reason people are dying in the streets – you're a disgusting drain on resources #stopoverpopulation #selfish parents

HannahBannanah:
ANGEL! This is the best news I've heard all year.

Congratulations sweetheart. Here's to your happy ever after xxxxxxxxx

fly-high-yoga:
im so happy you found the person who makes your soul smile

Abbi123:
beautiful news beautiful couple beautiful life x

tinamina:
ahhhhh so happy I don't have to keep this beautiful secret anymore!!! Expecting my wedding invite in the post ;) x

Nia YogaGuru:
@tinamina it's already on its way hunny haha xx

jojo_12:
women like you make me want to be sick you'd think no one had ever heard of feminism you're oppressed babe WAKE UP

matt22:
congratulations to the nicest girl in the world @tonybrown18 you better treat her right or you'll have me on your back ;)

nomorebabies:
can't believe you're still posting things like this – you should be so ashamed you're literally killing people you pregnant bitch #stopoverpopulation #disgusting

ginawilliamson:
gorgeous ring!!! Xxx

SpiritualAlice:

that baby is the lucky one having you 2 for parents! Don't listen to the hate comments lovely – you are amazing x

TheBridalShop:

Great news! We love to help out a new bride – let us know when you're ready to look for your perfect dress #weddingdress #visioninwhite

aDaM:

awwwww love this! xx

The photo shows her hand, clasped in his. The ring she's wearing is mine. Was mine.

Yes, I checked. No, it's not in your jewellery box anymore, Mother. I wonder how he knew I'd put it in there? I wonder when he took it – before he had sex with me, or after?

***

Dad's toolbox has a hammer, a screwdriver, some nails and screws. Hoping Greta will have the rest of the bits I need. Shoved a chair under the broken lock for now. Sent Billy back to Dorrie's. Keep him safe. I'm having another key made for the creepy, mystery door. A new lock. I've also replaced the light bulb down there. Makes it seem less eerie. And it means we don't have to walk around with torches all the time. I added it to my list after I fixed it. Just so I could cross it off. Cross something off. Make myself feel better.

The car has gone to sleep over Christmas. Takes me a couple of tries to get it started. I need to concentrate when driving. It's something I always forget to do. Sounds insane, but sometimes I worry the police will arrive at my door, my car caught on camera smashing into a wall, an animal, a person. And I would have no memory of it. I seem to blank out when I drive, just go through the motions. Same as when other people can't remember if they've locked the door, turned their hair straighteners off, turned off the stove. When they can't remember if they've plugged in an old radio, turned it on, left it blaring Radio One. That last one's quite specific.

I bet if I told a therapist I sometimes drive the same route multiple times in one night just to make sure I haven't killed anyone, they would link it back to my parents' deaths. It would be fun to tell them, just to see their face fall when I ruined their beautiful theory. I've been doing this long before my parents' car ended up flying the wrong way down a busy motorway. A long time. Since the first time someone died.

And here I am. Outside Greta's shop. Can't remember the drive here, yet again. I'll have to check carefully for death and destruction on the way back. I can already see there's no one standing behind the counter. Maybe Greta's been abducted by aliens, or kidnapped by gangsters, maybe the shop is a front for a drug smuggling ring. Stranger things have happened. To me. Literally yesterday.

My purse feels light as I take it out of my bag. Yep, only £20 left. And I took that from Billy's wallet. It's not good for him to have access to cash. I'm doing him a favour really – and he eats the food I buy, too. I'll have to drive out of the countryside to find a cashpoint. The idea makes my throat close up. I cough, grasp at the air. Must be allergic to anything busier than a small village now. Or probably just anything that reminds me of Tony.

The bell as I head through the door sounds the same. The strip lighting is the same. The peeling paint on the walls the exact same. The shelves are the same. It's the things on the shelves that are different. Thank God Billy didn't come with me.

Rows and rows and rows of identical green and white boxes, bottles, baskets. Filled with perfectly ripe fruit, perfectly portioned meals, perfectly smooth smoothies. Overly bright, glittery, glowing. Food shouldn't sparkle, surely? A banner hangs from the ceiling, green and white stripes, like some kind of alien's pregnancy announcement: *All New Entirely Natural Products – Buy Today!* The whole store is filled with them, branded products, all imprinted with a tiny, little golden tree. I realise for the first time what a terrible name that is. If you have to tell people your products are completely and *entirely* natural – honestly, totally and perfectly natural, literally nothing not natural in there at all, we promise, really – it makes it sound like there's something definitely *un*natural going on. *Methinks, the lady doth protest too much.* What's that from? Can't remember now.

The sheer uniformity of the products in front of me is unnatural. You can be too perfect, you know. I wonder if Billy had anything to do with this new line of ready meals – *perfect taste in just 5 minutes.* Healthy microwave meals, whoever thought we would get here? He probably had no say in these things. In possibly the most ironic turn of events in the history of mankind, Billy worked for their human resources department. Although his reaction to any mention of the company makes me think they really were sourcing humans to run experiments on. *Eat this green stuff and try not to vomit.* They couldn't pay me enough.

Entirely Natural oaty spelt bread – £7.50. Okay, they could pay me enough. And what the hell is oaty spelt? Sounds like a paint colour at one of those fancy décor shops. *Come on, darling, let's paint the drawing room Oaty Spelt, it'll look simply magnificent.*

"Clem. Hello." Greta stands behind the counter, appearing as if from nowhere, like some kind of grocery magician. Maybe she can magically lower these prices for me. At the moment I can afford:

One loaf of oaty spelt bread
One pint of organic completely totally absolutely organic milk
One packet of something called Perfectly Toasted Coconut Shards

Possibly the shortest list I've ever done. Also, 'shards' isn't the best word to use in relation to food. I like my meals to not sound like they're capable of slicing my throat open, thanks very much. Can something even be called a list if it's only got three things on it? Oh, sorry, even that is out of my budget by £1.50. These coconut shard things must be coated in gold. Or maybe they cure cancer. Bet they don't cure infertility, though, so what's the point, really?

"Greta. Hi."

She doesn't meet my gaze.

"New stock?" And the asker of the most unnecessary question award goes to…

"Yeah, got delivered just before Christmas."

I can't see any gaps on the shelves, no spaces at all. Either Greta is *extremely* good at keeping her shop endlessly stocked, or no one's bought anything over Christmas.

"That's great, Greta." Pause. "Do you have anything – ah – normal? You know, not *Entirely Natural* level of… price?"

"No, we don't stock other brands anymore, we have an exclusive deal with *Entirely Natural*, inclusive of all meals, store cupboard essentials and even non-food products. *Entirely Natural* caters for all needs."

Is she okay? She sounds like a robot. There's something in her hands, crumpled. Oh, she's reading from a piece of paper. A spiel she's been given to say to those who question, to people like me. And she's right, even the cleaning spray is now *Entirely Natural*. Not all bad then, bet that isn't allowed to smell like bleach.

"Right, well. That's great, Greta." Now I sound like a robot.

She shrugs her shoulders. She still won't meet my eyes.

I take a loaf of oaty spelt from the shelf, set it on the counter alongside a bottle of organic milk. Think I'll leave the coconut shards for now.

Greta looks at my crumpled £20 note. I probably shouldn't be using it here, it might have traces of cocaine on it, knowing Billy. Could it get Greta in trouble? Do they do random checks like that, just turn up to random shops and test their money for drugs? Would Greta then trace it back to us? A slick of sweat appears on my skin.

"Sorry, we're cashless now." The word sounds strange in her mouth. Yes, the cities have been cashless for years, but not the little village shops. And never Greta. She hates technology. It's why she refused to update her cash register even though it never closes properly.

She produces a sparkly new card machine from under the counter, holds it out to me as if it's alive. Alive and squirming. With some kind of horrific smell. I find my card, beep it against the machine. *Sale authorised – thank you for shopping with Entirely Natural.* Jesus, they've even expanded into card machines.

"Thanks, Greta."

She tries to smile. Fails. Turns and disappears into the back room. I wait a few seconds. She doesn't come back. Doesn't make any noise. I leave.

***

There's an alert from my bank on my phone by the time I get home. Banks are so paranoid. *Unfamiliar activity on your account. Company Name: Entirely Natural. If this wasn't you, please contact us immediately.* Chill out, bank. It was me. I know it's hard to believe I've bought food from a health company, but here we are.

Better hide these things from Billy before he sees the logo. Cute little tree. Embossed in white, like a ghost tree. It feels the same against my thumb on the plastic, the same long loops as on the envelope.

All that money, Dorrie. Just sitting there.

All. That. Money.

Hidden.

If she doesn't know I put it back, if it just sits there forever, then what? Do payment cards go out of date? Sitting next to old, canned meat and forgotten bread, mouldy and stale. But *Dorrie knows all,* that's what Dad would say. She already knows I put it back. She's just waiting for the right time to tell me she knows.

When I walk into the living room, I realise that day probably won't be today.

Gus is sitting on my sofa.

Billy is sitting next to him.

I drop the bag of *Entirely Natural* junk to the floor. The milk bottle immediately splits and starts leaking milk into the carpet. Cheap plastic. That's going to leave the worst smell.

"Clem, it's alright, love. Come, sit."

Dorrie's here. Thank God, Dorrie's here. My brother's death has been averted. No, Mother, I'm not being dramatic – have you never heard of an eye for an eye? Then again, you never accepted that it was Billy's fault in the first place, did you?

Dad did.

I did.

But not you, Mother. Never you.

If it had been me in that room, you would have – *It's her. She's the guilty one. She's always been strange, untameable. I tried my best with her, I really did.* You would have loved that. Lapped it up. Lived off the drama for months. But it wasn't me. It was Billy. The Golden Boy. Not so golden anymore. Even you have to admit that, Mother.

Right now, the Golden Boy looks like he's going to throw up. Gus looks like he wants him to. Or maybe like he wants to punch him, or a wall. Or like he wants to cry. Or all of the above. I want to do all of the above.

"Gus just thought he'd pop round with your Christmas present, didn't you, love?" Dorrie smiles at Gus. "He says he's sorry it's a couple of days late, but I told him you wouldn't mind, of course."

She's narrating the scene for us. Telling us what we would say if we could move, if our mouths worked, if we could use our lungs. As if we're in a play, as if this isn't real life. She directs me where to sit, hands me the gift-wrapped prop. This doesn't feel like real life. My head hurts. Dorrie shows me where to peel back the brown packing paper, stuck down clumsily with tape. The edges slice into the tender skin under my fingernails as I unwrap the box-shaped thing in my hands without looking at it, without feeling it, without feeling anything.

I can hear Gus's breathing, loud in the quiet room. Did Billy open the door to him? Did Dorrie invite him in for tea and biscuits? Did he react – what do you say in that situation? I have to know what happened. I have to ask. Have they talked? Has anyone? Or are we trapped in this place now, this world where Dorrie speaks for us?

"Well, hold it up, love, so we can all see what it is."

Do I even *want* Gus to speak? To regain that power, to contrast Dorrie's high notes with his own baritone. Because what would he say to Billy?

"Oh, isn't that just lovely?"

What does anyone say to the man who murdered their sister?

"A bird feeder. You know our Clemmie well, don't you, love."

Everyone's staring at me. I move my tongue around in my mouth. Dry.

"Thank you."

My voice isn't my own. It's coming from somewhere else. Somewhere outside of me.

Gus stands, opens his mouth, closes it. He leaves the room. I want desperately to leave with him.

"We'll have to buy some more birdseed to fill this with, love. I think you're all out."

The sound of the door slamming. I watch Gus stride back across to his house, disappear inside. I watch my little brother curl into himself on the sofa, start to shake. I watch the empty windows of the house across the street. I didn't get him a gift.

***

Dorrie makes porridge for tea. From real rolled oats. I don't know where she got them from. Not from Greta, that's for sure. She brings more milk over from her place. We sit and eat in silence. None of us looking at the other. I stare mostly at the radio, back on the counter. Escaped from its drawer yet again.

It wasn't really Billy's fault what happened. Except that it almost definitely was. All of it. They were his drugs. It was his vodka. Well, Dad's vodka really, but same thing. It was the classic story. Girl likes boy. Girl takes drugs in stupid attempt to impress boy. Girl passes out and chokes on her own vomit. Boy panics. Boy cries. Boy never forgives himself and enters into a downward spiral that terrifies family and destroys future.

It was what happened next that didn't stick to any kind of script you'll be familiar with. This village is very good at keeping secrets. Very good at knowing everybody's business but repeating none of it outside safe circles of known and trusted ears. Billy should have been arrested, should have faced consequences. Any other sixteen-year-old boy found with a dead girl in his room and a load of cocaine up his nose would have been. But Billy had something those other boys didn't have.

He had you, didn't he, Mother? And you're stronger than you look. Strong enough to carry a dead weight down one flight of stairs and up another in the middle of the night, all by yourself. Well, nearly by yourself.

What's that quote about secrets being valuable? Like money. *A bartering tool*, Dad would say. Strange word: bartering. Doesn't sound real. B a r t er ing.

They found her the next morning, in her own room instead of Billy's. Of all the things you made me do over the years, Mother, gripping her cold, dead ankles was the worst. Carrying her next door in the dark. Tucking her fluffy, yellow blanket around her neck. Gus's daddy always left the spare key to the back door under their blue flowerpot. He'd gone out for a drive with Gus that night. We watched them leave from our living room window.

Of course, the police interviewed us. But our mouths were super-glued closed with your spite, weren't they, Mother? It didn't help that Gus's family were already known to the police – his father suspected of 'neglect in a caregiver's role' after his daughter turned up at school with clothes that hadn't been washed in a week. A bad father, a lonely daughter and a son who likes to take innocent young girls into the backs of vans. No, it didn't look good at all.

Why no one ever suspected Mother of 'neglect in a caregiver's role', I will never know. She made me lie about Gus, to make them look like an even worse family than the police already thought they were. *White trash*, I heard one of the police sergeants call them. I said he put his hands on me, that he didn't listen to me, that he did things I didn't want him to. I wouldn't say rape, would I, Mother? Even though you wanted me to – said it would have more impact. But I wouldn't go that far. I just hinted at other stuff, nasty words, heavy-handedness – I mean, I had the bruises to prove it. No one would be able to say it *wasn't* Gus that gave them to me.

Dad died believing me. I only just realised that. He knew Billy messed up, but he didn't know I lied. He thought that part was true, didn't he, Mother? Because otherwise, he never would have let me do it.

It wasn't a complete lie. It stemmed from truth. So many lies do. Gus was strong, he did push me that night. The space in the back of his father's van smelt like peppermints. It was all I could focus on when he kissed me, grabbed my hair, pulled until it hurt. He told me what was happening, I was just expected to go along with it. It would have been easier to let it play out. But I didn't. I slapped him instead. I think he was more in shock than anything. He genuinely didn't think he'd done anything wrong. Which is definitely more worrying, now that I think about it. We didn't speak for a while after that. In fact, the next time we spoke was when I arrived at his house, my parents in tow, to perform our grief, our sympathy. To pretend we'd never seen her staring eyes, felt her cold, stiff skin. We had to watch them cry. We lived through the funeral.

The police believed our lies, Mother's lies. The coroner ruled accidental death. There were more interviews, of course, but they didn't find anything. I always thought it was amazing, at the time, that Billy didn't snap. Amazing they didn't realise her body had been moved. But maybe it's not that shocking when you really stop to think about it. Young girl, overdose, bad family. No one looked too hard.

Lips sealed – don't worry, Mother, they are. Or they were, until Tony. Idiot, Clem. You're an idiot.

We went on with our lives. I don't know how Gus's father did it, but he did. His neglect case was dropped, citing lack of evidence. Difficult to gather information on your suspect when the kid in question is dead. Always a strange man, Eddie. You would think he would bond with Greta, find some kind of shared pain or something. I don't know, I can't feel what they felt. But he didn't. Seemed to actively avoid her actually. Maybe he thought he'd been infected by her, drawn into her grief, cursed.

Gus went to a training course. Qualified as a plumber. I went to the city, started work as a freelance writer, then got my job at the magazine. Met Tony. Billy continued his downward spiral. Lost lots of jobs, lost more of his sanity. I think he's trying to forget her face with the partying. Sometimes I wonder if what we did for him actually made him worse. If he'd been made to own up to his part in everything, admit his guilt, maybe it would have helped him. They do say honesty is the best policy. It's way easier to live with as well. At least if you're honest from the start you don't have to worry about letting things slip, telling the wrong person – or the right person, depending on how you look at it.

But we carry on, don't we, Dad? We pretend we're a normal family. Pretend Billy doesn't need help, because even if he went to a therapist he wouldn't be able to tell them why he was there. What's done is done, as you would say, and no one's coming back. No matter how long we think about our memories, watch them flicker in our heads, we can't change them, so why bother wasting time? Move on.

Her name was Amanda.

PART FOUR

Another doorstep surprise this morning. No, not a dead bird. Makes a change, I know. A box this time. A large one. With a tiny, embossed tree on the side. Golden tendrils flowering outwards, delicate leaves. The detail on this thing is ridiculous, really. It's just a logo. Calm down.

There's no one outside, no unusual cars nearby to tell me who left it here. No note.

I take it inside, put it on the kitchen table. It looks funny sitting there, shiny and white against the old, scarred wood of the table, the old-fashioned kitchen. Country kitsch, an interior designer would probably call it, before announcing it out of fashion and gutting the whole thing to re-design it in ugly chrome and sparkle.

I use a pair of scissors to open the box, peel back the flaps at the top, before I notice it isn't addressed to me. Or to Dad. Or even to you, Mother.

"Billy?"

He's taken to lying down upstairs, actually underneath his childhood bed. He shimmies into the dust-filled space and spends hours staring at the coils of springs hidden there. Not the weirdest thing he's done, and we all know it could be so much worse, so I'm not questioning it for now. Annoying when I need him, though, he can't seem to hear anything when he's under there.

"Billy!"

I'm halfway up the stairs, then all the way up the stairs, then practically under the bed with him when I finally get a response.

That response is, "Uh?"

So eloquent, my baby brother.

"You've got a package. Downstairs."

His eyes look as confused as my head feels. It has to be something bad, obviously. No one knows he's here except me, Dorrie, Gus and Tony. I didn't send for anything, Dorrie wouldn't order something without telling me, Tony's so wrapped up in his own ego the idea of him buying a present for someone without the ulterior motive of sex is ridiculous, so the only person who could have addressed this box to my brother is our vengeful neighbourhood plumber. So, the conclusion is it's a box of anthrax. I probably shouldn't have brought it inside.

Billy looks as it, sitting there on the table, like it's a bomb. Another possibility, I suppose.

"Don't ask me who sent it, I don't know. Don't ask me why, I don't know. It was just on our doorstep."

Billy doesn't move.

"Are you going to open it?" Long pause. "Look, I'm sorry I opened the top, I didn't think it would be for you."

Although why I thought it would be for me, I don't know. Who would be sending me gifts? Maybe I thought it was something Dad ordered before he died. I can't have thought it was something *she* ordered, or I wouldn't have bothered to open it, would've just chucked it straight in the bin. I don't want anything of yours, Mother. I don't know what I thought.

If he doesn't open it in the next ten seconds, I'm opening it for him. I can't bear the suspense.

Ten

Nine

Eight

Seven

Billy clasps his hands together over his chest, like he's about to deliver an important address to the box delivery community. Or maybe he's praying. Ha, that would be the next thing, wouldn't it? Been waiting for the day my brother announces he's found God. Always think it's funny when people say that, like they've just found this old, bearded guy hiding behind some bins in an alleyway somewhere. Found him, guys! I found God. He was hiding again! Crafty old thing.

Six

Five

Four

Three

Tw—

So close. Billy moves quick suddenly, like he wants to get it over with, flings open the box, tips it so the contents fall onto the table. Plucks out a piece of card from the pile: a note, carefully typed in an increasingly familiar font. Billy's face does something strange and scrunched-looking. He makes a small *muhrr* noise and then wobbles like he's going to faint, holds the card out to me:

Dearest Billy,

We are so glad to see that your sabbatical is going well and hope you will accept this gift as a token of our thanks for all your family has done for us over the past few months. We understand this is a difficult time and would like to remind you that any hardships you feel we can help with, all you must do is ask for our assistance. We are always here for you, as a valued employee and trusted member of the department.

We look forward to welcoming you back to the office once you have returned to full health.

With many well wishes,

The Entirely Natural Team

It's a care package. A bloody care package.

I don't believe this. Last time I was off work sick the most I got was an email from my boss telling me I better be back by Friday because she needed the monthly report. Something which wasn't even my job. And I was *legitimately* off sick with food poisoning – from bad food I bought *at the work canteen*. Maybe it's a good thing they've started employing robots there – you can't poison a hunk of metal and make it spend seventy-two hours throwing up undercooked meat. My point is, *I* was actually ill. Billy just has no impulse control.

"I thought you said you got fired?"

My brother looks at me with those big eyes, shrugs his shoulders.

Infuriating. How has this happened? Someone please tell me why my fiancé cheating on me means he gets to have a baby with a younger, more attractive yoga instructor and I have to clean up my little brother's messes – both physical and otherwise.

I look at the crush of stuff on the table:

Apples
Oranges
Bananas
Raspberries
Cold Medicine – same as the one Gus gave me
A smoothie – 'berry burst'
Teabags – camomile flavour
Oat biscuits – whatever they are
A box of tampons – weird, must be a generic box they send out to all sick employees. Godsend all the same though. I'm down to my last one just this morning.
Another box of teabags – this time their flavour is listed as 'sleep/relax'. Tasty.
A packet of the famous coconut shards
A bottle of something called 'distilled rosemary oil – natural pain reliever'
Coffee beans – always useful when you don't have a coffee machine.
A bottle of something called 'lavender sleep oil'
A bottle of milk
And a large string bag of ripe clementines

"What have we done for them?"

Billy looks up at me, from his new position on the floor of the kitchen. "What?" His arms are huddled around his knees.

"It says: 'thanks for all your family have done for us over the last few months.' What have we done for them?"

"I – I don't know."

I'm quite the expert at knowing when Billy is lying – practice makes perfect, hey Dad? Right now, I'm ninety-two percent certain my brother is telling me the truth. But someone else isn't. Well, she hasn't actually lied outright, but she's – what's that phrase? I think about the expensive piece of plastic, hidden at the back of a cupboard. The £10k me and Billy have more claim to than anyone. The ridiculous amount of money that sits there, unused, untouched. Lied by omission, that's what she's done.

Haven't you, Dorrie?

***

See your sabbatical is going well. See? I sit up in bed. See.

Who packs a box of tampons in a care package for a male employee? That wasn't a generic gift, it had a personalised note. And who at work would have known Billy was staying with me? He didn't tell anyone where he was going when he left that party. Mainly because Billy didn't know where he was going when he left that party. I was a last-minute decision. Christ, I really wish I hadn't been.

See.

I told Gus I had my period. But he gave me the cold medicine because he didn't have anything else. Someone saw him give it to me. Someone saw me looking for tampons in Greta's shop. Someone saw me. Us.

Someone's watching us.

This lavender sleep oil does *not* work.

***

"So, no one actually said the words, 'you're fired'?"

"I told you, Clemmie, I can't remember."

"No, of course you can't. How convenient for you." I slam the fridge door closed with a *thunk*.

Billy sits at the kitchen table, hangdog expression fixed firmly back in place. The care package things sit between us.

"I just assumed that once they saw I was high, they weren't exactly going to keep me on."

A fair assumption to make.

"But you were high at the party, right?"

He nods.

"Then you probably weren't the only one. Have you not seen *Wolf of Wall Street*? Half the team will have been on something. Your boss was probably doing lines in the toilets. What are you always telling me? Everyone does it. Christ, do you not remember that finance firm you worked at? The MD ended up in rehab!"

He shakes his head.

"You can't just assume you've lost your job and not turn up for work, Billy. That isn't how the world works."

"They're not like that there. They don't do anything.

They're all natural remedies and hemp and yoga. My supervisor wouldn't even take paracetamol."

The sigh hurts my throat. I reach for the box of camomile tea.

"You want one of these?"

Billy snatches the box out of my hand, holds it against his chest.

"Seriously? What, you don't want to share with your big sis? Because it's *all yours*."

He shakes his head, starts to put everything back into the box.

I laugh. "You really are selfish, aren't you? You want the tampons too? Just give me two minutes, I'll go pull this one out of myself, you can have it straight back." I'm shouting now, it's loud.

Billy starts to cry.

I can't stop laughing.

"I told you not to use this stuff, Clem. I begged you."

"I should have known, you always were terrible at sharing. Everything your sticky little fingers touch, you just keep for yourself, you—"

"I don't want it! Any of it. I want it gone, out – I want to throw it out." He's shouting now, too. He's still shoving everything back into the box, fast, throwing things in, denting the boxes, ripping the packets, bruising the fruit.

"Oh, so just because you don't want it, nobody can have it?"

"We can't eat it, we can't – we can't have any of it!"

I can see what looks like hysteria swimming around inside his eyes. I grab the bag of clementines out of the box. He actually *snarls* at me, like a kind of wolf-boy, and

159

runs around the table, lunges for the bag. We both pull at it and end up on the floor, kicking and scratching like we're kids again. I half expect him to bite me, like he used to with his little milk teeth, leave tiny marks along my forearms. It never hurt, not really, but I would cry like it did. It hurts now. His arms are strong, his knee pushing into my stomach, spittle hits my face. He's a lot bigger now.

So am I. I shove at him, fist my hand, knock it against his cheek. His head snaps back and clips the edge of the table. He sucks in air, sharp, then makes a kind of groaning sound and falls away from me. His eyes look unfocused and when he pulls his hand back from his hair there's red all over his fingers.

I didn't mean to.

"Billy?"

He whispers, "Ouch", and leans back against the cupboards.

I grab a dishcloth from the side, soak it, put it against the back of his head. Pull it away: more blood. But not too much. There's not too much.

My breath feels funny in my chest.

"I'm sorry, sorry, sorry. I didn't mean—"

"You didn't tell me you could throw a punch." He twists his mouth into an attempt at a grin.

"This isn't funny."

"I know."

The bleeding is slowing, slowing, stopping. Mother's favourite dishcloth, the one with the blue polka dots, now has red dots as well. They're not quite as uniform as the blue ones. Splotches, rather than dots. They'll dry brown, not red. Crusty.

I check him for signs of a concussion. Do that thing where you get the person to focus on your finger, move it about in front of their face. I get him to close his eyes and his pupils dilate normally. Probably the first time in a long time they've done that.

He smiles.

He says he's fine.

He goes to the toilet.

I call Dorrie. I need her second opinion. And I need to confess, listen to my own sins said out loud, have them stain the air.

I will not be her.

I will not.

I will be better.

***

He doesn't have a concussion. We called Dr Robertson round, just to be safe. Oh yes, he does house calls now. For Dorrie, at least. She told him she had chest pain on the phone, then when he got here said she'd been mistaken, but whilst he had made the journey down, did he want a cup of tea? And a biscuit? Every cup of tea needs a biscuit, Doctor, it's no trouble. Billy was having a biscuit, to help with his headache. Oh, he had a nasty fall in the shower, blood everywhere. Oh, Dorrie was ever so worried. Oh, Dr Robertson, kind, kind man, would you mind just taking a look? Just so she could sleep tonight, without worry, just for his sister's peace of mind. Poor, poor, little Billy. He's so clumsy at times. And so soon after their parents, well... you know.

He fell for her simpering act hook, line and sinker. I thought doctors were meant to be perceptive. He checked Billy over, told him to be more careful next time, perhaps invest in a non-slip mat for the base of the bath, gave him some painkillers for the headache which had started to bloom and then he left. Insightful as ever.

I threw the care package out whilst Billy was in the toilet. I didn't want to look at it anymore. Sat there, its smug whiteness showing up the dirty floor, cupboards, doors, walls, sink. I put it in the bin in the kitchen, shoved it right down to the bottom. When I went back in later, someone had changed the bin bag. The care package had been moved to the outside bin, the lid weighed down with the brick Dad always used to hold the gate open. Well, I suppose it is windy tonight, we don't want another bin-tipped-over fiasco.

When I opened the bin to check, the little box of prescription painkillers was in there too. Unopened. Yes, of course I checked the tablets were all still securely in their little foil packets, I'm not stupid. They were. All sixteen of them. The box embossed with a little tree, golden leaves flickering in the light of the street lamp.

***

BREAKING NEWS:
Anti-Birth Riots Escalate Across London
Pregnant women live in fear for their lives
YOUNG WOMAN KILLED IN ANTI-BIRTH RIOT
Trending: #antibirth #stopoverpopulation #nomorebabies
Top Ten Reasons Why You Should Never Have Children

'NO MORE BABIES!' TOP DOCTOR BEGS WOMEN

Women in labour are being denied medical care – scandal or a step in the right direction?

DOCTOR DEATH: The Insider Story of the Doctor who Aborted Hundreds of Babies Without Being Asked. Read Now for Free!

Mother of Four Assaulted Outside School – 'my eldest tried to pull them off me. He was fearless.'

Liberate Don't Procreate! #anti-birth-rally

The Rise of Hidden Pregnancies – how to dress to protect your baby

TOP STORY: Manchester 'Anti-Birth' Attacks Leave 3 Dead

What is it they say? Stop 'doom scrolling', Clem.

Scratch, scratch, scratch. Oh, God.

    Scratch, scratch, scratch. The rats are back. Or the mice.

    Scratch, scratch, scratch. They must be. What else could that noise be?

    The floor is cold under my feet. Chill. Really need to YouTube 'how to fix a boiler'. It can't be that hard, surely? If I can fix a washing machine, who's to say I can't fix other things? Maybe that's my new calling – an odd-job woman. Or just an odd woman – think I've already got that one covered.

    I place my ear to the wall in the hallway. Slide my head along the wall. *Scratch, scratch, scratch.* There it is. Are they in the walls? Under the floorboards? Infesting the house?

    Scratch, scratch, scratch. No.

    It's coming from the basement.

    Of course it is – suitably creepy. Dead of night, check;

cold, dark basement, check; single woman alone and dressed only in her nightgown (read: flannel pyjamas), check.

It's so loud, just the other side of the door. I imagine taking the chair away from under the handle, pulling the door open, being engulfed by hundreds of red-eyed rats, their paws everywhere, their teeth nibbling my skin. There must be so many of them, to be making this noise. So loud. Or maybe it's just one massive, mutant rat – human-sized. Teeth bigger than my hand.

I've never wished for a box of rat poison more. Even you would consider it, Dad, with an infestation this big. Traps just aren't going to cut it.

Scratch, scratch, rattle. The handle shivers. The chair scrapes against the floor. This rat is trying the handle, trying to break its way out. It's succeeding.

I press my back against the wall as the chair begins to give up, move out of the way. As the door swings back. As the rat rears up on its hind legs, stands tall, towers over me. As it skitters out of the shadows. As its paws morph into a pair of huge hands, its large ears shrink back inside a thatch of hair, its snout resolves into a nose, mouth, beard. Of course, it's not a rat.

It's a man.

A man I know. A man who knew my parents, knew my family well. A man who could have known about the door in the basement, who could have known when we would be out of the house, who did know where Dad used to keep his dodgy old radio. A man, not a ghost, not the dead spirit of our vengeful mother. Not a murder of super-intelligent crows.

Just a man.

"Gus?"

He swears, teeters on the top step of the basement stairs. "God, Clem, you scared me."

I stare at him, wonder if he's ever heard of irony.

He stares back.

"Are you going to say anything?"

He shrugs his shoulders up towards his ears, places a hand on the back of his neck. Sighs.

He's been coming in here. Freaking us out, moving things about. Killing birds and throwing them around the house.

"I know you hate us, Gus. I understand it, sympathise with it, even. But those birds didn't do anything to you. You killed them to hurt me, but they didn't deserve that. They were alive, Gus. Alive."

"I would never hurt you, Clemmie."

"You have."

He steps nearer, lifts a hand as though to touch me.

I slap at his fingers, see them covered in gore, bird innards. He murdered those innocent creatures to get to me. Essentially, I killed them. I'm a bird murderer.

"Clemmie, please."

"When did you find out about the door in the basement? When you were doing work for Dad in the garden? When you were moving boxes around for Mother? How long have you been coming in here in the middle of the night? Before Billy arrived? Have you been watching me sleep?"

It's sarcasm when it leaves my lips, but the red bloom on his cheeks turns it into a genuine question. Makes me feel sick.

"Why the radio?"

A pause. Darting eyes. Twisted mouth.

"I knew it was your dad's routine. Thought it would freak him out, make him leave."

"Billy?"

Gus's eyes darken.

"You knew he was here. Before you brought me the bird feeder. You already knew."

Shrug.

"You're a good actor, you know. Should have been on stage."

"You don't need him, Clem. He's ruined you, ruined your life. More than once. Why are you letting him stay?"

He reaches again for me – I press hard into the wall, the peeling paint cold through my pyjama top. *Don't touch me.*

"He's my brother."

"He's nothing. Nothing like you, Clemmie. He's not your responsibility."

"He's my brother."

"He's a killer." A fleck of spittle lands on my cheek.

"He's my brother."

Gus growls – I don't think he's ever looked more like a bear. I've never been scared of him before, not really, even that night in the back of his father's van. But his bulk seems sinister amongst the shadows, when he has that look in his eyes, when this anger coats his skin. When I think about the fact he's been coming into my house, moving things around, watching me.

"And she was my sister. She would still be here. If not for him. We would still be *us.*"

He really believes that. He really thinks I would have stayed with him. That we would have had a proper relationship, married, had 2.3 kids and moved into his father's house. Just waited for his father to die and then moved into the big bed. Lived out the rest of our lives across from my mother, every action steeped in her judgement, everything dyed an ugly, purple bruise colour.

"I've never stopped loving you, Clemmie."

It should be a line from a romance novel, but here, in the dark, literally backed into a corner, this horrible rat-bear-man looming over me, it sounds like something from a bad horror film. A chill blows up from the open door of the basement, prickles against my skin. I think about the clementines, waving around down there. Their green leaves beckoning me forward, whispering, "*Clemmie, Clemmie, Clemmie.*" I hate them. Their perfectly orange skin, sweet innards, sharp juice. I want to mash them all into pulp.

Gus's hands grip my arms, circle my waist, snatch at my hair. *Stop, get your bird murderer hands off me. Get them off.*

I shove at him, push, pull. He grips me tighter, my wrists, face, neck.

"Clemmie, I love you."

He tries to kiss me, his lips are dry, his breath tastes like old tea, long grown cold.

"Please."

My pyjamas are loose. I'm not wearing underwear. There's probably some kind of cautionary tale about this – lying about something only for it to become true, years later. Only for it to actually happen and no one believe you. Karma. Or The Boy Who Cried Wolf.

I would be able to be more convincing now, Mother. I would be able to say it.

My skin is even colder now it's bare. I go to scream and find my throat has closed up. I wouldn't be able to make a sound, even if a huge hand wasn't barring my mouth.

"It's okay, Clemmie, it's okay."

Both of my wrists fit inside one of his hands, clamped together.

I can't move.

My body starts to go numb.

His tongue is wet, saliva drying cold on my face.

He shifts his weight, takes his hand away from my mouth to unzip his trousers.

I don't scream. I don't shout. I can't. But somehow, I wake up my legs. Right on the edge of the moment that could rip my world, my body, wide open from the inside out. I wake up my legs, bend my knee, and smash my foot into him. Again. Again.

Gus howls and falls backwards, against the doorframe. Pain in his eyes. A confused boy, unsure why I would do such a thing, unsure why I'm not happy with the attention.

I shove the heel of my hand up this time, hit him in the face.

I seem to be developing a reputation for making men's noses bleed.

He snorts and splatters blood up Mother's white walls.

And that could have been it.

That should have been it. But he stands again, and I know my body is done. I've gone limp, back against that wall. Those huge hands grasp my shoulder again.

"You bitch."

Blood covers his mouth, melts into his beard. I smell it, metallic against my skin. Fingernails cut into the soft skin of my face as he grabs at my neck, as he pulls out a chunk of my hair, the short strands limp in his fist.

"You're just like your brother," he snarls.

I feel saliva flood my mouth, so I spit it in his face. I don't know where I get the courage from. But he rears back, hurt in his eyes. As though I'm the one who needs to apologise.

His hands leave my skin.

We stare at each other.

He opens his mouth, like he's going to say something else.

Then there's a scream. Not me. Not him.

And then he's gone. Pushed away. Stumbling backwards. Hands flailing. Down the stairs. *Thud, thud, thud, thud, thud, thud, thud.*

Another shape stands in his place. A thinner shadow. A shaking body.

Cold hands pull my pyjamas back onto my limbs and my little brother places his slim body in front of mine.

I feel the rest of my body wake up, breath rushes in and out of my mouth, cold in my throat.

I wait for the next thing to happen, for those huge hands to close around Billy's neck, wait to watch the life be squeezed out of my brother's body.

But there's nothing. Except the silence.

I watch spots of blood slide down white walls.

The door to the basement hangs open, broken lock clicking in that cold breeze.

A soft sound. A gurgling noise.

I peer over Billy's shoulder and we move as one. I just need to grip the handle, just need to close that door. Maybe he's hit his head. Maybe he's out cold. Maybe, just maybe, we can get away. Get help before he wakes up. We can run to Dorrie's – she'll help us, she'll know what to do. She always knows what to do.

Billy's fingers are trembling as he presses the light switch.

Yellow floods the basement.

I really wish I hadn't fixed that light.

Gus lies against the set of drawers at the bottom of the steps, hands splayed either side of his head, arms wide like some kind of fallen angel. An angel in disgrace.

I really, really wish I'd moved those garden shears.

There's a man who lives across the road. My baby brother has accidentally killed both of his children. His daughter. And now his son.

Because Gus isn't out cold. Not with that much blood flowing out of his neck. Not with a pair of garden shears through his throat.

Glassy eyes stare up at us.

There's a lot of blood. Way too much. We watch until it slows, slows, stops. Until Gus's skin turns the same shade of grey as our own. Until we're sure he's dead.

Billy's hand finds mine, squeezes.

He clicks the light switch.

I swing the door shut.

We run to Dorrie's.

Dorrie will know what to do.

Dorrie always knows what to do.

PART FIVE

Blood: notoriously difficult to get out of clothes. We know this. Apparently, even harder to get off old, white, peeling paint. I scrubbed for three hours before Billy found the tin of paint in the basement.

Interesting design choice, to paint one wall of the hallway a mud brown colour. But needs must, I suppose. If anyone asks – but why would anyone ask, who's going to come visiting? Tony? Doubt we'll see him again after the nose-to-door incident. No, we'll be left alone here, with no one to call on us, with nothing to say. That's what Dorrie said. How she reassured us. The only person who might miss Gus is his bedridden father – he's hardly going to come round and ask to look inside our basement, is he? He's hardly going to be doing anything much within a few days. Probably starve to death.

It's funny, really. Death has become something that sits on my shoulders, follows me about. But I almost don't notice it anymore. You were right, Dad. When you keep busy, make lists, distract your brain, you don't feel its weight on your back. You can ignore the guilt. Painting's a good one to do, easy, repetitive. The noise of the roller on the wall. The strong smell of the paint – it covers up the metallic smell, the smell of the blood. His blood.

I've written this particular list in my head only. Obviously. I'm not completely stupid.

Clean wall
Paint wall
Bleach stairs
Bleach carpet
Bleach basement floor
Find somewhere to put body
Bury/hide/dissolve body
Bury/hide/destroy murder weapon
Act normal for rest of life

That last one can never be crossed off. I hate that. I can never throw this list out, can never get it out of my head. Also, I feel like it should be longer – you should need more supplies and have to do more things to cover up a murder. Was it this easy for you when you covered up Amanda's murder, Mother?

Sorry, Billy, not murder. Manslaughter. That's the word Dorrie used. It was self-defence, or sister-defence, I suppose. It's not as serious, there's no pre-meditation, no conscious thought of *I'm going to kill this person* – everything happens too fast, driven by passion, anger, fear. Yeah, sounds like Billy.

You get less time in prison for manslaughter. Which is good. I guess. But I think the fact we've conspired to hide the man-slaughtered body and carried out a full clean-up operation kind of makes us seem a bit more guilty.

It would be truly typical if Billy managed to take random drugs in clubs for all these years only to get arrested for killing someone. Sent to prison a murderer/man-slaughterer/whatever. I wonder if that would give him more or less kudos inside. What would be respected more? Well, he would sort of be both, so he might get double points.

He wouldn't last five minutes in there. Then I'd have to carry more death.

Christ, I hate the smell of bleach.

I didn't have to close his eyes. Didn't have to cover him up with one of Dad's blue tarps he used in the garden. Didn't have to watch him go from a person to a Thing, a body, a nothing.

Dorrie did that bit.

But she can't carry all that weight on her own. And we have to do it now. Before it gets light. Or the Thing will be in our basement for another whole day. Okay, we might not get actual visitors coming to the house, but it would arouse suspicion in even the most casual of window watchers if we waved, "Morning!", whilst carrying a huge, body-shaped package out into the garden and started burying it in the vegetable patch.

That's where we're going to have to do it. The rest of the ground is frozen hard, our spades wouldn't stand a chance. But the soil in the veg patch is soft, isn't it, Mother? I don't know how you did it, but thank you, for the first time in my life, I thank you.

Flump, flump, flump.

"Stop! You're just moving it around."

"Well, we have to get it out of the hole."

"You're putting it back in the hole! That's *my* hole."

"Well, this is *mine*. Your hole isn't even big."

"Excuse me?"

"There's no way a dead rabbit would fit in there, let alone—"

"Hush. Don't talk so loud."

Flump, flump, flump.

"You're ruining my hole."

"Shut up! No talking."

"I'm just saying—"

"You ruined my life; I get to ruin your hole."

"That's not fair, love."

"Oh, I couldn't be more sorry, really. I really, really couldn't. I'm *so sorry* that I might have hurt your feelings during our midnight *body burying*."

"I didn't mean it."

"We know, love. Hold this."

Flump, flump, flump.

"He just… fell."

"Shut up."

Flump, flump, flump.

"Where are we going to put all these plants?"

"No one cares."

"She would care."

"We'll just put them back, love."

"What?"

"Will you *stop* putting the soil *back* in my hole!"

"On top of his dead body?"

"Move it *out*, not *in*."

"We can't move the veg patch – people would notice."

"But… on top of his dead body?"

"Will you stop mentioning dead bodies, please? We're trying to be subtle. I know that word's not really in your vocabulary – so actually, maybe just *shut up*."

"You shut up."

"I would be able to, if you *stopped* putting your soil in *my hole*!"

THWACK

"Ow!"

"Shhhhh!"

"Hush, hush."

"She just—"

"Quiet now, love."

"Did you see—"

"Oh, calm down, it wasn't even that hard."

"Just shh! Come on. We need to get this finished."

Flump, flump, flump.

"She wouldn't like it. A dead body under her garden."

"I should have hit you in the mouth."

***

My hands smell of bleach. I feel like Lady Macbeth. Out damned smell. It burns into my skin.

"I didn't mean to, Clemmie. I didn't mean it."

I'm getting a strong sense of déjà vu, Billy. Stop. It's making my head hurt.

God, you're an idiot.

You did it for me.

So, I will do this for you.

It's what siblings are for, right?

Nothing says 'family' more than helping each other cover up a murder. And the two people who just helped me bury a body in my back garden are all the family I have left.

The new locks were easy to put onto the basement doors. Really easy. If only they'd arrived a day earlier, then none of this would have happened. Probably.

I lock the Narnia door tight with the new key. Push an old chest of drawers in front of it. Just to be safe. Head back upstairs, lock the basement door. Jiggle the handle. Just to be safe.

Safe. We'll never feel safe again.

I stash the key in Mother's jewellery box.

***

I can hear Billy talking to himself in the kitchen. This is it. The moment we've been waiting for, Dad. I think he's finally snapped. I'll be looking at 'homes' next. More money we don't have. And, no, I haven't been thinking about the envelope sitting behind Dorrie's tinned peas, thank you very much. Just sitting there. Nope. Haven't been thinking about it at all.

"No, she's not here right now… well, I don't know exactly. She's somewhere, obviously."

Maybe he's practicing for the courtroom. You know, for when he's arrested for murder. Or manslaughter. Or cover up of manslaughter. Or whatever. He needs the practice, for sure. Billy always has been a bad liar.

"What? I don't know anything about that."

Good, Billy. Just deny. Deny. Deny. Deny. We don't know anything about a dead body. We've never owned a pair of garden shears. The house smells of bleach because we like it that way. The windows are all open because we like the cold. No, Your Honour, we would never dig up our mother's garden, especially not in the dead of night, and definitely not to bury this dead body we don't know anything about. Definitely not.

Yes, we knew Gus.

No, we did not watch him die.

We don't know where he's gone. Maybe he just wanted to get away from his father, this village, his past. His father held him back, hollowed him out. It was never his plan to stay here for so long. Maybe he finally decided to go travelling.

Maybe he just went away. For a bit. Or for ever. Forever.

F o r e v e r.

I've always been a good liar. A great one. I had to be. Survival instinct, you see. If you can lie about something so effectively you believe it yourself, that's when you know you've succeeded. That's when you can call yourself a good liar.

Gus went away. He just went away.

I don't know why I'm staring at this wall, this brown wall. There's no reason for me to be staring at it. None at all.

I sound like a Dr Seuss book. Remember those, Dad? I loved those books. Mainly because she hated them. You would read them to us in secret, remember, Dad? To me and Billy. We would squash our laughter behind our hands, bury our heads in the bed covers. Remember, Dad, remember?

"I think she's busy… well, I can go look, if you like?"

What is he rambling about? Billy would be terrible in court. He would just cry. Might work – sympathy vote. Depends on who the jury are. Oh God, the jury. Can you be called up for jury service in a case with someone you know? Surely not. That would be wrong. Surely? Please. These are really the kinds of things I need to clue myself up on if I'm going to continue my life as a murderer. Murderess? Would I be called that now? Or is that sexist? I can just see Gus's father, sitting there, in judgement. Billy wouldn't just be locked up, he would be strung up. Hung, drawn and quartered medieval style. I would be made to watch. My punishment. The worst punishment.

"Do I know you – your voice sounds… huh?… No, no, no. I'm her brother."

I blink and spots appear on the brown wall. The smell of the paint and the bleach must be getting to me. Could that be toxic? Jesus, I didn't even check. You can kill someone if you mix toilet cleaner and bleach. Paint might be the same. My chest feels tight, my breath harsh, the breath of someone who's been poisoned. I feel sick, headache, stomach tight. My heart is beating in the base of my neck. All the typical signs of a body breathing in slow-acting poison. Or someone having an anxiety attack. Same thing, really.

If we are dying, at least we won't have to sit through the court case.

"Well, I'm just looking now, it – hello?"

Billy's frame fills the hallway behind me. His skin heats the air near mine. It's freezing in here. Maybe he has a fever – great, probably another sign of poisoning. His skin does look a funny colour. If he did what he did for me and I've killed him with paint-bleach fumes, I will never forgive myself.

"Clemmie?" His voice is sweet, childlike. Hard to believe this overgrown boy stood in front of me and killed a man the size of a grizzly bear last night. Even if it was an accident. He killed him. Just like he killed Amanda.

I try to smile at him. Act normal. We just act normal, don't we, Mother? For the rest of our lives. *The rest of our lives.*

Billy holds up my mobile – I must have left it in the kitchen. It must have rung. He must have answered it – he wasn't rehearsing his story at all. He was chatting away on the phone. On my phone.

"Who's Nia?"

3 missed calls: Unknown number

New message: Unknown number: Hi it's Nia Tony's partner? I really hope you don't mind me taking your number from his phone I need to talk to you please can you call me?

Who says *partner*? So smug. Just say fiancée. Or other woman. Or *womb.*

That last one was mean. Sorry.

"What did she say?"

"She asked if I was your boyfriend."

"What?"

"That's what I said." Billy smiles.

Why would she need to speak to me? We've never spoken before. Never been in the same room. I've never even met the girl. The girl who ruined my life. *No, he's the one who ruined my life. She was collateral damage. She didn't know about me.* Is she going to yell at me for breaking her fiancé's nose? *Oh God. What has he done?*

"What did she actually say, though?"

"Not much."

Like you then, Billy?

"Yes, but why did she ring?"

"Who is she?"

"She's no one. Why did she ring?"

"If she's no one, why are you making such a big deal—"

"Fine. Don't tell me. I'll find out for myself." I go to take my phone and Billy swipes it away. Playing keep-away like a kid on a playground. Piggy in the middle. I scrabble at his chest, but his arms are so long, it's ridiculous. How have I never noticed how long they are before? Surely, they're out of proportion with the rest of his body?

"Tell me who she is, and you can have the phone."

I stare him out. He stares back.

"She's Tony's new… woman."

Woman. Sounds even worse than *partner.* I sound like a balding, white man from the 1950s – "*She's ma woman.*"

Billy hands me my phone.

***

Nrrrrr, nrrrrrr, nrrrrrr

Isn't the noise of a phone ringing, the sound of the

other person not picking up, the most annoying sound in the world?

"*I'm sorry, the person you are trying to call is unavailable.*"

Correction: the most annoying sound in the world is that patronising woman's voice. The one who tells you no one wants to take your call. Not even your ex-fiancé's new woman.

New message: Unknown number: Sorry cant talk now

Typical.

Are you coming back to the city at any point??

Double question mark: desperate. And no, don't worry, Nia – there's no reason for me to come back. No reason for me to leave this village. Ever. Especially not straight after witnessing/covering up a murder. That would be stupid. Never run from the scene of a crime, right, Dad? It makes you look guilty.

I need to see you

What?

"Darling, I need to see you."

God, it's exhausting to be so in demand.

Dorrie is standing in my kitchen. Her shoulders are starting to hunch. I don't like that – makes her seem old. Well, I guess she is old. *Reminds* me she's old, then. I don't like being reminded of things I'm trying so hard to forget.

"I should have given you this a long time ago. I just… thought you knew."

I try to tune myself in to the conversation.

"Where did Billy go? He's not outside, is he?"

"I thought he would have told you."

"Seriously, I'm worried about him. He seems hot, too hot." I think he's getting worse.

"You two always shared everything. Daddy's little girl, that was you." Her eyes follow me over to the window. Her gaze heavy on my skin – it feels guilty. Makes me itch.

"I can't deal with him if he catches a fever – you know what a nightmare he is when he's ill."

"Clem, please, love."

I sigh, turn back to her. What now?

She takes a deep breath. Holds out an envelope.

"This better not be that money, Dor."

She looks puzzled. That envelope must still be stuffed in her cupboard. This is a different one – I see that now. No embossed tree. And a word, written on the front, in shaky cursive. My name.

Clemmie

My name. In your handwriting, Dad.

You always would insist on writing joined up, even though you were thoroughly terrible at it. No one could ever read what you'd written. No one apart from me. It would take me a while, but I would get there. So you never stopped writing like that.

Now you're writing to me from beyond the grave. I mean, obviously I know you're not. You clearly wrote this before you got in that car. But that's what it feels like, Dad. It's creepy, actually.

The envelope feels cold under my fingertips. Like it's been kept somewhere secret, somewhere hidden.

Dorrie swallows. "I'm sorry, darling. I should have given it to you before now. It just – it never seemed like the right time."

I can't breathe. The air has turned soupy.

"When?" It's all I can manage.

I can see Billy outside, no jacket, just a t-shirt. The wind is blowing his hair straight backwards, so he looks like he's caught in a wind tunnel.

"The day he died."

I can see my future: brewing hot drinks and clearing up snotty tissues. I don't have time for you right now, Dad. I don't have time for whatever this is.

What is this?

I place the envelope right in the centre of the table. I nod at Dorrie, squeeze her arm. I head outside to retrieve my now frozen little brother.

***

Cant talk on the phone anymore sorry x

A kiss. Really?

I really need a friend right now

She's forgotten who she's texting. She thinks I'm someone else. She must.

Do you know Chakras Café?

Of course, I know Chakras Café. It's where you go every morning to get a skinny chai latte – whatever one of those is. It's right across from the school where Tony teaches. It's where you both met. Believe me, Nia. I know far too much about Chakras Café.

Yes.

Meet me there? Tomorrow?

I place another blanket around Billy's shoulders, his skin like ice against mine. He needs another hot water bottle. I need to find somewhere nearby to get cold medicine. I need him to get better.

I knew this would happen. Idiot.

No

Those two little letters look harsh, just sitting there all alone. So, I add:

My brother's sick. Sorry.

I don't know why I'm apologising to her. God, this bitch really can wrap anyone around her little finger. I check back on her latest Instagram post. There's more hate comments. More nasty things than nice now. Maybe Tony's not commenting back enough – not tearing down her haters for her. I think that's what people call them – haters.

One person has posted a comment on the photograph of the grey squiggles:

Abort abort ABORT!!!!! #stopoverpopulation

Yeah, 'haters' sounds about right.

Maybe Tony's been drawn into a fight with one of them – maybe he's got himself arrested or beaten up or something. Maybe he's had some kind of brain aneurysm and decided to join the #stopoverpopulation crew, kicked her to the curb, as they say. Maybe he's dead – wishful thinking.

The baby isn't Tonys

...

I'll be outside Chakras at 11 tomorrow.

PART SIX

It's easy to forget about overpopulation when you're away from the city. It's so hot here. There's no *space*. Maybe you've finally made me into a country girl, Dad. I want to go home.

I saw at least three anti-birth demonstrations on the way here. Plus one that might have been a demonstration – or might have just been two guys screaming at each other in the street. Either way: inconvenient.

She'll be heavily pregnant by now – funny, that expression. I guess that is what it feels like. A heavy weight. Both physically and on your mind. I have a friend who said having a child was just signing up to a lifetime subscription of Worried Monthly. Okay, it was you who used to say that, Dad. Obviously.

Hope we don't get attacked. Imagine, if people just started shouting at her, poking at her ripe belly, random strangers. It would be my bad luck that she gets punched in the stomach or something the day I'm with her – I'd get dragged into it all. Typical. We might have to go to hospital. And how the hell would we explain that one to Tony? If he rushes in to rescue his damsel and I'm stood there: "Oh, hiya! Just ignore me. I'm not here, ha ha."

How is she going to explain any of this to Tony?

You would have thought I would have noticed her a mile away, huge belly, sweat standing at her hairline, blooming under her armpits. But she looks so different, I honestly didn't recognise her. Also, I was looking the other way.

"Clementine? Hi." She tries to smile but it looks more like she's about to be sick. She looks like she's going to try and hug me.

"It's Clem." I throw my hand out into the space between us. A friendly handshake instead. But I don't smile, so it feels more like we've just made some kind of business deal. Maybe we have. Maybe by even being here I'm entering into some kind of dodgy deal to promote secrets and sell lies.

She glances around, furtive, as though I've just palmed her some drugs. That reminds me, I need to get cold medicine for Billy. I've left him with Dorrie, so he'll be fine. He should be fine. His temperature was thirty-nine degrees this morning. Officially a fever. Dorrie offered to call Dr Robertson out again. How eager she is to fake a heart attack to medical professionals worries me. I said no. It was an executive decision. I was worried he would notice the smell of bleach. The brown wall. I was worried he would ask questions. I was worried he would say Billy was really ill.

"Should we…?" I point at the café.

"Yes, yes." She does the about-to-vomit smile again.

God, she can barely walk the bump is so big. She can't be that far along, can she? I'm too tired to do the maths. Brain fog. Maybe I'm getting Billy's flu. No idea how long they were sleeping together before I found out anyway.

Damn, keep forgetting it's not even his.

An annoying bell rings as we come through the door. How do the people who work here cope with that? Every single time someone comes in *bing, bing, bing.* Christ. Horrendous.

"I'll get these. What would you like?" she asks.

"Just a coffee, thanks. With milk."

"Oat, almond, soy or dairy?"

"Huh?"

"What kind of milk? Oat, almond, soy or dairy?"

I stare at her.

"Um… I'll just get you whatever they recommend." She vomit-smiles yet again, heads to the counter.

It's busy in here. Hot. I take my coat off, spy a spare table in the corner, head over. I put my bag on the other chair, stare at it sitting opposite me.

There's a message on my phone: *Dorrie: All fine here. Billy eating soup. X*

Good. I send a thumbs up emoji back. She won't know what that means.

"He'll bring them over for us." She hands me my bag, slots herself into the chair. With an extreme amount of difficulty. The swell of her bump makes my hands itch. I want to touch it.

"Cute tote. Where's it from?"

I only realise she means my bag ('tote' – who even says that?) because she's pointing at it.

"Ah… F&F?"

"Oh, is that the new season Versace?"

"It's Tesco."

"Oh."

Pause.

She fans at the back of her neck. "Hot in here, isn't it?"

There's a lot of pregnant women in here. Babies too. I fold my hands over my stomach. Breathe.

"So, it's not Tony's then?" I nod at her bump.

She flinches, blinks a lot. Then the tears come. I knew it. This was a mistake. Obviously. I should never have come here. I should have stayed at home. At home with my brother. Someone who needs me that I actually have a connection to. I'm a terrible sister.

"He doesn't know."

Obviously.

"But he's going to find out – I can just feel it. The baby feels it too."

Oh, Christ.

"The minute he holds her, he'll know. He'll know she's not his."

Looks like me and the baby have something in common, then. Nia's eyes meet mine and, for a second, I think I said that last part out loud.

Then she says, "What am I going to do?"

I look back at her. *How the hell am I supposed to know?*

A little boy tugs at the side of my jeans. Holds up a soggy, half-eaten biscuit.

"For you," he says.

I bind the sharp, hot feeling in my chest up and shove it down into my stomach. Cover it up by smiling into his sunny little face and saying, "Thank you. What a gentleman." I take the damp shortbread, place it on the table.

The boy's mother waves at me, mouths, 'Thank you'. She looks tired.

I wave back.

Nia is dabbing at her now red eyes with a serviette. She sniffs.

"Do you want kids?" She smiles. Innocent.

I'm going to be sick. It's far too hot in here. Surely, they have to provide air con or at least open the windows. Anything. Something.

"It's not as easy as just wanting them. For some people."

Some people lose the one person willing to go through IVF with them. That long, drawn out, agonising process. That expensive process. And some people take whichever man they want, regardless of whether he's the father or not. She destroyed everything I had because she could. Not because of a baby. Not really. She must have known, right from the beginning. Because if she had any doubts, if she thought there was any chance the baby growing inside her body might share Tony's DNA, she wouldn't be sitting here right now, her fat tears staining the blonde wood of the table. In front of me.

"Oh. Yes, of course." She knows she's said something wrong, *hit a nerve*, as Dad would say. And that nerve is raw. But she clearly doesn't know exactly *what*. Tony hasn't told her. She doesn't know what she did.

"I did want to say, Clem, that I'm sorry. For the way things worked out." She takes a breath, straightens her smock top over her bump, her boobs – they've got bigger with the pregnancy. They look great. Obviously. "I never meant to hurt you."

"I never thought you did."

"Oh."

"You don't owe me anything. I don't know you."

It's Tony that meant to hurt me – he's the one who knew I was sitting at home, waiting for him.

"Which is why I don't understand why I'm here right now, Nia."

She flinches again. Blinks again.

I think it's the first time I've actually spoken her name out loud. It feels strange in my mouth. N i a. Nia. Nnnnn iii a. Odd. It's so short. Small. She *looks* small. Ironically, with her huge belly. But she looks small. Her limbs are thin, bony, bendy, like a little tree sapling. Too much yoga, probably.

"I'm sorry." Even her voice is small. Quavering. I've only ever heard that word applied to old ladies before, their voices grown wobbly with age, and suddenly Nia seems much older than her twenty years. Then she seems old and young all at once. And I feel a vice tighten in my chest. The same vice I feel when I see Billy upset, or high, or sick. I touch my neck.

"One chai tea… and one coffee." The man smiles as he places our orders in front of us, apparently oblivious to the tears running down Nia's cheeks. To my clenched jaw. To him, we're just two girlfriends, meeting for a drink, excited about the birth. Or maybe a married couple, eager to meet their child. Or perhaps sisters, celebrating a pregnancy. Although probably not that last one. No one could possibly think me and Nia are related.

The man with our drinks is tall, bearded, wearing a

blue apron and a name tag that says LIAM. He places a small, green, clay cup with no handle in front of Nia. It's filled with a greenish coloured liquid. It looks vile. Smells worse. He places an empty blue version of the cup in front of me, along with a tiny red jug, also made out of clay, filled with milk. Mystery milk – whatever Nia ordered for me. Liam vanishes and I'm starting to think my coffee is some healthy, yoga, invisible kind when he reappears with some kind of contraption, all angles and harsh metal.

"Should be ready in a couple minutes for you." He beams again and places the coffee torture machine on the table. It all but obscures Nia from my eye line. *We're not in Kansas anymore, Toto.* The thing starts making a swishing noise and coffee starts to swill through the different tubes, starts to drip into a tiny filter at the bottom, to *plink* softly into the clay cup. Drop by drop. Literally. I'm reminded of the science experiment stuff in my parents' basement. I'm so glad I'm not paying for this.

I shift the whole thing to one side, wait for Nia to collect herself. Again. She's making quite a pile of snotty tissues there. Good to know even yoga goddesses produce mucus.

She curls her fingers around her cup but doesn't drink the stuff inside. I don't blame her.

"He came to one of my yoga classes."

For a second, I think she's talking about Liam. I'm about to say, "Oh, that's nice." Then I realise she's staring down at her own bump.

"We had a fling, a few months before I met Tony."

Fling – I swear, this girl speaks like she's from the 1950s.

"He was sweet, but kind of sad – the kind where you think you can 'fix them', you know?"

No.

"We got drunk one night, got careless. But it was only after things soured that I realised I was pregnant. Tony and I were already… well, you know."

Yes, Nia, I do know.

"But nothing physical had happened yet. I was going to tell Tony, but then time passed and we got closer, and we admitted we really liked each other. I didn't want to jeopardise a future that could be so beautiful by bringing up my past."

Wow, sensitive, thanks.

"Then he realised I was pregnant, and he was so happy. I just didn't have the heart to tell him the truth. He assumed the baby was his because obviously I'd not been too fussed about using protection."

Oh, *obviously*. I must be the only cheated-on fiancée who now knows the details of said cheating.

"You can't get more pregnant, can you? Ha. Ha, ha."

From her expression, I can't tell if it's a serious question or not. I shake my head anyway. Just in case.

"Why me, Nia? Why are you telling *me* all of this?" Of all people.

She just looks at me. Her eyes are a deep, rich brown. Like dark chocolate. She has those annoyingly long eyelashes us mere mortals could only dream of growing – of course she does. Probably puts some kind of argan, lavender, vitamin oil on them. Or something.

"Do you not have someone else you could talk to about this?"

"My parents are both dead."

Who would have thought I would have something in common with the wonderful Nia? Not such a gilded life, after all.

"And I don't really have many friends at the moment."

"What about all of the people commenting on your photos? Or is that whole profile just lies?"

It takes a second and then I realise what I've said.

Her eyebrows squeeze together, lips twist inwards.

Now she knows I've been stalking her online. Great. Nice one, Clem. Smart.

A tiny bell attached to the coffee torture machine makes a small *ting*. My coffee is ready. It's surprisingly hard to drink from a cup with no handle. And whatever this milk came from, it wasn't a cow.

I watch Nia over the top of my cup. I still don't know why I'm here, what she wants me to say, to do. Maybe nothing. I might just be a pair of ears, simply here to listen.

"I need your advice, Clem."

Or maybe not.

"You know Tony better than anyone else."

I would have gone for his mother rather than his crazed ex-fiancée, but I suppose it's an awkward conversation to have with your future mother-in-law. *Your first grandchild actually belongs to a random yoga class attendee – how do you think I should break the news to your son?*

"Should I tell him? I just don't know if I can lie for the rest of my life."

A brown wall, a set of steep stairs, garden shears.

"Sometimes we have to lie. Sometimes we don't have a choice."

I walked Nia back as far as my old flat, left her at the entrance. The concierge will make sure she gets back to the door okay. She's not my responsibility anymore. Neither is Tony. Neither is that baby.

I put her name into my phone on the train on the way home.

As I was driving from the station, she texted: *Thank you for today x*

I seem to attract people who should really be going to see a therapist. *I* should probably go and see a therapist. This whole situation counts as trauma, right? Am I a trauma survivor if I'm also a murderess? Sorry, murder*er*. Can you tell your therapist you killed someone and buried their body in your back garden? I don't think patient confidentiality extends that far. Christ, I wish it did.

I texted her back: *Good luck*

I know, I *know*. But she's thinking of telling him soon. She's going to need someone there, someone who understands what it's like to be on the receiving end of Tony's… well, she would probably call it 'negativity'. I would call it 'childishness', but both work. Although mine works better. It's more accurate.

My hand is bleeding. Just a little bit, but the skin over my right knuckles has split and is leaking bright red drops. Tiny little skin rubies. I can feel them tracking down the back of my hand as I stare at the road. Probably all that bleach, drying out my skin. All the hand washing. Lady Macbeth's hands must have been shredded into ribbons. Bet she bled all over her new queenly bed sheets. Must have been annoying. I bring my hand off the wheel and suck the droplets away. That familiar metallic taste. The smell hits the back of my throat. Even with that tiny amount, I feel my stomach twist. And I'm standing back at the top of the stairs, listening for a noise, any noise.

The road blurs. At least the salt in my tears gets rid of the taste of blood. It tastes quite nice, actually. Never tell anyone that, Clem. That's weird.

What are we going to do with all your fruit and veg, Mother? I don't fancy eating it anymore, not when I've been on first-name terms with its fertiliser. But we can't just throw it away, it's perfectly good food. Perfectly good. Maybe we could give it away. Greta could sell it in her shop, give people a cheaper choice, a choice other than *Entirely Natural*. It would be a nice legacy for you, Mother. You never were close with the community, were you? Bet you would have hated to share your food with them. Selfish. Well, I refuse to be like you: I'm going to make up some boxes tomorrow, take some round to the neighbours. Not Gus's father, though, that would be too far.

Would it?

Yeah, it would. Definitely.

I've driven home without noticing again. Watching my thoughts instead of the road. *You won't have hit anyone on the way, Clem. Just go inside. Just go home and go to bed. You don't need to go back. You don't need to check the roads. You haven't killed anyone… well, anyone else.*

Does it even matter if a murderer murders? How high does your body count have to be before you're labelled a serial killer? It would have been an accident, though, if I did hit someone. Just an accident. *No such thing as an accident – if you're unaware of your actions, then that's your problem.* Shut up, Mother.

Just looked it up on my phone: it's three. That is not that high. Well, it *is*, but it isn't. Billy is one person away from being a serial killer.

I forgot to pick up cold medicine.

***

Flyer through the door:

NEIGHBOURHOOD WATCH
Meeting Thursday 6pm in the Village Hall.
All welcome.
Nibbles and drinks will be provided by Greta.

Ha. No, thanks.

There's a message attached to the flyer. Stiff, pastel pink card attached with a bright pink paperclip:

Hope to see you both there.

No signature. Don't recognise the flamboyant, curling handwriting. Neither does Dorrie. Billy's asleep.

Weird. It should feel nice. To be invited somewhere. But it doesn't. It feels strange. Odd.

It feels like a test.

PART SEVEN

There's a dead crow on the back doorstep. I thought it was Gus that was leaving these around the house. It must have been him that decorated the house with their little bodies, right? Maybe I have another crazed, crow-murdering stalker. Maybe it just died of natural causes. Maybe someone saw us burying a body-shaped thing under the vegetable patch the other night.

It doesn't look like it suffered a natural death. It looks violent. Its stomach is swollen, its little legs sticking out at right angles. Its eyes are bulging, its beak stuck open, fear haunts its body. Looks like it choked on something. Something lodged in its throat. Probably plastic, it normally is these days. *Littering makes you a murderer* – you were right, Dad, it does.

Granted, not as violent a death as a pair of garden shears through the neck, but really, what is?

A stickiness coats the crow's feathers. Or what's left

of them. The bird's body is plagued by bald patches, dead feathers fanned out across the doorstep. From a distance it might not look like a bird, it could be a little rodent. A hairless rat.

"Hello, love."

I look up to see Greta making her way across our garden. She waves, picks through the frost on the grass in her blue wellies. They have little white stars on them. Cute.

I scrape the leaking crow corpse behind me with the heel of Dad's boot. Wave back.

I see her stare at the vegetable patch as she walks past.

The soil doesn't look disturbed. Does it? No.

"Hi." She's breathless. Our garden is bigger than most, but it's not that big. She should probably do more exercise. There's no way she does her 10,000 steps a day, standing behind that shop counter. Sorry, that was mean. Greta is nice. I should be nicer.

She waves. Again. Indicates her throat – trying to get her breath back.

I smile. Push the dead crow further back, back, back. Just hope she doesn't look down.

"Sorry… wow, this garden's longer than I remember."

I nod.

"Your mother's vegetable patch is still going strong, I see. Lovely tomatoes."

Why pick out the tomatoes? Because they're red? Blood red. We watch as an oversized crow flops down next to the plants, starts pecking at the crimson skin. Juices leak over its beak, sticky in its feathers, and I know I'm going to be sick.

"How can I help, Greta?"

We've swapped roles somehow. She's usually the one asking that question. I don't know what she thinks I have that I can sell to her.

"You should get a scarecrow. Keep the birds off the plants."

Since when has Greta been this chatty? I hear movement inside the house, pray Billy's shadow doesn't appear against the frosted glass of the door.

She turns back, peers behind me. She must have supersonic hearing or something.

I step forward. "Did you need something?"

She steps back. "Oh, yes, of course."

I bet it was her who posted that flyer through our front door, clipped that message to the front. Didn't realise she'd be the kind of woman who owned pink stationary, but okay. Things really have changed since I've been away, I guess.

"I just wondered if you'd seen Gus lately?"

I stop breathing. Greta's smiling face blurs and I feel like the crow trampled into the floor behind me.

"He didn't come into the shop this week and I know you two had been catching up recently. I thought you might know where he is?"

She glances behind me again, at the windows, and I know she thinks it's him moving around in there. That we've been doing more than 'catching up'. That he stayed the night. In a way, he did. He just slept buried under a few feet of earth with worms in his eyes and a pair of shears stuck through his neck.

More crows have landed on the vegetable patch, picking at the earth, swarming the soil.

"I know he's really been enjoying catching up with you, love. He was never the same after you left."

Before I know what I'm doing, I've rushed forward, arms flailing, voice screaming, batting at the crows, desperate for them to get away from the vegetable patch. From the shallow grave in my back garden.

The birds scatter in a flurry of blackened wings. Frantic *caws* slice the morning air. They'll be so confused, not used to this treatment from me, their friend, their bread-provider. But they have to understand – they were going to give us away. I stopped the crow-murderer, and this is how they repay me? They need to learn. If they want to live in my garden, they have to elect a new leader. They have to keep control of their crow-group. They have to choose a head for their *murder*.

"Clemmie? Clem, darling!"

"I don't know what happened. She just started shouting."

"Clem, what is it?" Long arms circle my waist, pull me back. "Clemmie, what? What?"

"The poor love, I think she was upset, the crows—"

"She's been under a lot of stress."

"Yes, yes, of course."

"What with her parents."

"Of course, I understand. Trust me."

"Clemmie, don't, don't." Soft hands come to my cheeks. Warm.

"It was the crows. They were on her mother's plants. Destroying them."

"Yes, yes, she's very upset. She hasn't processed it. Not at all."

"No, not at all."

"No."

A tall body carries me back indoors.

I watch as the crows cluster back over the plants, resume their breakfast.

The dead one is forgotten, crushed on the doorstep. Its feathers forlorn – greying and moulting in the morning sun.

***

So, I passed out. Guess I'm not doing as well with the whole cover-up-a-murder-and-lie-for-the-rest-of-our-lives thing.

Billy's no better. Worse, actually, after he had to carry the lump that was unconscious me back into the house. Apparently, he nearly dropped me twice. Dizzy spells. I'm quite glad I wasn't aware of what was going on. Would have been way too stressful.

Oh, and now Greta knows Billy is here. Which is just perfect. It'll be around the village in minutes. So will the fact that Gus hasn't been seen for days. Someone will probably go round, go inside to check on his father, find the old man dead melting into a puddle of his own goo. Then questions will be asked. Then the hard part will really start. Ha. Hilarious to think that this has been the easy part, right, Dad? I'm going to have to go to that Neighbourhood Watch meeting, do some damage limitation. Brilliant.

Also, the crows are angry at me. I know because they're doing that annoying squawking thing. They never used to do that when you were here, Dad.

Your letter is on the bedside table. Billy's opened it. He pretended he didn't know anything about it, but as I've said before, I can tell when that boy is lying. We all could, couldn't we, Dad? Also, the envelope is ripped. He's tried to un-rip it, to put it back the way it was, but he's done a bad job. Pretty much Billy down to the ground, right? He does things with good intentions, though. He was probably trying to protect me. And we all know how his protection of me ends, don't we? Or maybe he was just trying to make sure you hadn't written anything bad about him in there. You mustn't have, or it wouldn't be lying here, ready for me to read. He would have hidden it. Actually, the fact it's been left here, *placed* here, makes me think he *wants* me to read it. That it's important. If it wasn't, he would have just left it where he found it, in the kitchen. Or even just chucked it out, pretended he never opened it, that it never existed. Not sure if anyone's noticed, but that is kind of Billy's speciality. Cover it up, push it down, forget about it. And when you can't forget, take mind-altering substances that force you to forget. Clearly a bad system.

But I do kind of get it now.

Now that image of shears through a neck is seared into my mind.

The paper is thin, and my hot fingertips leave sweaty prints where they touch. It's not lined, and I can already see the writing spidering all over the place.

What did you write about, Dad? What could you possibly have to tell me? You were an open book.

You *were* an open book.

You *were*.

Please.

I can't bear it if you lied to me, too. If you were a liar. If you weren't *you*.

Dear Clemmie,

Nope, I can't.

Not right now, Dad.

Not right now.

I had a dream last night. I was picking fruit. Apples, pears, lemons, strawberries, blueberries, limes. Clementines. Then a pair of hands came up out of the earth, grasped my ankles and pulled me down, down, down, drowned me in soil.

Even my nightmares are predictable, boring. That's what Tony used to say about me. That I *plodded* along, always the same, keeping to the middle, never *changing it up*. I wonder how he feels about the woman who *changed it up* so much that she slept with someone else and passed their baby off as his.

She can't have told him yet. I've had no teary texts anyway.

I check my phone.

Yep, no missed calls.

He's not going to react well. I know that much.

I hope he doesn't come to me for emotional support. I can't deal with the both of them. I can barely deal with the one of them.

"Clemmie?"

Oh, Christ. I know I prayed to whatever it is up there that controls the universe, but when I said I wanted a child, I meant my own baby, not a Billy to look after.

"Clemmie?"

"What?"

That was too harsh, Clem. It's not his fault. It's probably *your* fault. You didn't tell him to keep warm, to wear a coat – how's he supposed to remember all on his own?

He did what he did for you.

God, he's the worst patient. He's stretched out on the sofa, blankets piled around him, hot water bottle, red nose, shivering. The bucket next to him is filled with vomit. His forehead is sticky with heat.

I take the bucket into the bathroom, pour the still-warm contents down the toilet. Does having a chill really make you throw up this much? Maybe it's the flu. I can't call Dr Robertson again, can I?

"Clemmie?"

"What?"

Better, Clem. That's a better tone. Kinder. Good.

"Can I have some water?"

I find a clean glass, fill it from the tap, hand it to Billy, then remember the rats and snatch it back off him. Brownish water sloshes onto his blankets.

He genuinely looks like he might cry.

"Sorry."

I take the bottle we filled up from Dorrie's tap out of the fridge, fill another glass with clean water, hand it to Billy. I watch him drink. Watch him cough. Watch him blow his nose on one of his blankets.

"Clemmie?"

"Yes?"

"Am I like Tony?"

"What?"

"Am I a bad person?"

Oh, God.

I shake my head. "No, Billy, you're… you're fine."

"I left…" His breath rattles in his throat. "I left her."

"It wasn't your fault, Billy. You panicked, you were so young."

"No, no, no." He shakes his head.

"She was already dead. There was nothing you could have done."

He looks at me with big eyes. "Not Amanda."

Huh?

"There was a girl."

Oh, Christ.

"She was perfect."

Oh no.

"And I left. I left her alone."

Oh, God.

"I'm a bad person, Clemmie. I just left her."

He starts crying. Like properly crying. Actually, this must be what people call 'weeping'. It's very wet.

I should say something. Tell him he's not a bad person. Tell him it's fine, that this woman is probably fine, that she's better off without him. Undoubtedly. He would not make a good boyfriend. Although, I probably shouldn't tell him those exact things – might make him feel worse. I decide to stay silent. It's usually the best way with me. Otherwise, I end up saying things I regret. I think it might be why my head is so loud inside – because I don't let much of the noise out of my mouth. It's just stuck.

I stroke my brother's hair instead.

She won't have been perfect. It's all just hormones,

chemical reactions in our brains. Believe me, I know. She was just a normal woman.

I don't say this out loud either.

Instead, I boil the kettle, refill his hot water bottle. Swap him this for the snotty blanket. I contemplate putting it in the washing machine. Put it in the outside bin instead. It's chilly outside and by chilly, I mean absolutely freezing. To the point it burns my skin.

There's someone standing at the end of the garden. Watching.

For a second I think it's him, that he's dug himself up, that he's coming for his bloody revenge. Then I realise the shadow is too short, too slight. It's a woman, definitely. Dorrie? No, I can see her moving around in her kitchen, her lights blazing across the field that separates our houses. Greta? No, too thin. Not that Greta needs to lose weight, just that this shadow is thinner than thin. Waif-life almost. Like that of a small child. Anyway, why would Greta be hiding in the shadows, watching our house? She has a shop to run, she—

They've gone. Whoever they were. They've gone. Into the night.

I stand and stare at the treeline for another few minutes. I turn, head back into the house.

***

The village hall is packed. I didn't realise this many people lived in the village. Have they all been shipped in from the nearby towns?

Really wish I didn't have to be here.

Dorrie's over the moon. Apparently, she's sick of coming on her own because she always gets sat with Sarah-from-over-the-way, and Sarah-from-over-the-way is intensely boring and every week talks to her about her hummus dip which every week she brings and every week no one eats.

I can't believe these things happen every week.

That smell hangs in the air that always hangs around in these places. That kind of damp coldness. That one that eats its way into your clothes and clings to your hair. It mingles with the smell of antiseptic cream, which we all know is the smell of old people, and the smell of stale sausage rolls. They must have onion in them. There's a whole platter of food, spread out on a trestle table covered in a white cloth. There's even a couple of cartons of orange juice, paper cups, paper straws. Very environmentally friendly.

Some of the stuff is clearly homemade. You can tell because some of the cakes and bakes have people stood next to them, smiling inanely and nodding encouragingly at anyone that looks at their food. Greta must have provided the rest of the stuff. Must have used her leftover stock she's not allowed to sell anymore because none of it is *Entirely Natural* – first time in months I've seen so much food and not seen that familiar golden tree. I should have brought a bigger bag, I could have hidden baked goods in it, taken them home for Billy.

We shouldn't have left him on his own. I told Dorrie it was a bad idea. She said if I wanted him to stop behaving like a child, I need to stop mothering him. I agreed to it on the condition he texted us every thirty minutes with updates. I deleted all the contacts from his phone except mine so he can't call any of his friends. His 'friends'. They'd probably try and treat his cold with three tabs of acid and a Jägerbomb.

He has to tell me if he feels worse and he has to ring me if he sees anyone outside the house. If he falls asleep, the whole system falls apart. I also locked him in the house. The last thing we need is a flu-addled Billy roaming around, terrorising the local villagers.

I check my phone.

New message: Billy: still fine eating chocolate I found in the back of the cupboard

Great. God knows how long that's been there. Probably been nibbled by rats.

Dorrie tenses beside me. "Oh, God, brace yourself."

An older woman walks over to us. Well, I say walks, hobbles would be more accurate. With the help of a bright red walking stick. Her skin is more wrinkled than Dorrie's, her hair completely silver, her eyes a milky blue. She looks like an old woman from a storybook. Like she's literally stepped out of the pages of a child's story. The thing we need to work out is if she's the kindly old lady who takes the little orphans in out of the kindness of her golden heart, or if she's the one who locks them in a cage and then feasts on their pure flesh.

"Dorrie, lovely to see you."

"Yes." Dorrie nods. Then doesn't say anything else. She suddenly becomes very interested in the orange juice.

The woman smiles at me, all gums, no teeth.

I smile back.

Dorrie carefully inspects the label on the orange juice.

"You're John's girl, aren't you?"

I hear Dorrie's sharp intake of breath beside me. Who is this woman, Dad? Why is she saying your name?

"Would you like some food, Clemmie?" Dorrie asks me, shoving a plate of cocktail sausages under my nose. I shake my head and take a sticky cup of orange juice instead, try to keep my smile in place.

"Clementine, that's it! I hear your brother is home. Unwell is he, poor mite? I remember the both of you as tiny little things, you know. Funny ones, you both were. No wonder I suppose, living with *her*... Well, you're the spit of your dad, aren't you?"

"Ignore her," Dorrie hisses. Then she raises her voice. "Come on, love, let's get you something to eat." She moves along down the buffet, filling a paper plate.

The woman follows us. "Oh, yes, you must eat. All you young kids are far too thin these days. Have you tried the hummus, my dear?"

Ah ha. "You must be Sarah. It's lovely to meet you."

She beams.

I decide I quite like Sarah-across-the-way. When she mentioned you, Mother, her lip curled. She's clearly a good judge of character.

My phone buzzes in my pocket.

New message: Billy: making myself a cup of tea where are the teabags?

Bad idea. Hot water and Billy do not mix.

Clem: in the cupboard next to the fridge left hand side be careful with hot water!!!

Billy: will do x

I look around the room and realise I'm the youngest here by at least thirty years. The majority of people have walking sticks, greying hair, wrinkled skin. Bony hands grip cups of orange juice, thin lips open to chew mini cucumber sandwiches, feet in orthopaedic shoes shuffle towards the nearest chairs. Most of the women have that creepy make-up that old people put on, when they outline everything too harshly and end up looking like Yzma from that cartoon with the crazed llama.

There are a couple of younger people, mainly men – must be people's children and grandchildren. They look bored out of their minds. They stand around, gazing into their cups of orange, clearly wishing they were holding a pint.

I try to smile at the guy nearest to me. I don't recognise him. He looks a bit like Tony so we're not off to a good start, but I'm prepared to give him the benefit of the doubt. He gives me a kind of sneer and turns away. Fine. Never mind. *Young people are so rude these days, there's something wrong with your generation, really there is.* No, Mother, get out of my head. I will not become like you. I will not.

Sarah is chatting to Dorrie – obviously the subject of conversation is her hummus. Apparently, she's added lemon this time. It's completely changed the flavour structure. I didn't realise Dorrie's eyes rolled that far back in her head.

Buzz.

New message: Billy: where are the mugs?

Clem: Top cupboard above oven

Clem: I'm sitting next to a woman whos obsessed with hummus x

Billy: Ahhh Sarah?

Clem: youve heard about her then?

Billy: Dor mentioned her once or twice

He's put a smiley emoji at the end. For some reason the little yellow face makes tears cloud my vision.

"Oh, here we go." Sarah's voice is bright with expectation. "Heeere we go." She grips my arm like an excited child.

The group goes quiet.

I look up to see a young woman enter the hall. She's dressed in a pink skirt suit, low pink heels, dark bob, bright, even smile. She's carrying a tiny briefcase. She's pretty, but in that overly perfect way some women are that makes them look just a bit scary. A bit *unreal.*

People stop browsing the buffet, move to their seats, settle themselves in. It feels like we're at school and the teacher has just entered the room. All conversation has dropped away to a low murmur, a scraping of seats, and a strange *fizz* has entered the air, a kind of hot thrill. I think it might be anticipation.

The woman – girl, really, she must be younger than me – steps up onto the small stage that has appeared at the front of the hall. I seem to remember standing on that stage as a small sheep, cotton wool stuck in my hair, waiting for you to come through those doors, Mother. It should have been enough that Dad was there, but somehow it wasn't. You always made your non-presence felt, didn't you? My little sheep heart shattered.

"Is this seat free, love?"

Greta.

I nod. She sits down beside me, gripping a copy of the flyer between her fingers. Her knuckles are white.

"Did you send us that note?"

She looks at me, confused. "Sorry, love, what?" Her voice holds a tremor. She keeps glancing towards the stage. To the woman standing there. The woman now unpacking her tiny briefcase, taking out pastel pink sheets of paper, pastel pink pens, bright pink paperclips, lining them up on the table in front of her. Pink stationary.

"Never mind." I shake my head.

The woman finishes unpacking her unnecessarily tiny briefcase – seriously, why is it so small and how does she fit all that stuff in it? She locks the case, stands it up on the table. The side facing us has a golden embossed tree decorating the surface.

Dorrie's hand reaches across and pats mine. She takes the cup of orange juice from my grip, places it in on the floor. It's only when it's out of my hands that I notice the stickiness on my skin, the pool of orange liquid on the floor. I must have squeezed the cup so hard, it split.

"Good evening, all." The woman's voice isn't loud or commanding, it's not particularly strong. It's light. Girlish, even. And the hall instantly falls silent at the sound of it.

"I recognise most faces here tonight. It's lovely to have you all back here again." Her smile stretches even wider, until it takes over her entire face. She's just a mouth and teeth standing in front of us. "But I can also see we have a number of new faces here. So, for the benefit of those who don't know: my name is Helen Higgins. I'm here on behalf of *Entirely Natural*, the wellness brand that puts you at the heart of everything we do."

The woman (apparently Helen Higgins, which is quite simply the most ridiculous name I've ever heard – and my name is Clementine) stares directly at me as she delivers

212

her marketing spiel. I try not to judge people on their appearance and frequently I fail at this. But this woman is beautiful. Actually, stunning. She could be a model – although she probably doesn't have the height for it. Even with heels on, she's shorter than me. And that's *short*. But the way she uses her face, the way she never lets that smile slip, it makes her ugly. This tiny girl stood in front of me is without doubt one of the most terrifying people I've ever met.

"I know we're all joyful to welcome Clementine tonight." She spreads her hands, and everyone's attention turns to me. There's general murmurs of appreciation and a man I vaguely recognise leans forward and grips my shoulder, nodding, smiling. I feel like I might have unwittingly entered a cult.

"I'm sure we all agree it's a huge shame that William cannot be here tonight, and we all wish him a speedy recovery."

William? Oh, she means Billy. No one ever calls him that. I still expect an outcry at the mention of his name. But no one reacts. One woman even nods, mutters, "Oh yes, yes."

I'm definitely in a cult.

"Now, down to tonight's business. First on the agenda…" She consults her pink pages with what feels like unnecessary enthusiasm. "Ah, of course, Greta. Please, come forward."

I watch Greta's legs shake as she takes the steps up to the stage. Everyone applauds as she stands next to Helen.

"As of today, your very own village shop is now stocked completely with *Entirely Natural* products. And that's all thanks to Greta here, who has worked tirelessly with us to ship in new stock and redecorate her lovely shop. Three cheers for Greta!"

Greta looks as though she's going to be sick as huge cheers go up around us. Her whole body trembles as she gives a teary smile. Helen shakes her hand, gives her a small envelope and guides her towards the edge of the stage. As she sits back down next to me, I can smell the sweat on her skin, see the tiny golden tree embossed on the envelope's edge. I know that envelope is the same as the one Dorrie tried to give me. I know it contains a thin piece of plastic charged full of too much money.

Helen turns back to her pink papers, calls out more names, shakes more hands, gives out more envelopes:

"Jane Babson. Jane has begun stocking *Entirely Natural* products in the local pharmacy, supplying your own Dr Robertson with the best medication money can buy!"

"Peter Liamson. Peter's son joined the *Entirely Natural* head office this week, thanks to the encouragement of his loving father."

"Anna Cousins. Anna joined *Entirely Natural*'s distribution team this week, helping us spread our products through the local communities!"

Even Sarah-from-over-the-way-Beeson gets a mention: "Sarah helped spread the word about *Entirely Natural* this week through her letter writing campaign, targeting local councils."

It takes her an age to make her way onto the stage. She waves her walking stick at the crowd in glee when she receives her envelope, huge gummy grin on her face.

It's when Helen calls for Angus Thompson that my throat completely closes up.

"Angus? Has anyone seen Gus tonight?"

Murmurs throughout the hall, shaking of heads. Greta twists round in her seat, worried eyes searching the crowd of people. Dorrie pulls my hands into her lap. I think I'm shaking.

"Well, Angus did a wonderful job this week helping Greta get her new stock situated in her shop. Greta, if you take Gus's envelope, you can give it to him, yes?"

It's the first time I've heard a small break in Helen's voice, a small annoyance: something is out of place, something hasn't gone perfectly according to plan.

She recovers frighteningly quickly. Her perma-smile never wavers.

"Clementine Finch."

She really knows how to pull a crowd back.

Even Greta turns back round to beam at me. "That's you, love." She pushes me towards the stage as people begin to applaud.

I walk on numb legs up towards Helen. I take her outstretched hand with my numb fingers. I turn to face the cheering crowd with my numbed brain. They're clapping like I've won an award. Helen steps closer, hands me an envelope, her fingers close around my wrist, face pushes close to mine. Cold.

"I'm so glad you're here, Clementine. You should be very proud of your mother. She's done a great thing. I'm sorry for how things ended."

The crowd's shouts ring in my ears. People are on their feet, clapping, some are even crying. Dorrie sits at the front, hands clasped in her lap, looking up at me.

What did you do, Mother? What did you do?

Something's wrong with my legs, a *buzzzzzzz* drifts over my skin. I need to get off this stage. I need to leave. It feels like my bones are vibrating. It's only once I've staggered back to my seat that I recognise that *buzzzzzzzzzz* as my phone vibrating in my pocket. *Billy.*

I rip my phone from my pocket, but no, it's not my little brother. Nia's name lights up my screen:

2 new messages: Nia: thank you for meeting me. I really appreciate it x

No more messages from Billy. Nothing at all. He was supposed to keep checking in. A cold feeling closes in around my throat. Why has he not been checking in? I send him a message.

Clem: everything alright?

Helen is now leading some kind of chant, they're stomping their feet, synchronised moves.

No message.

I call him. No answer.

I push past Sarah-from-over-the-way, make for the door. People try to grab me, shout something in my face. I can't hear them. I can't hear anything. I have to get out, get to Billy. Something's happened. Something bad. I can feel it.

Where are the mugs?

I remember standing on that chair, reaching for Billy's favourite mug. The legs slipping against the tiles. I could have broken my neck.

Where are the mugs?

Why the hell do we keep the mugs in such a stupidly high cupboard, Dad? Why the hell didn't I move them?

I call him again. No answer. Again. I look at the little, yellow smiley face he sent me. I can feel my heartbeat under my skin. Panic is lodged in my throat. Terror scratches along my skin.

I break out into the cold, dark air.

Where are the mugs?

I feel that same flip deep in my stomach as when I stood on that chair. See my little brother wobble, fall.

Dorrie lurches out of the door behind me. "Darling, what is it?"

"This is your fault! I should never have left him. *You* should never have *made me* leave him."

"Billy? What happened?"

"And for what? To come here to this – this – what is this? Some kind of twisted awards ceremony!"

She tries to speak, to say something else, but I can't stay here any longer. I turn and start to run. And run right into Dr Robertson.

"Miss Finch. Congratulations." He nods to the envelope still clutched in my hand. "So good to see you here tonight. Hashtag stop overpopulation, right?" He grasps my shoulders, smiles, nods.

For the first time I can make out what the group in the hall are still chanting: "no more babies, no more babies, no more babies."

Dorrie reaches her hand out towards me. She knew about this. She knew what this was. I can tell by the expression on her face. Guilt.

I pull myself away from Dr Robertson's grip.

I need to get to Billy.

PART EIGHT

The corridor is cold. Like always.

A nurse smiles briefly at me as she strides past. I recognise her from last time. I wonder if she recognises me. I'm here so often they should have a chair permanently reserved for me. They could put my name on it. Clementine Finch – perpetual waiter.

The walls seem whiter than normal. I don't know why.

The smell of bleach makes the inside of my nose fizz. Or maybe it's the tears that are doing that. Their saltiness, not content with eroding my eyeballs, has switched to my nose. I'll lose my sense of smell next.

Why they made us come here after your accident, I don't know, Dad. True, doctors can do amazing things – fuse a bone back together, help un-crack a skull, restart a heart. But I don't think even they could un-burn bodies.

You know, I overheard this woman at your funeral, Dad. I don't know who she was, where she came from.

I didn't recognise her face. But she must have known Mother well, because she said, *A fitting end if you ask me, they always did say to burn the witch.*

Swish. I look up to see if it's the doctor pushing his way through the swing doors. But it's just Dorrie.

I let her sit next to me. My tears stain her cardigan a deeper purple. What colour do they call that? Mauve?

She prises my hands away from the wrapper, scrunches the paper up into a tiny, tiny ball and shoves it into her handbag. It doesn't work, the heat of my hands melted the leftover chocolate and now it's dried onto my skin. He was eating chocolate. Happy. All he wanted was a cup of tea. That chair, slipping against the tiles. I see him in my head, over and over, slipping, falling. And I'm never there to catch him.

Dizzy spells. Just from his cold. Nothing to do with the thin white lines I found decorating our coffee table, right, Dad? Nothing at all.

He needed me. I'm never there when he needs me. Never there in time.

I don't know how hard he hit his head against the kitchen counter. All I know is when I got home my little brother was sprawled on the floor, his blood leaking into the grout. And he wasn't moving, wouldn't wake up no matter how loud I screamed. And I screamed very loud.

His phone is all smashed. I'll have to get him a new one. Please, let me have to get him a new one.

Swish. The doctor still isn't here. It's another nurse coming through the doors this time. He's pushing a very elderly man in a wheelchair. They're chatting, like old friends. They probably are – the older man looks very at home here, like he's lived here a long time. Both men nod at us as they pass.

Dorrie nods back. I don't. I'm busy making a list in my head of everything I need to do when I get home. It helps. To think of the things as chores, things I can complete, things I can do and then forget about.

Clean up the sick – side note: this task is becoming a too regular occurrence in your life, Clem

Clean up the drugs – we can't have a newly painted wall, an out-of-bounds basement AND a cocaine-covered coffee table. That really would be too suspicious

Clean up the blood – splatter is an issue

Clean the sofa – might have to strip the cushions of their covers and have them professionally cleaned

Check the whole house for more drugs – flush any I do find down the toilet

I think it was cocaine, anyway. That's the only one I know of that people make into those neat little lines. I'm convinced he puts more effort into making those lines perfectly straight than he puts into anything else in his life.

I gave the little bags of white powder to the A&E nurse. I don't know if this means they have to tell the police. But surely if they know what he's taken, they have a better chance at doing their jobs. At saving him.

Films and books and things always make it seem like hospitals are forever busy places, never quiet, never empty. But this one is. It's very empty. It was last time as well. Maybe everybody else knows something we don't, maybe other doctors can un-burn bodies. Okay, that's not really true. The hospital is busy. The A&E waiting room is very busy. But we're not in the A&E waiting room. We're in this corridor. Which is the corridor we were in when they told us about you, Dad. We're in the corridor where they tell you the bad news.

Swish.

***

Dear Clemmie,

I hope you never read this letter.

It's genuinely the hardest thing I've ever had to write. I know you'll be rolling your eyes reading that and saying, "cliché, Dad", but it's true.

I have always loved your mother. I know you had a difficult relationship, and in part I blame myself for that. But she did care for you, in her own way. She can be a good person. Which is why I can't understand why she's made the decisions she has. I told her we didn't need the money and that I would find another way, but I think she just got sick of waiting.

The loans weren't her idea, I need you to know that. They were mine. I got us into this mess, and I wanted to get us out. I made the decision to take out the money, for your brother and for you, because we love you.

I need you to remember that, Clemmie. We love you.

Sorry. I'm not explaining myself well. I've written this letter so many times and I've got ink all over my hands.

I can't see another way out, Clemmie. I have to stop her. She's become obsessed.

A woman called Helen came to the house. She said she'd heard about your mother's career, her knowledge of science, the breakthroughs she had when she was working for the government. She brought back all those things I thought we'd left behind when I convinced your mother to leave her job. She said she wanted your mother to work for Entirely Natural – *she'd make it worth our while, pay off the debts, give us a lot of money, even give Billy a job at the company.*

At first, I thought it would be good for her, a nice side project, something to keep her busy when I was out of the house. Too good to be true, I suppose.

I didn't realise what she was putting into the food at first, I promise. If I'd known, I would never have let her give it to us. I don't really care about me, I already have you and Billy, and you're all I need. But you're young, you could have got married, had children. I hate that she's taken the best thing that ever happened to me – having the both of you – away from you. But she thought she was doing the right thing, protecting you, your futures. She became obsessed with this overpopulation nonsense, convinced herself that any more children would

222

ruin the world, would mean certain death. In her way, she was trying to save you.

She developed a formula. I don't know how – you know I've always been rubbish at these technical things. I'm not a thinker, not like your mother. She's a genius, Clemmie. But they – this Helen woman and the people she works for – they took her genius, and they used it for themselves. They convinced her that the answer to this overpopulation crisis thingy was infertility, that mass infertility was the only thing that would protect the world and that we could put something in the food, make it subtle. They promised no one would need to know she had anything to do with it.

I told her they were crazy. That we couldn't just sterilise people without them knowing, but she wouldn't listen. You know she never did listen to me. And she got involved in these meetings, with everyone from the village, ranting and raving like some kind of weird cult.

I should have stopped it earlier but honestly, I never thought it would get to the stage where they actually went ahead with it. Apparently, her formula is nearly ready to be rolled out and they're going to put it into their products, the food and the drink. They were actually celebrating last night, her and Helen, drinking champagne in our kitchen. It wasn't Entirely Natural *champagne because Helen doesn't eat or drink anything* Entirely Natural. *I think that tells you everything you need to know.*

Don't let Billy eat any of the food, Clemmie, or any of the fruit and veg from the garden. It might not be too late for him. And it's not even just the fertility thing. Your mother rushed this through, because they said we couldn't have the money if she didn't get it done. And she wanted the money for you and Billy, to make sure we had something to fall back on in case either of you ever needed it. It was done out of love, Clemmie, you have to remember that – and so is what I'm going to do. It's because I love you, all three of you. And I can't let this happen.

It's the only thing I can think of to do. I know it will be hard for you, but you and Billy have each other and I know you will look after him. You're the strongest person I know, Clemmie. You're my brave, brave girl.

And this way you won't have to worry about the debt. All of that will go away as well, and you and Billy can get on with your lives. You can both have your futures.

We've had our time, your mother and me. And I've done everything I wanted to in this life. I will miss you and your brother, of course I will, but I always said I would die for my family. That's my job as a father, as a parent you have to give up everything for your child, even if that means sacrificing yourself. All I wanted was for you and Billy to have the chance to feel that love, the kind that makes you fearless and terrified all at the same time. You would have been such a great mum, Clemmie. If I'd known she was putting that poison into the food she served us both, I would never have let you eat it. I'm so sorry.

I need to stop her. And it will be quick, I promise.

We won't suffer and maybe if I do this now, no one else will either. They won't be able to use the formula without her. It's not stable yet and only she knows how to make it work. Without her finishing touches, there's no telling what this thing could do. They need her. And whilst your mother is alive, she will help them.

I have to stop her – I wish I didn't have to do this, but there's no other way. Believe me, I've looked.

My little Clemmie, my fellow birdwatcher, my daughter.

I love you.

And I hope you can forgive me.

Dad x

P.S. – if you can, take care of the birds for me.

It was deliberate. You did it deliberately. You didn't crash. You turned the wheel, you sped up, you drove into the oncoming traffic.

On purpose.

You killed yourself, on purpose.

You killed her, on purpose.

You killed all those other people, those strangers, *on purpose.*

And with that letter, you just killed my dad. You killed the man I thought I knew.

And you were wrong, by the way, Dad. Debt doesn't die with you. It's passed on to your executor. Guess who that lucky person is?

You think she was a good person. But she put it in the clementines. She filled my namesake with poison. She could have chosen any fruit, but she chose clementines. On purpose. Good people don't do things like that.

But I guess you wouldn't know, would you, Dad? You wouldn't know how a good person thinks. Because you weren't one. I'm starting to understand, you *never* were.

***

I hate myself.

For all of those nights I wished Billy wasn't here. That he would leave me alone. That he would go away.

I would give anything to clean some sick off the floor right now.

I've stopped trying to muffle the crying with my pillow. What's the point when I'm on my own?

He never told me quite how cold it was on this sofa. Even with the blankets. He never asked to swap, to have my bed, even for one night. He just slept here. He accepted it.

I hate that I had to wash everything. It's taken his smell out of the fabric, taken his shape out of the cushions. Everything just smells clean. I hate it.

Knock knock knock knock knock knock knock knock knock knock knock knock knock knock

That's not Dorrie. She's not that insistent. And she always comes to the back door. Everyone from the village does.

It's an outsider. Must be.

And it can't be Tony or else I would have heard his car. Even Nia would have come here in a taxi. Whoever it is, they walked here. Yep, I can see their footsteps striding through the frost on the path, a neat line, a low heel.

"Clementine."

A terrifying smile. Helen Higgins.

"Wonderful day."

I look up at the darkening sky. It's freezing and spitting with rain. I knew it. This woman is clearly delusional.

I stare at her.

She stares back.

It takes a while, but she breaks first.

"I heard what happened. I'm so sorry, Clementine."

I will not cry in front of this crazed pink woman. I wonder if that's the same pink skirt suit she had on at the cult meeting or if her wardrobe is just full of carbon copies of the same outfit. I wonder where she's staying.

"Your brother was a very valued member of the *Entirely Natural* community." She tilts her head and pouts her pink painted lips out. I think she might be trying to look sad. She's failing. Miserably.

I don't say anything.

Her eyes are a very bright blue. They're probably contacts. No one's eyes are that blue. Surely.

"It's such a shame for the company to lose him in this way. He did brighten up the office. Sparkly little thing." She smiles. Again. "I brought you these – with our condolences." She produces a huge bouquet of lilies from somewhere, pushes them into my arms. They're wrapped in purple tissue paper, and they stink.

She reaches out, pats my hand with hers. Cold. "I know it's hard right now, but things will get better. I promise."

"He's not *dead*!"

I drop the flowers on to the floor, watch their orange pollen stain the front step.

Her smile doesn't slip. Of course it doesn't. But I can tell she's annoyed. Not upset – annoyed. It's something about the way her eyes look into mine.

"No, of course not, Clementine. But he is very ill."

I think I finally understand what the phrase 'she had a voice like cut glass' means. Her words hurt. Feels like she's slashed my wrists for me. I wish she would stop saying my name.

"I did wonder if I could pop in for a few minutes, Clementine." She toes at the dropped lilies with the edge of her pink, suede shoe.

"You're not taking my mother's research."

That must be what those notebooks full of spidering scribbles and numbers are in the basement. I own everything in this house. It was left to me in the will. She doesn't have a claim over any of it. They needed my mother, they needed her mind. Well, now she's gone and they can't have her memories.

She smiles, shows me those whiter than white pearls again. I close my lips tight over my own coffee-stained teeth.

"Oh, Clementine." She makes a huff sound that I think might be how she laughs. "Don't worry, I'm not here to take anything from you. I don't need to. Your mother gave me everything we needed before she died. She wasn't as naïve as your father thought, you know. In fact, the new range is already in circulation."

The cold air burns my throat. My stomach definitely has something small and hot inside it, curling and writhing. Maybe I have a tapeworm. It's painful.

"No, no, I just wanted to take a look at that wall. How did the brown paint work out for you?"

The edges of my vision go fuzzy. She can't know. She can't possibly know.

I think of the shadow, stood at the end of the garden, watching.

Oh, but she does know.

She saw.

She saw everything.

I stand back from the door, to let her into the house.

But she doesn't step forward.

Instead, she reaches into her pink pocket, brings out yet another stiff white envelope, a tiny golden tree embossed in the corner.

My hand reaches out.

And I take it.

"I knew you'd make the right choice, Clementine. This should take care of the outstanding debts, Billy's rehab."

"Rehab? He doesn't need *rehab*, he's fine."

She just smiles at me.

"He doesn't have a problem." My voice sounds small, childlike.

Helen turns, starts to walk back down the path. Then she stops.

"Oh, and don't worry about the other... matter. We can make that go away. Easily. As long as you leave everything to us. You just stay here, Clementine. Live your life. Forget about all this."

She reaches the gate, then turns back to deliver the final blow.

"You're more like your mother than you know, Clementine."

Ouch.

***

It snowed last night. The fallen lilies have dissolved into a mulchy, half frozen mess on the front step. They smell even worse now.

I decide to leave them there.

One way to deter visitors.

I have to scrape the ice off the windscreen. Can't find one of those little scraper things so I just use my hands. It hurts.

Need to concentrate whilst I'm driving this time. Then again, if I do hit someone, I can just scrape them up off the floor and drop them off at A&E before I head to the intensive care ward.

I can't believe I'm heading to the intensive care ward. Or maybe I can. Should have been obvious this was going to happen, Clem. You stopped paying attention. You left him alone.

It's your fault.

Like everything.

I can't get his blood out of the grout. Yes, Mother, I have tried everything, stop judging me.

BANG

Oh God.

Oh God, oh God, oh God.

I've hit something. Run something over. It's dead, whatever it is. Definitely, definitely dead. I felt the wheels go over its body, crack its bones in half, burst its lungs. If it's a person, I only have to kill two more and then I'm a serial killer. It can't be that easy, surely. It can't be that quick.

The car makes that annoying *ding, ding, ding* sound as I open my door, step out. It's misty this morning, the air thick, maybe no one saw me, maybe I can get away with murder.

Again.

The radio did say visibility was low. Is that a mitigating circumstance? Could I win sympathy from the jury with the fact that Billy is in hospital? Probably not, considering he's also a murderer.

I could just take the body, bury it in the veg patch. With him. Keep all your secrets in one place, then you know exactly where they are. Or are you meant to spread them out? Because if someone finds one, they'll find them all. And whoever this is trapped under my wheels, they don't deserve to be stuck with him for all eternity. They didn't do anything wrong. It's me that's the wrong one.

If I have my license taken off me, how will I get back and forth to see Billy? He's got Dorrie, but it's not the same. Or maybe he prefers her. Maybe he hates me. That would make two of us.

There's blood. On the front wheels. There's blood.

Oh God, I'm like him. I'm like my dad. Lethal behind the wheel.

It wasn't deliberate, I promise. I swear to you.

There's blood.

And fur.

There's fur.

It's a rabbit.

Or it *was* a rabbit. It's now a mangled mess of fluff.

I hope it's not someone's pet. I can't see a collar. But then I can't see anything resembling a face either. Or a body. Or paws. Now that I look closer, I'm not sure it was a rabbit. Maybe a fox, a hare, an extremely large rat? I hope it wasn't the last one. Then again, if I've killed it, there's at least one less of them scurrying about. Getting under people's wheels. In people's water tanks.

There's nothing I can do for it now. Whatever it is. Was.

I get back in the car.

My hands shake.

I cry. Again. My eyeballs are definitely going to rot from all the salt. Why is no one else talking about this? I feel like it's something we should be warned about.

I close my eyes and think of perfect, orange clementines. Something else we should be warned about, right, Mother?

I take such a deep breath it hurts the back of my throat. I open my eyes. I put the car into gear. I can't take an obliterated maybe-rabbit to the hospital. Not if I want them to concentrate on Billy.

***

Back in the bad news corridor again.

No one else here, again. I should be happy about that. Less seriously ill people should be a good thing. But it's not. Not when it's your brother laid at death's door.

I liked that saying when I was little – 'death's door'. It always made me think of a little black door, in that white waiting room of limbo. A tall, thin figure in a long, black robe popping his little skull out every so often, calling a name. Welcoming them in. He seemed nice in my head, Death. Nicer than the angels, anyway. They always seemed righteous to me. And how do they keep their robes so clean? Very suspicious. Death seems more down to earth – I feel like I could have a good chat with him. He would definitely send me down, rather than up, so I wouldn't even have to make small talk with the angels. And at least it would be warm, down there. Up in the clouds always sounded cold to me. Bit like this corridor. You would think they'd want their patients to be comfortable. It's nearly as cold as the cottage in here.

Voices. I can hear voices. People talking.

He's awake.

I start running.

I drop my bag and multicoloured things spill out across the floor. Keys, tampons, lipstick that I forgot was in there, chewing gum, mascara that I haven't used in months. Difficult to wear mascara when you keep crying it off. My phone hits the ground. Definitely smashed. I don't stop.

I round the corner, push through the door into Billy's room.

I don't understand the picture in front of me.

It wasn't Billy talking. It was Dorrie. And Helen. It was Dorrie talking to Helen.

Billy isn't in the bed. He isn't sat on the uncomfortable blue chair in the corner. He isn't standing at the window. He isn't in the tiny bathroom linked to the room. He isn't anywhere.

"Clementine. How lovely to see you again." That whiter than white smile.

If I still had my bag full of heavy things, I would throw it at her head.

Dorrie's been crying. I can tell from the red patches around her eyes. Why has she been crying? Where is he?

Please. No, no, no, no, no, no.

I don't want to need those lilies.

I try to speak but my throat feels clogged. I just point at the empty bed, the smooth sheets, the hospital corners.

Helen clears her throat. Keeps that smile in place.

Then Dorrie sees my face. "Oh darling, no. He's fine, he's okay, he's fine."

The floor comes up to meet me. For such a tiny woman, Helen is surprisingly strong. She lifts me up, steers me over to the uncomfortable blue chair, sits me down. She must be wearing a lot of perfume, she smells pink.

"Yes, Clementine, this is truly a joyful day."

Why does she speak like that? She's definitely from a cult, she's quoting their religious text.

"Where is Billy?"

My voice doesn't sound like me.

"He's okay, love. He woke up a couple of hours ago, they've just taken him for a few scans and things. He'll be back soon." Dorrie smiles at me through what I now know are happy tears.

"He's been awake for a couple of *hours*, and you didn't call me?"

If they had called me earlier, I wouldn't have hit that maybe-rabbit.

"It all happened so quickly, love. And I knew you'd be here soon anyway." She tries to take my hand, I pull away. Why was the strange, pink cultist here but I wasn't? That's not fair. He's my brother. Mine. Not hers.

I can see the contents of my bag spilt over the floor in

234

the corridor. I should really go and get everything. There's a letter amongst the stuff. The one from Dad. Forgot I put that in there. Need to get it back before someone else picks it up and reads it. Too many people have already seen it. Dorrie probably has. Billy definitely has.

Billy's read the letter.

He knows. He knew. This whole time.

Everyone knew but me. Right, Mother?

"Clemmie?"

He's in a wheelchair, his head wrapped in a thick bandage. Pale, thin, alive. Now that I know he's okay, I kind of want to push his wheelchair out of this second-floor window. He smells like hospitals. And bleach. Makes it hard to go near him.

I feel him smile inside my hug. He's cold, like always. I need to take better care of him. He's my responsibility, *my* little brother. He doesn't have anyone else. I'm taking us away from here. Somewhere new, somewhere where there's no cult meetings in the village hall, somewhere safe. We'll get away from these people. Dorrie can come if she likes. Somewhere where he doesn't have access to drugs. Somewhere even more remote than the village. Somewhere we can make our home. Away from the memories, the dead bodies and the poisoned clementines growing fatter in the basement.

I pull back, look at his eyes. His pupils are normal. His eyes are pretty, really, very blue. Calm. Then they go wide.

"Hello, William."

My brother's entire body stiffens. He stares at Helen.

"Oh, don't worry, your place with us is safe. The job will be kept open for you until you're better. You're a very

235

valued member of our team, William. I'm just here to make sure you're okay."

Billy looks like he's going to throw up.

The doctor who wheeled him in is speaking to Dorrie, explaining something, pointing at various papers. He looks serious. But then, what doctor doesn't? It would be wrong if they were beaming all over their faces, telling you it's terminal and they can't operate. Dorrie nods.

"Oh, I'm to give you this. Don't worry about the money, it's all paid for. All you need do is find someone to drive you there." Helen hands my brother a shiny booklet. Looks like a university prospectus. "I'm sure your sister wouldn't mind." She turns her thousand watt smile back on me. Those teeth can't be real – they practically blind you if you try to look directly at them.

Why would *Entirely Natural* pay for my brother to go to university? They can't possibly think by being in an academic environment, it's going to unlock some kind of genius, passed down from his mother. Can they?

"Sorry, ladies, I'm going to have to ask at least one of you to leave. We're not really allowed more than one visitor at a time."

The doctor is wearing a name badge: *Dr Simonstone*. He's young, looks fairly normal. But then so do a lot of the people who were at that cult meeting the other night. I think *I* look fairly normal. So really that means nothing.

"No apology necessary, Doctor. I was just leaving." Helen bats her eyes, and the young doctor suddenly goes all smiley. What is the matter with men? Seriously.

"I wish you a speedy and joyful recovery, William. Dorothy, lovely to see you, as always. Clementine." Helen nods at each of us in turn. Her eyes linger on mine, she leans in close. "I hope you'll consider The Retreat, Clementine. I think it will be good for your brother. You know we'll take care of payment, take care of the both of you, for as long as is needed. You need do nothing. *Nothing* at all."

The retreat? I peer closer at the prospectus. It's not a university. It's a rehab centre.

She says the words in a voice that makes the doctor gaze at her, as though she were some kind of angel. But as we know, I don't trust angels. And I know what she really means. This is why they've been giving everyone cards charged full of cash, this is why they've guaranteed Billy a job at their high-profile company, this is why she's really here in my brother's hospital room – they're buying our silence.

***

The doctor gave us a load of pamphlets:

The Dangers of Drugs
How to Cope with Addiction
So, You Think You Have a Problem With Drugs?

Apparently, they found high levels of cocaine and LSD in my brother's system. Guess we can't keep pretending he's fine anymore, hey Dad?

Billy has slept all morning. Apparently normal, the young doctor says. I don't really care if it's normal or not, as long as he's alive.

Dorrie has spent the morning baking coffee cake, trying to cover up the dank smell that has started to rise from the basement. No idea where it's coming from. Maybe there's a damp patch somewhere. Maybe it's a reaction to the fact it housed a dead body. The house is rebelling. Don't worry, Mother, your precious clementines are fine.

Your less precious Clementine has spent the morning adding up the money on the cards inside the envelopes. It's taken that long because I have to keep checking the amounts written on the plastic cards. Dorrie must have found the envelope I hid in the back of the cupboard, because that one's here as well – £10,000. £50,000 in the one Helen gave to me at the cult meeting. Another £53,000 in the one she gave me at the front door yesterday – an oddly specific amount. £113,000 – meant to be an unlucky number, isn't it? Thirteen.

I wonder how much she paid you, Mother?

I checked the online banking, the debts they left me with – £50,567. And twelve pence, to be exact.

The rehab centre they've recommended is £2,500 a night. I can't believe we're talking about a *rehab centre*. That's not language I need to use in my life. It's something other people need, something other people have to deal with. Not me. Not my little brother. Not our family.

I don't know quite how I've deluded myself into thinking that we're normal people.

Helen said they would cover all costs, she said they would clear the debts, and every week, I'll get another envelope.

All I have to do is nothing.

And if we do nothing, we don't even have to worry about the body buried in the back garden.

They found his father yesterday. When we came back

from the hospital the police were parked next door, the paramedics pushing a black plastic body bag into the back of the ambulance. I tried my hardest to disguise the blood and fluff of the maybe-rabbit still plastered over the car's front wheels.

If someone dies because of neglect and that neglect only happened because of something you did, are you their murderer? Because that means my little brother is officially a serial killer. I wonder if there's any kind of mitigation with that definition if all three dead people are members of the same family – and if that family are intensely annoying. Were. Were intensely annoying. Probably not. Might actually be worse.

We got an invite to the funeral this morning. Disturbingly fast turnaround, if you ask me. Must have had them all ready and printed, just ready to be handed out. People around here are morbid. I didn't see who dropped the invitation off but judging by the block-heeled footprints in the frost, I think we can all have a good guess. How is she not cold in that pink skirt suit? That blazer can't be very thick.

"Clemmie?"

I head straight to the bedroom – I've moved Billy in here, so he can have the bed. The sheets are twisted up and covered in sweat, but there's no sign of him.

"Clem, love?"

Dorrie.

Now I can hear Billy coughing. They're in the kitchen.

Dorrie is sitting him down at the table, stroking his back. He looks up at me with worried eyes. His bandage needs changing again. Rusty red.

"You're on bed rest."

"Love, you need to see this." Dorrie points out of the window at the garden. My first thought is the veg patch – there's a hole where it once was, an empty, gaping hole, and the soulless zombie of the man we killed is standing staring at us, revenge in his eyes.

But no, the patch is flat, the veg still thriving. It's not the body of Gus I need to worry about, it's the little bodies of the dead crows that lie scattered across the frost.

The whole flock. The whole murder.

My breath sounds loud in my own ears. I open the door, step outside, the frost bites into my feet. Cold, little teeth.

Their liquid black feathers have turned a dead white-grey. Their shiny, bright eyes permanently open. There's no one here. I think of Helen, standing at the bottom of the garden. I think of Gus, letting the creatures into the cottage, leaving them to starve to death. I think about his gift at Christmas. But the bird feeder is still full, only a few seeds have been pecked away. Because why would they eat the tiny, boring seeds when there's a smorgasbord of fruits right there? You killed them, didn't you, Mother? This whole time, it was you.

Yes, their beaks are sticky with some kind of red goo – juice. From the berries. From *your* berries, Mother. I move closer. Yes, the berries have little pockmarks in them, where pointed beaks have gorged on the flesh.

I pick up one of the bodies, cradle it in my hands. Its feathers disintegrate under my touch, leave a layer of dust on my hands. My teardrops land in the bird's bald spots.

"Love." Dorrie appears at my shoulder, makes me put the corpse back down on the grass. I want to cover them

240

with something, leaves, or soil. I could bury them under there, with him. Maybe their ghostly forms would peck out his dead eyes. He deserves that.

"She did this."

Dorrie nods, her eyes watery.

"She did all of this."

They didn't do anything. They were innocents. Just like us. Just like those people on the motorway, driving their cars. But you didn't save the birds either, did you, Dad? I thought you loved them. But then, I thought you loved me, too. But you let me eat her experiments. For years.

You're the reason I'm not a mother.

We have to tell someone, anyone. This stuff is lethal, we can't let them roll it out to the public. We could go to the press. It would be a scandal; it would blow up. There would be more riots. There would be an investigation. Everyone's opinion of you would be confirmed, Mother. I think that would be the best part.

I can see Billy standing in the doorway, he reaches one arm out, as though he wants to touch me. But I'm standing too far away.

He needs that retreat.

You made a vow, Clem. They saved him, now you need to put *him* first. *He* is your responsibility, not these other people, these strangers you don't even know. You don't owe them anything. If they choose to buy *Entirely Natural* products, on their heads be it. Who eats something so trustingly anyway? Who drinks something just because the adverts say it's great? No one can trust anything nowadays – people should know that. It's not my fault people have blind faith.

No one else would turn down this amount of money. And none of it is really anything to do with me. Just because they were my parents, doesn't mean I'm responsible for their actions. Should be the other way around, really. I'm their child, we're their children, they shouldn't have left us their mess to deal with. I shouldn't have to make these decisions.

It's nothing to do with me.

Nothing at all.

But Billy is.

I need to read that retreat booklet. Find out where it is at the very least. I wonder if they allow siblings to stay. I'm not leaving him on his own again. Not now. Not ever.

I walk back inside and steer him back into bed.

I think we all deserve a cup of tea. I'll clean up the dead birds later.

PART NINE

I watch Dorrie's bent back as she makes her way around the garden. Picking up the little bodies, putting them carefully in a basket. We've decided to dig a mass grave at the end of the garden. At least we can dig this one in the daylight.

I turn back to the booklet in my hands. It's shiny, blue and filled with pictures of smiling people. Their grins have a slightly demented feel to them, like Helen's.

We fully support all your needs here at The Retreat. From specialist treatments, to diet-specific meal plans and fully-trained therapists on call 24/7, we want to help not only cure you, but allow you to thrive. Your time at The Retreat will allow you to unlock your true potential and fully engage with the world around you. Join us today to begin your new life.

Again, I'm getting cult vibes. Maybe this isn't the best idea.

And what kind of therapist isn't fully trained, anyway? That shouldn't be a selling point, it should be a base requirement, surely. I suppose the kind of therapist I would be able to pay for without stupid Helen's help might not be what you could call 'fully trained'. Or even 'partially trained'. Or even 'therapist'.

Because it would be me.

Without Helen's help, I don't just have no money, I have minus £50,567.

And counting.

49.9% APR.

I need to talk to you

…

I think I've made the worst mistake

…

Of my life

…

Leaving you

…

Can I see you Clemmie??

…

Please

Tony. He must be drunk. Maybe she finally told him.

***

Is it worse to go to the funeral of the man you indirectly killed, or worse to stay away? I mean, they're both bad options. It's a bad situation.

Dorrie thinks we should go. She should be a political campaign manager. She always thinks of the optics, how things would look – to who, when, how, who will be there, who won't be, what they would say to each other and to strangers if we went, and what they would do if we didn't.

I guess village life is a kind of cult in itself. Even without omniscient, pink leaders, synchronised chants and deadly food and drink. Christ, I swear I'm living in a dystopian film. Maybe the next person to appear on our doorstep will be the producer, complete with his camera crew and adoring fans, telling me I've won, that I've beaten the show. Gus will appear, covered in fake blood, my parents with their bodies unbroken, their debts non-existent, the research meaningless. Helen will remove her creepy smile and put on normal clothes. Billy will reveal he's been sober for two years. Nia will remove her fake bump and Tony will return to bended knee.

Or maybe not that last one. I don't know about that last one.

"Well done, Clementine! The viewers love you! Such heart, such drama! You're an instant star!"

No, I would hate to be famous. Everybody knowing your business.

Even in my fantasies, I have a constant sense of dread.

There's definitely something wrong with me.

My hair has started growing out weird, mainly in tufts above my ears for some reason. I look insane. Probably accurate.

***

Really should have seen this coming.

He has always had the worst timing.

At least Billy is still asleep. He doesn't need to know about this. About any of this. No one needs to know about any of this. As far as everyone outside this room is aware, the following things never happened:

I looked out of the window and saw a stupid, sporty car.

There was a knock at the door.

I noticed seven missed calls on my phone.

I opened the door.

I let him inside.

We talked.

He cried.

We had sex on the newly cleaned sofa (side note: the dry cleaners in the nearby town are going to think I have some kind of OCD problem).

We slept.

He told me he'd made a mistake.

He told me that she told him that the baby is not his.

I feigned surprise.

He slept again.

I stared at the ceiling for four hours.

I made this list in my head.

Yet another list I probably shouldn't write down anywhere. Great. Again, that means I can never throw it out. I have to file it away next to the murder clear up lists inside my brain. It's really getting cluttered in there.

Tony's hair is going grey at the temples. It's shiny in the sunlight coming through the kitchen window. Weird.

Yes, my hair may look crazy, but at least it's still a normal colour. I wonder if the stress has turned it that shade. Saying that, if grey hairs were down to stress, mine should have all shrivelled up and fallen out weeks ago. Maybe even months ago. He must just be getting old.

"Clemmie?"

I bolt upright, scramble for my clothes on the floor.

"Clemmie?"

Christ, don't come in here, don't come in here, do *not* come in here. My brother does not need any more trauma in his life. It might make his brain implode. Also, the doctor told him to avoid stress. He even said it with a completely straight face, so I think he was serious, and it wasn't the hilarious joke I first assumed it to be.

"Clem? What you doing?" Tony holds a sleepy arm out in my direction. "Come back."

I really need to stop collecting needy men. They're a drag.

"Stay here. Don't move." I shove his arm back under the blanket. Billy's sick blanket, I've just now realised. Lovely. At least I washed it.

"What?" He's laughing. At me. Again.

Why am I like this? I mean, it's obvious there's something wrong with me, but I keep going back to *him*? Really? Okay, so he's not the baby's biological father, but that shouldn't matter. If he really loved her, he would be that baby's dad just the same. Being a father and Being A Father, being someone's dad, they're not the same thing. At all. But clearly he doesn't love her, does he? Or he wouldn't be here. With me.

His nose has pretty much fully healed, just a purplish bruise left. He told me last night he thought it was hot that

247

I almost broke his nose. Why I didn't run screaming from him then, I will never understand. Come on, Past Me, that should have made you stop, made you think. What kind of psychopath thinks random violence is hot? I guess, most men who watch those crazy action films. And some women. Women can be attracted to violence too, Clem – don't be sexist now.

I step out into the hallway, slam the door behind me, just in time. Billy is in front of me, wrapped in yet another blanket, bare feet, shivering.

"Can I have more painkillers yet?"

"No, Billy. Not yet."

"But my head really hurts."

He's jittery – is this withdrawal? The doctor told us to keep the pain meds to a minimum. I've already given him too much.

I push past him down the hall. Inside the bedroom, the sheets are twisted on the bed, sweat patches on the mattress.

I think about the body laid naked on the sofa in my kitchen right now. About the fact that the hands attached to that body took my ring from my mother's jewellery box and slid it onto the finger of a woman carrying someone else's baby. How did my life end up as an episode of Hollyoaks?

Billy's scratching his arms. Drawing blood. I touch his hands, still them. His eyes look sad when they meet mine.

"When can I have more paracetamol?"

I look at him. "When did it get this bad, Billy?"

"It's – what? I'm not – it's not bad," he stutters. "I'm just asking. I have a headache… I did just give myself a concussion." He tries to smile. Fails.

"Yeah, because you 'overbalanced.'"

"What are you saying?"

"I'm saying you have a drug problem, Billy. You were doing lines of coke off our coffee table, you had LSD in your system, you're jittery and weird and practically scratching your skin off your arms!"

I grab his hands again, pull them away from his skin. His fingernails have blood underneath them. Looks like he's got a pink French manicure.

"The doctors think you need rehab."

He looks down at his arms, as though he's seeing them for the first time. "It's just itchy," he mumbles.

I feel tears gathering behind my eyes.

"Clem, what's going on?"

Oh, fantastic. Don't worry, Tony's here everybody! What could be better? For Christ's sake, could he not have thought to put more clothes on? Pretty sure I bought him those boxers. Does he wear them when he's with her, too? Or did he dig them out of the back of his drawer for this very occasion? Does he still keep his underwear in the same drawer?

Focus, Clem.

"You." Billy's eyes narrow as he takes in Tony's shape standing in the doorway. I feel the air in the room start to shift. This is not good.

Tony smirks, looks Billy up and down, takes in his unwashed hair, his shaky limbs. "Detox looks like it's going well."

"Okay, Tony, why don't we go and talk in the kitchen?"

He leans against the doorframe, smiling at my shivering brother. He's enjoying this.

"What is he doing here?" Billy asks.

"Nothing. Tony was just leaving."

"Oh, nothing? It didn't seem like nothing last night," Tony says.

Please. I can't cope with this right now.

"I think you should leave." My brother's voice shakes, but his eyes are dark, stormy.

"Oh, really?"

"Yes, you need to get out of our house."

"I think you'll find it's actually Clem's house. According to the will."

Why do I tell Tony these things?

"It's not surprising. I wouldn't have left anything to you either if I were your parents. You'd probably just sell it to buy drink or drugs," he says.

"Tony, leave it."

"No, Clem. You're too soft with him, he needs some tough love."

"How would you have any idea what he needs?"

"Just, *shhh*, Clem – I've got this." He pushes past me, comes further into the bedroom. I see something in my brother's eyes shift when Tony puts his hands on my shoulders.

"Don't touch her," he says.

Tony just laughs, walks right up to Billy. I pull at his arm, and he shrugs me off, quite hard. I stumble back. I see the moment something snaps inside my little brother, wonder if this is the same look he had in his eyes that night at the top of the basement stairs.

"I said, *don't touch her!*" he yells. He starts to pick things up, throws them in Tony's general direction. Just cushions, pillows, a small, blue, plastic pen pot with no pens in it. Small things. They won't actually hurt. From the way Tony reacts, you'd think my little brother was chucking a selection of knives directly at his head. That man really needs to get some perspective. He starts yelling back hysterically, until both men are shouting at each other.

"Tony, calm down."

"Calm down? He's attacking me. He's deranged!"

"He's not deranged."

"You're a psychopath, your sister was right about you."

"Tony, stop."

"Me? He's the one chucking things at my head!"

Billy pushes his face right down into Tony's. Really *down* – wow, I hadn't realised how short Tony was until Billy stood next to him. He's like a lanky attack dog, poised to draw blood.

"I should kill you. You left Clemmie alone, you hurt her. I should *kill you.*"

"Yes, well, you're good at that, aren't you?"

Billy rears back, turns to me. Betrayal slides over his face.

"That was years ago," I say quickly. "He didn't mean to. It wasn't his fault she died." Emphasis on the *she*.

Billy looks confused, scared, *cornered.* Just don't say anything, don't say anything else. Of course, I didn't tell Tony about Gus – does he think I'm mental? He means Amanda, he only means Amanda.

"That's not what you told me before." Tony's smile is horrible, twisted. Smug. But Billy's fist wipes it straight off his face. I did not see that coming. It almost seems like

Billy didn't either. He's staring at his hand as though it hit Tony smack in the mouth all on its own.

Tony swears, starts screaming at us both. Then he lunges for my brother.

My body moves instinctively, pushes in between them.

Limbs flail, then I hear Billy scream as my head is slammed into the doorframe. I always thought it was just an expression, 'seeing stars', but little flashes of light actually filter across my vision. My body feels light, like I've drunk too much wine, or vodka, or gin. The floor comes up towards me.

Tony's eyes are huge, shocked. He didn't mean to, he was going for Billy, he's so so so sorry. Like the fact he was intending to hit my brother and not me would make it any better. It was an accident, just an accident.

Billy screeches like some kind wild creature and grabs Tony by his greasy hair.

The stars still decorate my vision as the two men tussle on the floor. Their shapes blur into one as pain blooms across my forehead. I think I might be bleeding.

Tony could be lucky number three, the next body to tip my brother over into serial killer territory. Please, no. He's not worth it.

"What on earth is going on in here?"

Dorrie's slight body appears in the doorway, like some kind of miracle.

We all fall silent.

Small rivulets of blood dribble down my face, fall onto the wooden floorboards. They make a nice pattern.

Dorrie sits me down on the sofa. Dabs at my head with clumps of tissue. I must be bleeding. Either that or they've started making red kitchen roll. She's saying something, but I can't really hear her. I'm just watching Billy. Sitting across from me. Worry in his eyes, his nails pulling at his skin. I want to reach out, stop him, but he's too far away.

"Why is he still here?"

"It was an accident, Billy. He didn't mean it."

"He slammed your head into the doorframe!"

"Okay, but it's not like I'm laid at the bottom of a flight of stairs, is it?"

I hate this. I feel like *her*.

Billy looks like he might cry.

"You don't like him anymore, though. Do you?"

"No."

He grips at my hand. I see a flash of doubt flicker across his eyes.

"You don't need him, Clemmie, you have me."

"Billy, you're hurting me."

His gaze drops to our linked hands, and he quickly releases his grip.

"Sorry. I'm sorry."

His long fingernails have dug into my flesh, leaving little half-moon imprints. I feel the now faded bruises along my arms throb in recognition.

***

"He has to go."

"I just don't know if it's the right place."

"What are you talking about? It looks amazing."

"Yes, but—"

"And you're saying they'll pay for all this?"

"Yes."

"Just because he's employed at their company?"

"Yes."

"Because they 'value him'?"

"Yes."

"That is a bit weird, Clem."

"You just said it sounded good."

"Yeah, but that is strange – come on – *him*?"

"Okay, Tony, you've made your point."

"Woah, woah, you're still bleeding. You need to stay sitting down."

"Oh, and whose fault is that?"

"Watch it! This suit is new."

"It's alright, I know a good dry cleaners."

***

How did you do this, Mother? I've had no sleep. I don't know which is worse: pretending I can't hear my brother crying in the bedroom or listening to Tony whining about a child that isn't his child and how unfair his life is. Tony is definitely more annoying. I know that much.

I don't say anything, just stand up and head outside. I need a break. I can still see his lips moving through the window. He hasn't noticed I've left the room. How has this man been engaged twice? What is wrong with Nia and me, as women? Because it's something serious.

Something is different about the garden. The fizz has gone from the air. That spark. It feels colder out here, if that's possible. The air: it feels dead.

Is it the crows, buried in their mass grave near the fence? Is it him? Affecting this world from the other side.

No.

It's the veg patch.

I suppose it could still be him, he is trapped under there now. But somehow, I don't think it is. I think this is you, isn't it, Mother? I don't know why – but then I never understood you. You're like that Greek goddess, is it Demeter? Killing all the crops because we aren't paying you enough attention anymore. Actually, I think Demeter killed everything because her daughter was dead. She was so angry that she couldn't keep her daughter, her grief made the world desolate. You would never be so loving would you, Mother? Well, you have my attention.

I know fruit and veg aren't supposed to grow in the dead of winter, they aren't supposed to contain poison either. But they definitely aren't supposed to look like that.

Or smell like that. Like curdled milk.

"You should really clean that away."

"Christ, Tony!" My heart jumps inside my chest cavity. Did you hear him coming, Mother? I didn't.

"I know she's dead, Clem, and that's very sad, but you were never that close to your mother anyway. It's not like keeping some rotten vegetables is going to make anything better."

I poke at the sludge congealing on top of the now frozen soil with the toe of my socked foot. Strings of black goop stick to me. I half expect it to shudder itself to life and start running up my leg, curl around my waist, drag me down to join him.

"Plus, they absolutely stink."

I reach down and dab at it with my finger. It's like tar. This stuff is swimming around in our innards. It'll soon be swimming in the innards of everyone. Swimming in Tony's innards too.

"Ew, Clem, don't."

Ew? He sounds like a teenage girl.

"I told you ages ago there was something wrong with them things. They shouldn't have been growing like that in the middle of winter. I don't care how good of a gardener your mother was. I'm telling you, get rid of them." He sighs. "I'm going back inside."

I don't know why he's telling me.

How do you get rid of toxic tar food anyway? Is it recyclable, Mother? We need to be kind to the planet, you know. Just killing all the future babies isn't going to solve everything. Even if there are no more humans born for a while, we still have all of the ones that are alive right now. There will still be a climate crisis, an overpopulation problem. You haven't fixed anything. All you've done is remove the possibility of more Greta Thunbergs being born. You've basically destroyed our chances. There really is no Planet B.

I can feel Tony shivering next to me. Still standing there. In his shiny shoes.

"There was fruit as well."

"What?"

"In the patch. She didn't just grow vegetables. There was fruit, too."

He stares at me. Shakes his head. Then he turns and walks away.

***

The image is of a sunset.

Generic. Yet again.

At least my life is varied. If I used my Instagram, at least people would get a kick out of it: rats in a water tank, murder, dead body, midnight burial, dead crows, detoxing brother, another dead body, pink cultist, envelopes embossed with trees, tar sludge stuff. See. Interesting. And that's just a small selection.

But, no, Nia's gone with a sunset.

The caption says: *When it feels like the world isn't looking out for you, remember, tomorrow is a new day.*

Yeah, a new day – a whole new opportunity for things to get even worse. More death, distoom and gloom. Distoom. *Dis-tooooom.* Is that a word? Maybe I mean 'doom'. Doom and gloom. And distoom. I like it. I'm keeping it. If it comes up in Scrabble, I'm claiming it as a word. Billy won't know any better. The state he's in right now, I could tell him the sky is green and the grass is blue and he'd believe me.

If I leave that tar sludge out there much longer, maybe the grass really will turn blue, and sprout tentacles, and start eating the neighbours. Well, the ones we haven't already killed.

Billy's gone small and shivery again. He says he doesn't need to go to the retreat. I don't blame him. He's probably terrified the creepy cultist perma-smile will transfer to his face if he spends too much time *among them*.

Join us, join us, join us.

I wish someone would make Tony leave. I've tried asking nicely. Then I tried asking not so nicely. Neither worked. Apparently, he's 'here to save me from myself', which is a completely meaningless sentence and doesn't get us anywhere. A meaningless sentence from a meaningless man.

Thank God Dorrie turned up when she did. I wonder if Billy would have got so angry if she'd been here in the first place? Maybe it's me.

Tony is picking his teeth over my mug of tea. I watch Billy's disgusted face turn from pale to sheet white. I swipe the cup away from him, pour the rest of it down the sink. Try not to see the bits floating at the top. What the hell has he been eating? Try not to be sick. How many times has he picked his teeth over mugs of my tea before and I've never noticed, just carried on drinking it? Uuurggh.

"So, what's the plan here, then?"

Three pairs of eyes turn to stare at Tony.

"I just mean, you can't all three of you stay here for the rest of your lives. Locked away in the provincial town, staring at the big, wide world from behind panes of dusty glass." He speaks in a kind of sing-song voice that makes me want to punch him in the throat.

"This is a very in demand real estate area I'll have you know, young man."

Go on, Dorrie.

"I mean, come on, Clem. You don't want to stay stuck here. You know that! The whole time we've been together, all you've done is complain about this place."

"That's not true."

It is.

"It is."

"Things change, Tony. We can't all have exactly what we want when we want it. We're not all you."

"What's that meant to mean?"

Meant to mean. Ha. Rhymes… I think. It sounds nice, anyway. Rhythmic.

"Clem is being responsible. Although I doubt you would know what that means, dear."

Remind me to always get Dorrie on my side in a fight. The woman is stone cold savage.

"You're not together anymore," Billy whispers.

Tony stands up from the table, comes to join me at the sink.

"Come *on*, Clemmie. Seriously? You want to stay here? With these people?" He leans close, starts to whisper. "You, Clementine Finch, want to spend your days stopping a mental junkie from smacking you in the face and drinking tea with a simple-minded old lady?"

Anyone would think he *wants* me to throw hot tea over him. I mean, the kettle is right there. I stare him out.

"The heating doesn't even work. You don't even have a proper bed!"

"Didn't seem to bother you last night." I lower my voice too, but I'm pretty sure I see Dorrie smile. Ears like a bat, that one.

"You're not together anymore," Billy repeats.

"What?" Tony turns to look at my little brother, annoyance radiating from him.

"You said, 'the whole time we've been together', but you're not together. Not anymore." Billy's voice is monotone, his eyes fixed on a long groove in the kitchen table. I think it's where I used to pick at the soft wood as a kid.

Tony does something strange with his jaw. I think his mouth is trying to find something clever to say, but his brain has come up blank. He turns to me, points at Billy, as though I'll defend him. Ha! Now that is funny.

"He's not wrong." I shrug.

"No, he's right," Dorrie says. "Pretty strange of a man to overstay his welcome at the home of an ex-partner, wouldn't you say, Timmy?"

"It's *Tony*."

"Oh, silly me." She smiles, sweeter than honey. "But then, I'm just a simple-minded old lady, aren't I, dear?"

His jaw does that thing again.

Billy slowly moves his gaze up until he's staring at Tony, dull eyes locked on his face. It is kind of creepy.

Tony lasts exactly twelve seconds. Then he storms out of the kitchen.

I smile at Dorrie.

She smiles back, pats my arm, then my cheek. She nods at me. And there it is. Confirmation.

I'm doing The Right Thing.

I sit next to Billy.

Breathe.

"Would it work?" Billy asks.

"Would what work?" I sigh.

He pulls a now crumpled brochure from under the

table. *The Retreat*. He strokes its glossy cover with shaking fingertips.

"I don't think I want to feel like this anymore."

It's the saddest thing I've ever heard anyone say. I cocoon my arms around his thin shoulders. And I feel pride rise in my chest like liquid gold.

***

We should not have come here.

We should *not* have come here.

"We shouldn't have come here."

Tony squeezes my hand. A squeeze that means *shut up*. Everyone's staring.

Funerals are weird. We're literally all congregating around a hole in the ground whilst a slowly decomposing body is lowered down into it, in a little wooden container. And a guy in a dress is chanting words. Sometimes people join in the chant, nodding, clutching at their hearts, teary. Again, cult vibes.

The last time I stood like this, over an open grave, it was illegal. I actually think that felt more normal. This shouldn't be a thing we do openly in society. It's creepy.

The only thing worse would have been if Billy came. I couldn't deal with two overgrown men-children right now. I think Tony only came so he could wear his new suit to an event. Whether a funeral can be termed an 'event' is still up for debate. I say no. Tony says yes. Obviously. Billy was too busy picking at his skin – that's his new thing. He says there are things crawling about under there. With all the stuff he's pumped into his body over the years, I wouldn't be surprised. Dorrie just made me a cup of tea. She stayed home with Billy. I'm not sure how that worked out. She was the one who said we had to go. But, come on, it's not like I could leave Tony to look after him. That would be worse than if I left him home alone again. I would come back to two more dead bodies.

"I wish your suit was black."

"It's navy, same thing."

"No, not *same thing*. Otherwise, they would both be called black. They're not. One's called navy. Know why? They're *different colours*."

Tony gives my hand another 'shut up' squeeze. Why am I holding his arm?

Sarah-from-over-the-way is next to us. She keeps shaking her head when the priest says nice things about Gus's father. She gets it.

"Sarah is wearing black."

"Shhh." Tony is staring intently at the service, sombre face out in full force. He loves to play a part. The Loving Boyfriend. Here to support me at the funeral of a man I barely knew and what I did know about him, I hated. I wonder if everyone else remembers the fact he didn't come to my own parents' funeral. The joint cremation. Probably not. They were all too distracted by Billy.

"Strange that Gus didn't come to his own father's funeral, don't you think?" Sarah leans over to me. I can see a faint line of sweat along her top lip. It makes the little moustache she's got going on there more obvious. Why she's sweating in the winter, I have no idea. She's painfully thin – the hand gripping her cane frightens me. If she's not careful, the bones are going to pop through her skin, spray the frosty path with bright blood. Her skin might tear, rip further up her hand, along her arm, up towards her chest, split down her legs, across her face, until she's just a bloody bag of bare bones. She might shed it like a snake, grow new skin in its place.

I blink and she's looking up at me, her skin still covering her insides. Thank God. Who imagines things like that? Me, apparently.

"I always said that boy was odd." She nods sagely. "He never liked my hummus."

I make a noise in the back of my throat. Watch the priest.

They're lowering the box now. I hate this part. I always worry they're going to drop it and the dead body will come spilling out, blank eyes staring. I blink again and the box is gone. Down inside the hole. Forever.

At least we didn't have to sit through the actual service. It was closed, family and close friends only. Well, close friends. No family left.

People begin to slowly move forwards, grab handfuls of soil from a little dish at the front, throw it down into the hole. Again, weird. We can't just let one person deal with the burial, no, everyone has to be involved. We all have to share the blame. I wonder if it goes back to the times when lots of people used to get buried alive? Just in case someone got trapped down there, everyone was guilty, not just one poor schmuck. Apparently, they used to have bells next to graves, so if you woke up and found yourself buried alive, you could just pull the bell, and someone would come to dig you up again. It was someone's whole job to listen out for the bells, help the wrongfully buried. My life may not be brilliant, but at least I don't have to do that to pay the bills. No, I just have to lie to the entire country about the safety of their own fertility.

And the dead crows.

Perhaps, the safety of their own lives.

Maybe the grave un-digging job wouldn't be so bad.

We're near the front of the queue now. Queuing to sprinkle dust on top of a dead man. I must be gripping Tony's arm too hard. He's trying to prise my fingers away. I let my arm drop. Nope, that's worse. I retake his arm, softer this time.

He smiles down at me. No, Tony, that's not what this is. Not at all. You're only here because I can't do this on my own. If I could have substituted you for Dorrie, I would have. If I'd known Sarah-from-over-the-way was going to be here, I would have sent you back to the city last night.

We're closer now. Close, closer, closest.

I think I might be hyperventilating. I'm not doing the *act normal* thing very well.

Tony looks at me funny. Clears his throat.

"Quick burial, isn't it?"

Oh, God. He's decided to *make conversation*. Kill me.

"Didn't he only die a couple of days ago?"

"Oh, this whole shebang has been planned for months, love." Sarah beams up at Tony. She's already told me twice she thinks my *gentleman friend* is *very handsome indeed*. It's been twenty minutes.

"We were just waiting for the old git to pop his clogs. Took his time, I must say."

I get the vague impression Sarah didn't much like Gus's father either.

"Wow... kind of creepy."

"We forward plan in this village, dear." Sarah smiles. A little too wide.

Yeah, we forward plan for the sterilisation of the human race.

She looks like an old Helen when she smiles. I don't like that.

"I'm surprised they managed to get the body processed that fast."

"Christ, you can't talk about someone's dead body at their funeral, Tony."

"I'm just saying—"

"Well, it's to avoid that questing thing, isn't it?"

We both turn to Sarah.

She looks back at us.

"Questing what?"

She waves her hands about. "You know, that thing. When the alien men came to the house. After they found the anoninon."

I blink. Maybe she's speaking a different language.

"Clementine knows what I'm talking about."

I don't.

"You *know*. The alien men. In the white suits." She points at her own skinny body, pulls an imaginary hood over her head. "The foreign-sicks."

How are we not at the front of the queue yet? People have stalled. There's a blockage up ahead. A woman is crying, wailing, throwing more and more soil into the hole. Calm down, love. Leave some for the rest of us. We want to join in, share part of the guilt too. Although, I probably carry more guilt than the others. I have to carry Billy's, too.

"Do you mean forensics?"

What? Forensics at Gus's house? I feel my heart speed into overdrive. It's lucky we're at the graveyard because I'm about to have a heart attack. Turn this *whole shebang* into a double funeral.

"Yes! That's it."

I translate in my head:

Foreign-sicks = forensics. They must have come and gone before I got back from the hospital with Billy.

Anoninon = anomaly? It must be anomaly – they don't usually forensically investigate non-anomaly deaths.

Questing = ???

"Between you and me… and also you, dear." Sarah beckons us both close. Her breath smells like stale tea. "I think Helen organised it. Made them go away. To make sure we don't get any unwanted attention in the village, at the meetings, you know. She's so brilliant." Her eyes go out of focus, hover at a spot over my shoulder.

I don't dare turn around in case she's there. I wonder if she would wear a black skirt suit for a funeral, or if she only owns pink ones. Now, that really would be inappropriate. At least Tony didn't come wearing one of those.

Got it. *Questing =*

"Oh, you mean an *inquest*."

Yes. Thank you, Tony. I forgot about him doing that thing where he finishes my thoughts. Infuriating. How does he get inside my head? Creep.

"Oh, whatever it's called." Sarah waves her hands about again, snapping out of her cult-admiration trance. "Ah, my turn." She almost skips forward to take a handful of soil from the little dish. Maybe she *would* have skipped if she could. I don't think her knees would allow it.

266

"Who's Helen?"

"I don't know," I lie. "Probably someone that lives inside her head."

Tony snorts. Tries to pass it off as a sneeze.

We watch Sarah sprinkle her palm full of soil over the box in the ground with what can only be called panache. She grins at the priest with her crooked teeth. He looks frightened. He probably should be. I bet her funeral will be a lot more complicated for him to deliver than this one. She definitely has songs planned.

Okay, our turn. It's easy. Simple. See, Tony can do it. Everyone's just waiting for you now, Clem. Just take a handful of the soil, that's it, surprisingly warm but fine, it's fine, everything's fine. Now, just throw it in. Just hold out your hand and open it over the grave, over the wooden box, over the dead body. The edges of my vision go fuzzy. My heart is too tired, it can't keep going like this, it's going to stop. Just like his heart stopped. Just like Billy stopped Gus's heart.

A paper bag of *Entirely Natural* medicine, resting on a side table. *It's my father's medicine. It's not proper painkiller, it's that all-natural stuff.*

An anomaly. An inquest. Forensic investigations.

I think Helen organised it. Made them go away.

They may have had this funeral planned for a long time, but it wasn't natural causes that killed Gus's father. It wasn't Billy, or me, or Dorrie by proxy – dead because we killed his son. It wasn't even Gus, which is apparently what the majority of people here believe. Mainly because he's not here. (Side note: thank Dorrie for making me come here – if I hadn't, they might have thought the same of

267

me, they might even have thought we planned it together, that he's waiting somewhere for me, a Bonnie and Clyde situation. That would have been truly horrific.)

It wasn't any of us.

It was you, Mother.

You and Helen.

It was your formula in that medicine.

He was a sitting duck. Or crow.

Tony's hand covers mine, tugs my fingers apart, gentle, making me drop the soil. Done. It's over.

He leads me away, arm around my waist.

People are whispering. About me, no doubt. Great.

Home. I need to go home.

I need to check on Billy.

I don't know where Sarah's gone. Don't know anything except the feeling of Tony's arm on my body. Christ, I hate myself.

There's a figure standing at the entrance to the graveyard. Petite, until she turns sideways. A pregnant figure. People are staring, whispering, full on pointing. The figure's shoulders are up around her ears, she's clutching something in her hand – a phone?

I reach into my pocket: *27 missed calls.*

Oh no.

Tony tenses beside me.

Is that—

"Nia?"

***

Tony lied. He said he only came for the funeral, to support

me, to help me through this difficult time. Mourning the death of a man I didn't even like who Tony didn't even know was dead until this morning.

I'm amazed she didn't see through it straight away. Because who plans to wear a navy-blue suit to a funeral?

"I tried to call you."

"I know. I'm sorry." There is a pause. It's quite long. I don't like it, so I say, "My phone was on silent. We were at a funeral."

"I know." She nods.

"I didn't ask Tony to come. He just—"

"I know."

Yet again, I am a terrible person. I don't mean to be. It just seems to happen. Maybe I did something bad in a past life. Must have been pretty horrific. To warrant all of this.

Warrant. Good word.

W a rrrrr ant.

A war on ants.

"Clem?"

"Sorry?"

She's been speaking to me, and I haven't listened. Again, bad person.

"I said, can't we go to your house? It's cold here."

We're sat on a bench, in the park, near the coffee hatch. I can still see the graveyard in the distance, church spire sticking up above the trees. You used to bring us here, didn't you, Mother? I remember sitting on the grass, picking daisies, making chains to drape around Billy's little neck. You sipping your Americano. Until you told me I was killing the innocent flowers. I've never picked a flower since.

There's nothing growing here now. Everything's covered in a thin layer of frost and Nia is only wearing a thin cotton dress, a jacket that doesn't close over her bloated stomach. The dress is Zara, maternity. I know because I bought it for myself, back at the beginning, when I thought the line on the test meant nine months later I'd be holding a small version of myself and not just a bundle of snotty tissues.

She must be nearly due by now.

She's enormous.

Tony is sat at the next bench along. Far enough away that he can't hear us, but close enough to pretend he isn't watching us. Trying to read our lips. We've angled our bodies away from him. Unfortunately, that means she's very close to me. Very close. Her bump resting between us.

Tony looks at her stomach like it's something alien. Has he always looked at it that way? Would he have looked at me that way if things had worked for us? If I'd got pregnant. Like he'd only just noticed that she was currently two people instead of just one. Maybe he *has* just noticed. He always was chronically unobservant.

Telling, I think, that he chose an Americano from the hatch.

My latte is too hot. Burns my tongue. Great, I'll get those little bumps now, inside my mouth. It hurts already. I should have waited.

Nia didn't want anything.

Good job, really. I doubt the hatch does vegan oat milk chai green lattes. Judging by the taste of this one, they barely even do normal lattes. I take another sip. Breathe through the heat on my tongue.

"I'm sorry to just turn up like this."

Yeah, it's not *great* timing.

"It's okay."

"Tony freaked out when I told him, you know." She points to her stomach.

I don't look at it.

"And then I was on my own and I didn't know what to do. I kept thinking, what if, what if, what if something goes wrong, something bad happens, and I'm alone. And I know you shouldn't do that – what's it called? – catastrophise – but I can't help it. I think it's the hormones."

Okay, Nia, we all know you're pregnant, that's obvious to anyone with the power of sight, you don't have to go on about it.

"It's fine, honestly."

She smiles a wobbly smile at me. Makes a point of shivering.

We are not going back to the cottage.

That would be too weird, the both of them under the same roof, *my* roof. Dorrie asking questions, making tea. Having to try and hold a conversation, the three of us speaking. And who knows what kind of state Billy's going to be in when I get back. He didn't want me coming to the funeral, cried about it all morning.

It's not my fault she didn't bring enough layers.

I forget how warm it is back in the city, everyone crammed in together. Probably feels like summer there.

Welcome to the country, Nia.

I take my coat off, wrap it round her shoulders. Snuggle it round the bump. Her bump.

She starts to cry.

God, sorry it's not designer. You can't have everything, woman.

I can feel Tony watching us. See his eyes out of the corner of mine. I should have made him sit further away.

He doesn't come over, try to comfort her. He does not deserve this woman. Or her bump. I'm glad the baby's not his. But not for the reason people would think – so I can't say anything, obviously.

I sit in silence and watch her cry.

Maybe me and Tony *were* made for each other. I'm as bad as he is.

Bundles of clothes on the floor. The sofa sagging under our shared weight.

Clementine Finch is a horrible person. Me. I'm a horrible person.

The latte has made me feel sick. I balance the cup on the arm of the bench.

Nia cradles her bump with her arms, rubs at it.

"I can't do this on my own, Clementine."

"You'll be a great mother."

Why did I say that? I don't know that. I don't know anything. That sentence means nothing. It's like when people say, "don't worry everything will turn out alright", or, "it gets easier." No, it won't and no, it doesn't.

"You think so?"

"Yes."

Liar.

The amount of photos I can already see her uploading to Instagram of that poor child. I am a liar, liar, pants on fire.

She smiles again.

"Well, you can't be any worse than my mother." I try to smile back. At least that much is true.

Nia shakes her head. "No, your mother must have been a lovely woman, to have raised you."

Yuck.

This girl is naïve to the point of insanity.

"No, she was a horrible person. She used to lock me and my brother in the basement. She resented us, me particularly, because we took her life away from her. We were unwanted. All we did was cause problems for her. Especially me."

"Oh." Nia's face has turned pale.

"She wasn't a very maternal person. She once told me she wished I was dead."

She actually gasps, puts her hand over her mouth, like a cartoon character.

"It's okay, I won. She's dead now."

A pause.

"Oh. Right."

Do you like my description of you, Mother? I think you'll agree it's fairly accurate. Maybe a little too sugar coated, but here we are.

A shadow falls over the bump. A Tony-shaped shadow.

"Look, I've thought it over. I think the best thing we can do—"

We – as though we're a team, all in this together. I don't think so.

"—is for me to take you back to the city, to your parents'. Clem, you'll be alright with Dorrie for a few hours. Then I'll come back here, help you sort out the rest of the cottage."

"No. I'm not going anywhere with you."

"Sorry, your parents?"

"Well, you can't stay here."

273

"I thought your parents were dead."

"You don't decide where I stay or don't stay, Tony. It's up to Clem."

"What are you talking about? Her parents aren't *dead*. They live in Marylebone. We went for dinner at their house last week... they have a pool."

What?

I look at her.

Her cheeks turn a flattering shade of red. God, she's beautiful. She pulls at the waistband of her dress.

"Why would you tell me your parents were dead?"

"Why would you do that, Nia? You know Clemmie's parents just died in a horrific road accident."

Yes, thanks for the reminder, Tony.

I keep looking at her.

She tucks her face into the collar of my coat.

Her voice is tiny when she says, "I wanted you to like me."

What?

She shrugs. "I thought if we had something in common, a point of similarity, you would like me more. I thought it would help us connect. Shared experiences, you know."

"But it wasn't a shared experience. Your parents aren't dead. They're alive. Living in a house with a pool, apparently!"

"Please don't shout at me, Clem. I'm sorry. I didn't mean to cause you pain."

'I didn't mean to cause you pain.' Really? What a pointless statement. Because she has. I hate it when people do that, apologise without apologising. It's a real skill, actually.

Bitch.

What did she expect? That we'd be best friends? Buy each other those matching necklaces that you slot together and have long, chatty sleepovers? Share gossip about Tony's skills (or lack thereof) in the bedroom.

Looking at her tear-stained face, yes, I think she did think that.

Mental bitch.

Another one who needs therapy.

"Do you know how destructive that is? How heartless? You could have set Clemmie's recovery back months."

"Oh, you mean heartless like cheating on your fiancée and getting another woman pregnant, do you, Tony? Oh no, sorry, it's not yours, is it? I keep forgetting."

Also, 'my recovery'? Rude.

Tony stares at me, his jaw doing that weird chewing thing again. Then he says, "I'm on your side here, Clemmie."

"No. You're not. You gave up the right to be on my side when you left me for someone younger, prettier and more successful, with a fertile womb and shiny hair. Seriously, how do you get it like that? Is it Argan oil? Because I tried that, and it just made my hair greasy."

Nia peers at me through her tears, rubs at her bump. "Erm, no, avocado oil."

"See, Tony? I didn't even know there was such a thing as avocado oil."

"Clem, what are you even talking about?"

"I don't know!"

We have become those weird, shouty people that others avoid in parks. Another step towards my transition into Country Bumpkin Spinster. Ten points to me.

"Okay, this is ridiculous. Nia come on, you're coming with me. I'll drive you out to—"

"I'm not going to my parents."

"Stop being a spoilt brat, at least you have parents to go to!"

"So do you, Tony. They live on the Isle of Man. No pool though."

"Shut up, Clem!"

Again, rude.

I hold my hands up in surrender.

"Why do you both always have to be so difficult?"

"Oh, I'm so sorry, Tony. Are we too opinionated for you as women? Do we ask for too much? Things like fidelity and trust. Should we just be silent, meek, stay at home and cook – would that make it easier for you?"

"Stop being a bitch, Clementine."

"Oh, it's *Clementine*, now, is it?"

"Erm… guys?"

"You'll be calling me Miss Finch, next!"

"You're being a child."

"*I'm* being a child? You're the one telling Nia where she can and can't go. What, because she's your friend, I can't play with her?"

"Guys, I think—"

"What does that even mean? You don't want her staying at yours anyway!"

"How do you know that? Did you ask me?"

"It's pretty obvious!"

"Guys!"

We turn to Nia. The girl looks terrified. The bottom half of her dress, the bench, the floor, are soaked. Oh my

God, she's wet herself. I knew babies weakened your pelvic floor, but I thought that was *after* the birth.

Birth.

Oh.

"I think my waters have broken."

Looks like we will be having that sleepover after all.

***

I don't know how much time we have. I've never witnessed a birth before.

Nia rang something called a 'doula', which turned out to be a woman with a loud voice who told her to 'embrace the truth of her pain' and 'settle in for a life-affirming wait' before she reaches her 'dilation potential'. I don't trust her.

I think we should be on our way to the hospital, but she insisted it was too soon and you can't argue with the woman in labour.

We can't stay in the park, clearly, so Tony is driving us back to the cottage.

I sit in the back of the car with her, try to do breathing exercises and pretend I'm fine with the fact that all the different parts of my life are about to smash into each other. I don't know if her squeezing my hand means I'm helping or not, but she hasn't asked me to stop. Then again, maybe she just can't speak through the pain.

It's going to get worse. That much I know.

Much worse.

Why am I involved in this? I swear, if one more soap opera-y thing happens to me, I will start to believe I'm cursed. Probably by you, right, Mother?

She seems to be struggling to breathe. Is that normal? I don't know if that's normal. Can't ask Tony, he's having his own hyperventilation problems. God, it's not even his child. Useless.

He better not crash this car.

She hasn't brought anything with her. No pyjamas, no birth plan, no bag filled with various baby things for the hospital. She hasn't got the baby carrier she bought for the drive home, baby's first outing. She hasn't even got a toothbrush. She only has her tears, me and a panicking not-the-father-of-her-baby.

Not the best situation.

And one that's about to get even worse.

As we pull up outside the cottage, I can see Billy standing in the front garden. He's not wearing a coat. Why is he not wearing a coat? Come on, Dorrie, get it together, I left you in charge for a reason. He must see Tony in the front of the car because he turns tail and practically runs back inside the house.

"Okay, stay here, I'll go and get some of my things."

"None of your things will fit her, though."

Lovely, Tony, helpful, thank you.

"No, I have to get out, I need to walk around." She's gasping, body shuddering.

Should it be this bad this fast? God, I wish I had more experience with this kind of thing. Or maybe I don't.

I help her out of the car so she can shuffle up and down the path. I don't want to let go of her hand. She might fall.

Dorrie comes hurrying out of the house. "Darling? What's – who is – oh, my love, is it your baby on the way?"

"Yes. She's in labour. This is Nia – Tony's—"

What? Girlfriend? Ex?

"This is Nia."

Dorrie nods and I feel safe, calm.

"I'll get some things together," she says.

I can see Dorrie making her own list in her head. Good, because I don't have time to make one of mine.

Tony hasn't moved from the car. His hands grip the steering wheel, his knuckles white.

Nia shuffles. I walk beside her. Back. Forth. Back. Forth. Back.

There's a crash from the doorway. I look up to see Billy, hands empty, tray of brownies on the floor in front of him.

"Oh darling, you spent so long making those." Dorrie is holding a bag, presumably full of the *things* we can take to the hospital. I'm so glad she packed it, because I don't actually know what the *things* need to be.

"He made them for you, love. An apology gift." She smiles at me.

Billy's face is blank shock. He must have really put a lot into those brownies. Probably the first time he's made any that don't contain drugs. Well, now they contain bits of grass, frost and gravel. Yum.

"Billy, it's okay. It was a lovely thing to do. Thank you."

I feel Nia gasp beside me, a sharp twist of my hand, her nails digging into my skin. We need to get this girl to the hospital. A woman giving birth on my front path is the last thing I need – the neighbours really don't need anything else to gossip about.

Billy's mouth opens, closes, opens. Then he says, "Genia?" A whisper. His eyes mist and his hands are shaking.

279

"Who, love?" Dorrie asks.

Genia?

"Billy?" Nia's voice shakes.

Nia. Genia.

He came to one of my yoga classes.

There was a girl.

We had a fling, a few months before I met Tony.

There was a girl.

He was sweet, but kind of sad.

There was a girl. She was perfect.

The kind where you think you can 'fix them', you know?

I left. I left her alone.

We got careless.

Don't let Billy eat any of the food, it might not be too late for him.

I just left her.

It was only after things soured that I realised I was pregnant.

There was a girl.

She was perfect.

Oh. God. No.

Tony leans out of the car. "Are we doing this thing, or not?"

No. No. No.

They stare at one another.

Please someone tell me I've got this wrong.

"Billy?" she says again. She lets go of my hand, walks forward. Touches his face.

He stares at her bump. Reaches for her. Then pulls back. Looks like he's going to pass out.

Then he smiles.

Nia seems to have forgotten she's in labour. She seems

to have forgotten about Tony sitting behind her in the car, Dorrie standing there with the bag of things, and about me. She seems to have forgotten everything apart from my little brother, the man from the yoga class, the *fling*, the one she thought she could fix.

The father of her baby.

***

It's a squeeze, the five of us in the car together.

She's moaning now, a low animalistic sound – but it is a lot less dramatic than in the films. Maybe she's using some kind of yoga mastery voodoo. She's not swearing at any of us or squeezing the blood out of anyone's hand. Her and Billy's hands seem to be fairly loosely linked actually, their fingers entwined – for now, anyway.

I really wish I'd sat in the front.

Billy's eyes are wide.

I don't know what's happening, but neither one of them has taken their eyes off each other since Billy dropped that tray of brownies on the floor. It's like something from a film. Why do I get soap opera insanity and they get critically acclaimed romance novel? Technically, they're the bad guys, the side characters – the needy younger brother, the fallen woman. But I guess that's only if I'm the protagonist and I'm probably not.

I never am.

I am apparently going to be an auntie, though. Which is… that.

I mean, I assume. Neither one of them has actually confirmed nor denied. They're probably going to have to spell it out at some point because I don't think Tony's connected the dots. Whoever tells him will have to use simple words.

The A&E department is heaving when we pull into the parking lot.

"Bloody thing!"

"No use shouting – it's a parking barrier, dear, it can't hear you."

Tony glares at Dorrie, then glares at the parking barrier, then at me. I don't know why it's my fault that the machine isn't working, but apparently it is. He doesn't notice the linked pair of hands right next to me. That will be my fault, too, when he eventually finds out. Obviously.

"We'll just get out here. The entrance isn't far. You can walk?" I turn to Nia.

Her teeth are gritted, her cheeks red, but she nods. We help her clamber out of the car, waddle to the automatic doors. A nurse sees her struggling and rushes out with a wheelchair, starts chatting about dilation and pain relief. It's not even too late for her to have pain relief. It's always too late for the pregnant woman to have pain relief in films.

Nia is one of the golden people though, remember, Clem? Her life goes the way things are *meant* to, in your head. She gets what she asks for and, probably because she's beautiful, people fall over themselves to help her. She gets the men she wants, the baby she wants – she even gets the non-dead parents she pretended she didn't have. And from the look on his face, apparently she now has my brother as well. I know she's in pain and yes, I should be sympathetic, but God, I hate her. Why can't she leave me alone? Stop taking the only things I have left – you already have so many people you can call yours. She'll be after Dorrie next.

They take her immediately through to a private room. Billy goes with her.

"And this is Dad?" I hear the nurse ask as they head down the corridor.

"Yes." The same answer from both of them, at the same time, in the same tone.

Aha. I was right.

I hate being right.

Or at least, I hate being right about this.

"Why has *he* gone with her?"

Tony and Dorrie appear behind me. I wonder if they got the parking barrier to work or if Tony had one of his hissy fits and just drove round it. Or through it. I should have stayed in the car with them – I would have loved to have seen Dorrie's face.

"Because he's the baby's father, dear," she says.

Well. They are small words.

Tony makes an *uhhg?* sound. It's a good job we're in a hospital, because he looks like he's going to pass out.

We guide him to an uncomfortable, blue, plastic chair, make him sit. The people just arriving probably think he's been through some kind of horrific trauma.

"Come on, Tony – you were just saying the other night how glad you were to be free of her, free of the baby."

How you really wanted me, my baby. The baby I can't have. I know that was just to get me into bed – or sofa, I suppose – but it can't hurt to make him feel a bit worse. Well, it can't hurt *me*.

We'll be here a perfect amount of time – not too long and not too short. The baby will be healthy and adorable and probably grow up to be a model or actor or singer or something equally glamorous. Nia will have no scars and the smoothest birth possible, and she'll lose the baby weight stupidly fast. She will be the best mother because she's the best at everything because she's Nia.

I don't think I'll ever be able to think of her as Genia. It doesn't suit her.

Anyone would expect – because I'd thought all of those things, all of those spiteful, jealous things – that something terrible would happen. The baby would die. Nia would die. Billy would pass out in the delivery room and immediately overdose at one of his parties, unable to cope with their deaths. I would be sat back in the quiet corridor again, the bad part of the hospital. And I would be alone. But when we're called into the delivery room, the midwife is calm, collected. And the little family in front of us are perfect.

It's a girl.

I've bought a small brown bear from the hospital shop. Its nose is horribly squashed. Nia tears up when she sees it, goes back to squeezing my hand. Her other arm encircling the little bundle.

Billy hasn't noticed we're in the room. He's stopped gazing at Nia, started gazing at the baby. His daughter. Without even speaking to him, I can tell he's completely head over heels. He's found someone even more perfect than Nia. He's found the love of his life.

She is perfect.

Tony didn't come in with us. He stayed in the waiting room. I'm hopeful that if we stay in here long enough, he'll get sick of waiting and decide to head back to the city. Alone.

Dorrie is crying, cooing over the bundle.

My eyes feel horribly dry.

"Do you want to hold her, Clemmie?"

No.

Four expectant pairs of eyes turn to me – yes, even the baby is looking at me, with her perfectly blue eyes. With my brother's eyes.

I can't.

"Here, love." Dorrie pulls a chair close to the bed.

I sit.

Nia places the bundle in my arms.

If this was a nice story, I would feel intense love, utter completeness – I wouldn't care that I couldn't have a child of my own because I could find fulfilment through this child, lavish this child with love, adore this child.

But this is not a nice story. This is my life.

So I feel numb.

I feel nothing.

Only a warm heaviness – should a baby be this hot when they're born? I guess she was just inside another human.

"We're calling her Nadia."

We. They're a 'we' now.

They're a three now.

"She's beautiful, my love." Dorrie's voice is low, quiet.

I feel like I might scream. Just to see what they would all do.

I thought babies were meant to cry. Why is this one just staring at me? With her massive eyes. With Billy's massive eyes. Bit creepy.

I can hear my heartbeat inside my head.

Actually, I don't think that is my heartbeat, it sounds suspiciously like words, like chanting. Oh great –

apparently, I now have schizophrenia on top of everything else. Are you meant to listen to the voices or not? Probably not. Definitely not in my case. I can't trust myself at the best of times. We all know that.

If I'm now insane, I should probably hand this newborn baby back to its mother.

Nia cuddles the little bundle close, tucks the brown bear close to her head. I don't know if I would do that personally. God knows how many sick children have sneezed on that bear during its lifespan in the hospital shop.

I walk over to the window instead. Look out.

Those voices aren't inside my head. I see that now. They're outside my head, outside the hospital.

Protestors.

Anti-birth protestors.

Outside the hospital, the hospital we're in, the hospital Nia has just given birth in.

The hospital containing Nadia.

They're marching in a circle, wearing what appear to be cagoules and waving blue placards with words on them:

We Should ALL be Anti-birth

No More Babies!

STOP PROCREATION

Selfish Mothers Will Kill Us All!

Stop KILLING our PLANET

NO MORE BABIES! (again, but this time in capitals)

BIRTH = DEATH

That last one is very clever, I have to admit. Horrific message, obviously, but good use of words. At least they're inventive with their slogans. Their English teachers must be proud.

There's a couple of the tougher-looking nurses heading towards the group, the purple sleeves of their scrubs rolled up. The protestors see them coming and their chanting gets louder, nastier.

I do not like the look of this.

I like it even less when one of the protestors, a small man (it's always the small men) in a red flat cap punches one of the nurses.

I never thought I would be this glad to see Tony again, but when he walks through the delivery room door, I almost hug him. Almost. Our getaway driver.

"We need to go," he says.

Oh, really, Inspector Gadget? What tipped you off?

"What do you mean?"

Oh, Nia. Oh, poor, innocent Nia. You could never conceive of the people outside this window right now, could you? Not in your post-birth bubble, not in your perfect world where nothing bad ever happens to you. Not in Nia-land.

The chanting is getting louder, less cohesive. I guess it's not really chanting anymore, more like screaming, more like the sound of flesh bashing against flesh.

"I hate to agree with Tony, but we need to leave. The back way. Make sure no one sees us."

Dorrie hurries over to the window. "Oh, Lord."

Billy follows her. His face turns sheet white. "I'll get a wheelchair." He practically runs out of the room.

"I'm not leaving. They said I can stay the night."

"Sweetheart, we have to go. There's some people out there, protestors. A fight."

Nia shakes her head. "I don't care. They can't get in.

287

The staff won't let them in." She buries down further under the thin covers. Tony's right, she is a brat. Does she not get it? We're trying to help her keep her perfect life, stop it from being shattered. We're trying to save her baby.

"The staff are semi-conscious," I say.

It's not a lie – one of the nurses is laid on the floor outside, blood on his face, protestors gathering around him, chanting. He's not moving.

Billy re-appears, a doctor by his side, pushing a wheelchair.

"We need to get your little one out of here, Ms Jones." She pulls back the sheets.

Nia looks small in the bed, too small to have just given birth. Is it possible she's started to lose the baby weight already? Surely not.

Genia Jones. Apparently, Nia's mother had the same strange impulse to give her child a ridiculous name as you did, Mother. And as Helen Higgins' mother.

There's a loud smashing noise. A cheer. Then footsteps, running ones.

"Okay, let's go." Nia hands the baby to Billy, levers herself into the wheelchair.

Oh, *now* she changes her tune.

Billy tucks Nadia inside his jacket and the doctor starts to wheel Nia down the corridor. We follow, close, quick. I think we left the bag of things in the delivery room. Another crashing sound. Another cheer. I think they're smashing windows. No time to go back. Somewhere a woman screams, high, sharp. Our little group starts to run.

"This way," the doctor says, ushers us down a smaller

corridor, the same as the others but with less doors, less lighting.

A shout behind us. I turn to see a tall woman, her face twisted, a large baseball bat in her hand. She swings it, hits the fire alarm.

Can a baby go deaf from such a loud noise so soon after their birth?

"It's this way!" the woman screams, beckons to other bat/mallet/garden utensil-wielding people behind her. One man has a metal bar. They're heading for the maternity ward.

This doctor better know where she's going.

None of us speak as we hurry down the corridor. Tony is clutching the car keys in his hand. We just need to get to the car, drive away, get out of here, get back home.

Home.

Home is a forty-minute car journey away – that's if we can get to the car, parked in the car park, right next to the baying mob.

I hear the smash before I feel the glass on my skin. A window implodes and a rock hits the linoleum floor in front of us, missing Nia's head by less than an inch. Billy pulls his jacket tighter and now I can hear her crying over the alarm. Baby's first fear.

I wait for someone to jump through the broken window, waving a baseball bat, but no, nothing. Dorrie peers around the window frame, tiny cuts pepper her skin. She turns back to us, shakes her head. Keep going.

There's a door at the end of the corridor now, a little one – it looks like it's getting smaller and smaller as we head towards it. I feel like Alice in Wonderland. If some weirdo hands me a

289

bottle of 'drink me' juice, there's no way I'm taking it.

The doctor pulls a key from her pocket, unlocks the tiny door. "This leads straight to the staff car park – take my car." She presses a key fob into my hand. Tesla. Nice. "Get her out of here, both of them – go somewhere safe."

"Come with us, my love," Dorrie says.

"I can't." She shakes her head. "Go, go." She practically pushes us out the door – literally pushes in Nia's case. Then she slams the little door shut. I catch a glimpse of her terror before it closes.

We're in an indoor car park. Lights flicker on automatically as we make our way forward. I start clicking the fob randomly until we see a red Tesla's lights flash on, off, on in the far corner. Bingo.

We don't have a car seat, just Billy's jacket. And that's got slivers of glass on it.

Tony tries to reach for the key fob, and I shove his hand away. I'm driving.

It smells like sherbet lemon in the car. A small lemon air freshener hangs from the rear-view mirror. The seats are buttery leather.

Nadia's cries are loud in the small interior. Less of a squeeze than Dad's old car, but not what you'd call roomy.

I make sure everyone has their seatbelts on (the soap opera/romance novel might have turned into some kind of dystopian nightmare, but that's no reason to forget about basic safety – might even be more of a reason to remember it. No use surviving a mob attack if you die immediately afterwards in a car accident) and pull out of the car park.

No one speaks. We listen to Nadia. She's definitely questioning why the hell these insane people have brought her into this insane world. It's a good question.

Is it better to speed away, fast as possible, or to drive slowly, draw no attention? Would it draw more attention to cruise slowly by? Probably. I choose fast.

The barrier is down.

A big man with a red face slams into the side of the car – he has blood all over his hands, smears it across the passenger window. He's mouthing something through the glass: "*Help. Help, help.*"

I keep driving. I don't even think about it. I was wrong – I don't feel nothing towards Nadia. If this man ruins our chances, if he draws the crazy people over here, if he puts her in danger, I will kill him myself.

I speed up. He falls away from the window, his shouts behind us now.

"Clem, the barrier," Tony says.

The hospital entrance blurs past.

"Clem? Clem!"

I smash through the barrier. Can't believe I'm taking driving tips from Tony – guess all those years of watching his road rage have paid off.

I angle the car towards home.

Home.

The nurse I saw on the floor is still there. Still covered in blood. Still not moving.

***

It takes Dorrie a grand total of eight minutes to get Nadia to sleep. Well, I guess she has had a very tiring first day in this world. We've dressed her in a flannel tea towel. It'll do for now to keep her warm and also doubles as a nappy.

We're staying at Dorrie's. Obviously. There's no way baby's first sleep was going to happen at the cottage, with its below-freezing average temperature and rat-infested walls. I made sure of that.

She's making this little snuffle sound as she sleeps, like a small marsupial. Billy made a little makeshift crib out of cushions and blankets. Looks a bit like the forts we used to make as kids. Only softer and more carefully constructed. Made with love.

We're sitting in a circle around her, watching her sleeping, breathing, existing, Nia half-asleep on Dorrie's shoulder. Empty cups of tea in front of us. Because, of course, Dorrie made tea the minute we got in. It gave Billy something to do with his hands, other than picking at his skin. I can feel the *need* coming off him now, like static. How did I not notice how bad he's gotten? I am the world's worst sister. He's not doing his pleading routine anymore though. He's silent.

The Tesla is parked outside. That'll give the neighbours something to really gossip about. Maybe they'll think Dorrie's got a flash new man.

I watch Billy's face in the low light of the lamp. Watch him watching his daughter.

My niece.

"I'll do it, Clem," he whispers. "The retreat. I'll go. For her."

She's only been here for a total of six hours and this kid's a miracle worker.

I reach for Billy's hand, squeeze. He squeezes back. And he means it. I can feel he means it. And I love him for it.

***

I see her face on the television in the morning, whilst I'm drinking my second cup of tea. The doctor who helped us, who saved us.

She's dead.

Stabbed.

With a metal pole.

Through the neck.

Brings back some bad memories. Garden shears are sharper, though. Less blood, surely.

Twelve dead. Seventeen more severely injured. Mostly women and children. Plus, the nurse on the ground in the car park.

"John, our correspondent, is at the scene. John, are these horrific attacks characteristic of what we can expect to see as the anti-birth movement gains even more followers?"

"Well, Sandra, I do think we all need to be aware that this kind of hate is spreading – and spreading quickly. This group is impassioned, desperate to spread their message and, as last night shows us, they will stop at almost nothing."

"Should we be worried, John? Should we be keeping our children at home? Our wives, and female relatives?"

"There was indeed a deliberate focus on attacking women and children last night, Sandra. Reports are coming in about the injuries, and sadly deaths, perpetrated inside this hospital behind me and there is a disturbing level of violence involv—"

I mute the television. I can hear Billy dragging his suitcase down the stairs. He doesn't need to hear this.

No one should have to hear this.

"All packed?"

"Yeah."

"Ready, then?"

"No." He smiles.

He's kept his promise. I thought he might change his mind in the cold light of the morning, but he's still going. He twists the retreat programme in his hands – it's all creased, crumpled. I notice the skin around his nails is ragged and bleeding. It looks sore.

I think I'll drive him there in the Tesla. Clearly the doctor doesn't need it anymore and I'm sure she'd want it put to good use. If you have to go to a rehab centre, might as well arrive in style.

"What is that smell?"

It's that damp smell again – I'm sure it's coming from the basement. Not that I've been down to check. Obviously. I tried, last night. On one of my breaks from baby watch. But got to the top of the steps and all I could think of was *garden shears, garden shears, garden shears*. Of course, now I'll also be thinking about a doctor and a metal bar, a fire alarm. Straight through the neck. Who invented necks? Who decided they were going to balance the centre of who we all are on a long, thin structure that is apparently distinctly easy to snap, block or sever? Whoever it was is an idiot – I don't care if they're omnipotent or not. Don't put important, heavy things on top of wobbly, delicate things – that's like architecture 101.

"It stinks."

"Well, there's another positive."

"Huh?"

"I'm sure there's no bad smells at the retreat. And I bet

they have heating twenty-four-seven. And fruit and veg that don't contain poison." I say the last bit quietly. There's no one else in the house – Nia and Dorrie are next door, staring at Nadia – but you can never be too careful. We all know walls have ears. Our walls more than most.

Billy looks at me with those huge, blue eyes. We've never actually spoken about it, I realise now. Never actually said anything to each other, just carried on with the knowledge that we know, we both know. That Dorrie knows, too. But at least she doesn't have to think about the fact she's related to the people who did this. Billy gets it.

"What's going to happen, Clemmie?"

Ah, the million-dollar question. Quite literally a million dollars (well, pounds) if I tell him the answer inside my head – probably more than a million, in time. Depends how long we live, I guess. And if this retreat works that might be longer than we all thought in Billy's case.

"Nothing."

He's going to say something. Make the argument, *that* argument, the logical one – the right one. I can't let him.

"Nothing will happen, Billy. You hear me?" I walk up close to his face, his scared face, his brave face. "We say nothing and nothing happens. You get better and you come home to Nadia. We all stay here. I can fix up the cottage. Start my own kitchen garden – a real one. We're safe here."

"But Genia – her parents—"

"I'll handle that. We can just tell them *Entirely Natural* goes against the principles of the yogi master." I place my hands together, bow to him. "Namaste."

He tries not to smile, fails.

"I'll look after them until you're back. Me and Dorrie will. I promise."

He hugs me, long, hard.

He's all bony so it kind of hurts. Sharp elbows. But I hug him back. Then I drive him to the retreat. Or *The Retreat*. When the woman with the kind face in a pink nurse's uniform says it, she definitely pronounces it as though it has capitals. *The Retreat*. She also talks about *check in*, as if it's a hotel, as though Billy's going on a nice little mini-break, five-star accommodation. Maybe if I think about it hard enough, I can pretend he is. They do have a pool.

He waves from the entrance as I drive away, surrounded by pink nurses, all smiling.

And it's fine.

It feels safe.

It feels good.

This is the right thing to do. The Right Thing.

***

Garden shears.

Blood.

Neck.

Dead eyes.

Blood.

Metal bar.

Neck.

Blood.

The sound of a fire alarm.

The THUD, THUD, THUD of a body falling down a set of steps, the smack of flesh against concrete.

Click. I snap the light on, open my eyes. Nothing there. Nothing.

Apart from that smell. Obviously.

I know what it is, Mother. You don't have to tell me. It's pretty clear.

I still haven't moved the sludge outside, where the veg patch used to be. It's frosted over now. I'm hoping it turns to some kind of toxic mulch, filters down through the earth and chokes his dead corpse. If you've murdered someone, you might as well make their afterlife as unpleasant as possible, right? Otherwise, what's the point?

The steps chill the soles of my feet. I stare down at them, my stripy feet. Then I look up.

Yep. I knew it.

The yellow-orange orbs have gone. In their place shrivelled, black globs of goo. Wow, check out that alliteration. I should have been a poet.

Maybe you should have been a poet, Mother. You would have been terrible at it, yes, but it would have been less destructive than what you have done. What you're still doing, from beyond the grave.

I've brought some rubber gloves with me, from the kitchen. Who knows what that stuff would do to me if I touched it with my bare hands. Looks like it would burn. I don't want stripy fingers as well as stripy feet.

There's a plastic box down here, filled with old action figures. Presumably Billy's. I don't remember ever playing with them, anyway. I empty them out onto the floor. Sorry, guys. Although the floor is probably a better place to be than under a pile of toxic goo. I'm sure they agree.

God, it's cold down here.

I start by picking them off one by one, throwing them in the box with a sticky *thunk*, but it takes too long and the fingers of the gloves start sticking together. It would be better to just cut them off at the roots, throw the whole plant away. It's not like I want to keep them, want them to re-flower, produce more. I need something sharp, pointed. I think about the shears, buried under the veg patch, nestled next to what's left of that neck. Would have been useful.

I search the basement, find an old trowel. That could work.

Their soil is strange, slippery, clumped together. I don't know why I'm surprised.

This is quicker. I just need to get rid of them. I don't care how – throw them in the bin, spread them over next door's lawn. I could bury them – that does appear to be my speciality. Just get them out of the house. Get her out of the house. This place isn't yours anymore, Mother, it's mine, ours. And I'm going to make it better.

I'm going to make it home.

PART TEN

"Genia, darling!"

A very thin, very posh woman is standing in Dorrie's living room. She looks both thrilled and horrified at the same time. When her daughter announced she'd had her baby and was staying with friends, I don't think this is quite what she had in mind. I mean, we don't even have a pool.

Nia's parents have been here less than twenty minutes and I understand why she told me they were dead. They're not as bad as you, Mother, but they're not far off. Their judgement is at least disguised as love, but it still hurts. You can see it in her eyes.

Nadia has cried from the moment her grandparents arrived. This kid has smarts.

Tony brought them. Of course he did. He said they deserved to meet their grandchild. I don't know if they know he's not the father. From the way Tony's acting, I don't know if he remembers he's not the father. Smugly proud is the only way I can describe it. He keeps touching the baby's head. I feel like slapping his hand away. Has he never heard of the soft spot?

"Here we are. Please, sit, sit." Dorrie brings the tea over, gestures at the sofas.

Nia's mother looks like she would rather sit on a crocodile. She does that thing that posh people do with their noses when they hate something, kind of squeezes it up until it wrinkles, as though she's smelt something horrible. She should try coming down into our basement.

Nia's father is large. His voice is the deepest thing I've ever heard, feels like it's reverberating through my soul whenever he speaks. Which is not often.

"Well, darling. This is *nice*." Nia's mother has an uncanny ability to make words like *nice*, *quaint* and *cosy* sound like scathing insults. It's a skill, really.

"Unusual eyes," her father says. Ugh, shivers through my bones – he sounds like he's speaking from beyond the grave. Probably just years of smoking expensive cigars and drinking port. I assume. I don't know what posh people do with their time. Investment banking? Polo? Yacht maintenance?

These people definitely have a yacht.

I'm actually amazed they managed to raise such a nice person. And that's nice in the real sense, not in the disguised insult sense.

"Yes, I wonder where the blue comes from. Tony, your eyes are hazel, aren't they?"

Yep, they don't know. Great.

Everyone looks at Nia. Then at the baby. At her eyes.

"Who wants milk?" Dorrie holds up her milk jug – the

300

one shaped like a cow. The milk comes out of its mouth. I loved that jug as a kid, played with it, made it walk across the table, towards my bowl of cereal.

"No, thank you." Nia's mother purses her lips. "Oh, darling, we brought you some things. Tony mentioned you didn't have anything with you." She looks pointedly at the old nightie of Dorrie's her daughter is wearing – it's pink with small flowers decorating the collar. I think she looks beautiful – then again, she would look beautiful wearing a potato sack. Clearly her mother doesn't think so.

"You know, just because you've had a baby, doesn't mean you can't wear make-up, darling. I didn't think to bring any… you know what, you can borrow some of mine." She says this as though it's some kind of great honour. Why, I don't know – she looks like someone spilled a load of black ink across her eyes. And she's wearing too much blusher. Unless she's just very warm – but, no, then that thick layer of foundation would have melted off. She produces a large, pink bag from somewhere, starts laying things out on the sofa next to Nia.

"Mum, you really didn't need to—"

"Oh nonsense, darling. It's just a few bits, from me and your dad."

Baby things. Tiny outfits, booties, bonnets. They look straight out of the 1950s. Nia will hate them. I hate them. Billy would laugh at them. Even Dorrie looks horrified.

I look away, if I catch her eye, I'll start laughing.

Still, more things are coming out of the bag. Then I notice something. On the side of one of the bottles, the one labelled *soothing nipple cream*. A small, golden tree.

"Sorry, what's that?" I ask.

"It's for Nia," her mother answers, without looking at me.

"It's *Entirely Natural*?" My voice sounds strange, far away.

"Of course, from their new baby range. All natural ingredients, darling. I know things like that are important to you." She pats Nia's leg.

Nia reaches forward, starts to read the side of the bottle. She nods.

Her mother produces more products from the bag, more creams and lotions and potions. More potion-like than she realises. Made by a real-life witch. Each and every one printed with a tiny, golden tree.

I remember Helen's words: *The new range is already in circulation.*

I'm going to be sick.

I stand up. Everyone looks at me. Even Nadia stops her snuffly cries, stares at me. With those gorgeous eyes. Those eyes I promised Billy I would take care of. That I promised myself I would protect.

I can't do this.

"Clemmie? What's wrong?"

I can't speak. I don't know what to say. I want to scream and wrench the things away from her, all the bottles and tubs and tins of stuff. Black, shrivelled globs of gunk hanging from dry leaves in the basement. In my basement. My fault. This is my fault.

"Darling, why don't you help me with some more biscuits, for our guests. In the kitchen." Dorrie carries the untouched plate of biscuits over to me, guides me out of the room. She shuts the kitchen door behind us.

We talk in whispers:

"I can't do this."

"Darling, don't panic. We don't know for sure—"

"We do know, Dorrie. We do. Don't pretend we don't. We *know*."

"I'll throw the things out, after they're gone."

"Then they'll buy more. Nia will buy more. You heard them, she loves entirely natural stuff – she loves *Entirely Natural* stuff."

"Then we tell her."

"Are you mental? 'Oh, sorry, Nia, forgot to mention your baby's other grandmother was a raving lunatic who tried to poison and kill everybody, we're in a cult and you have to join as well now. Just pledge allegiance to the pink crazed ones and we won't murder your baby.'"

There's a pause.

"Okay, fine, so we don't tell her."

I roll my eyes.

"I promised I would look after them for him."

"I know, love."

"Dorrie – what do I do?" I can feel the burn of tears behind my eyes.

"I don't know, love. I don't know."

This is your fault, Mother. This is all your fault.

***

I feel like a criminal. Me and Dorrie, again in the dark, again getting rid of evidence.

At least we're not burying things this time. All the digging gives me back ache.

Nia hasn't opened any of the things her mother brought. We put them in a plastic bag, hide them in the basement. If she asks where they've gone, we're going to gaslight her and say she must have put them somewhere herself. Yes, we are horrible people, that has clearly been established. Keep up.

They wanted her to go back with them, to the house with the pool. She said no, that she wanted to stay here a bit longer. Said it would be better for Nadia, to have stability, to not be taken from one place to another in the first days of her life. She needed peace and quiet. Plus, the air was better here, further away from the city. And there were less riots, less attacks on hospitals. Less attacks on women and children. She didn't say any of that to them, though.

"She's going to have to go back eventually," I say, now.

Dorrie nods.

"Then what?"

"I don't know, love."

I don't know why I keep asking her and expecting a different answer. Dorrie always knows what to do. Not this time. Actually, it would probably be quite worrying if she did have an answer for this specific situation – would mean she'd experienced something similar before.

We're going to have to say something.

I know it. Dorrie knows it. You know it, Mother. You planned it this way, didn't you?

I don't know what will happen to Billy. They'll probably kick him out halfway through the treatment. Not great.

I don't know what will happen to any of us.

I don't know.

"Hello, Auntie Clemmie."

God, I wish she wouldn't call me that.

She waves Nadia's hand at me.

Nadia looks at me with her big, blue eyes. Again. God, I wish she wouldn't look at me like that. Like she knows.

"Nia, I need to speak to you."

I've brought the paperwork from the basement, all your notes, Mother. She won't understand them. I don't understand them. But I know what they mean. And they look official – they'll help me. Help me convince her I'm not lying, that I'm not making this up. Because when you say these things out loud without pages of evidence, you sound like a crazy person.

"Look at her looking at you. She loves you, Clemmie."

This will not be easy. There's a baby-shaped distraction in the way.

"Nia." I sit on the edge of Dorrie's bed. "I have to—"

There's a small, white bottle on the bedside table. Tiny, golden tree. *Soothing nipple cream.* We must have missed it when we were cleaning everything away. My skin goes cold.

"Did you just feed her?"

"Yeah." She sounds half-asleep.

"Did you use this?"

The bottle is open.

The new range is already in circulation.

I can't breathe.

"Oh, yeah. She seemed to like it."

I stare at the tiny human in front of me. Think of the

black, sticky tar swimming through her insides. What have you done to her, Mother?

What have we done?

My fault. My fault. My fault.

The Right Thing to do was The Wrong Thing. I have done The Wrong Thing.

I am a horrible person.

"Nia, I need to speak to you. And I need you to listen."

I will make this right, Mother. I will not let you get away with this.

I will tell everyone.

***

New message: Unknown Number:

Hello, Clementine. How are you? Well, I hope.

I've just received some disturbing news regarding your brother. Apparently, he's finding the programme at The Retreat rather difficult – causing disturbances, disrupting the classes, refusing to take his medication. I want to reassure you that I have my very best people on it.

He would benefit from a visit from his sister. It would be my pleasure to make you welcome at The Retreat. And I can do that. As long as you stop.

You know what the deal was, Clementine. You say nothing, you do nothing, you leave the task of making this world a safer place to us. I don't think it's a big thing to ask of you – especially as, without our help, your life and the lives of those you love could be made, shall we say, unpleasant.

And I would truly hate for little Nadia to have a bad impression of us.

I do hope that nothing bad happens to your brother. You know how much we value the both of you here at Entirely Natural *– how we think of you as family.*

Think about who you're talking to, Clementine. I don't think you want to do this.

Kind Regards,

Helen Higgins.

ENTIRELY FAKE:
NEW ARREST IN ENTIRELY NATURAL SCANDAL

A new arrest has been made in the developing scandal surrounding 'wellness brand' Entirely Natural.

William Finch, 20, an ex-employee of the global enterprise, is the son of disgraced scientist Dr Marilyn Finch, the woman behind the terrible scandal. William Finch was arrested at holistic wellness retreat, The Retreat, last Wednesday night at 9:03pm on charges of fraudulent claims and pre-meditated violence towards the public. Finch attempted to disguise his mother's true, terrifying goals and used his influence at the company to push her dangerous formula through to the production stage. He also falsified test results and bribed officials in order to ensure the poisonous nature of the formula was not discovered.

Finch, thought to be a member of extremist group #stopoverpopulation, had reportedly been a resident at The Retreat for more than a week at the time of his arrest. The company paid for his place at the centre after he was found to have a serious and debilitating drug problem. Instead of instant dismissal, his colleagues agreed to enable a month-long programme at The Retreat to try and help Finch overcome his addiction. A previously close colleague, who would like to remain anonymous, told us: "In the eyes of many, this makes his betrayal all the more terrible. We were trying to help him, and he threw that back in our faces. He tried to harm not only the company and its reputation, but also our wonderful customers. It is truly unacceptable and has really hurt a lot of us who once would have considered him a friend."

Finch has also been linked to the disappearance of Angus Thompson, neighbour and Entirely Natural volunteer. Thompson, 29, vanished from the area around the same time as Finch moved back to the family home. Local woman Sarah Beeson commented: "He was always a shady character – the two families had issues with each other, ever since Gus's sister died. Billy was involved, we all knew it. We could just never prove it. I'm glad he's finally got what's coming to him." Click here to read the full story.

Helen Higgins, Entirely Natural representative in Finch's area, told us: "Everyone is horrified that this has happened. Dr Finch was able to use the current fear surrounding the anti-birth riots as a smokescreen to infiltrate our laboratories and deceive our head scientists. She is a truly contemptible individual with unspeakable ideas, and we are sorry to have ever been associated with her. We would like to thank our loyal customers for sticking by Entirely Natural as we weather this storm."

Entirely Natural would like to reassure customers that all contaminated products have been recalled and destroyed.

All of their products are completely safe and contain nothing but natural ingredients.

Finch's sister, Clementine Finch, was not available for comment.

There's a dead bird on my doorstep.

There often is nowadays.

This one doesn't have a head. That's new.

I kick it onto the new neighbour's lawn. It lands with a soft *splat*. Their problem now. Hopefully they'll think it was a cat. Fluffy little monsters. Or even better they'll decide to move – always an option. A particularly good option if you live in this village and don't want to become part of a cult.

I pick up the paper from the step and there it is, right across the front page. Your letter, Dad.

You didn't know I had it, did you, Helen? Or, at least, you didn't think I would actually send it to the newspapers, that they would really publish it.

Lines jump out at me:

A woman called Helen came to the house.

This Helen woman and the people she works for, they took her genius, and they used it for themselves.

Everyone from the village, ranting and raving like some kind of weird cult.

Her and Helen, drinking champagne in our kitchen.

It was done out of love, Clemmie.

It wasn't, Dad. But this was. Not love for you, or for her, but love for Billy. And also hatred for Helen. Obviously.

I wonder if Tony's seen it by now. He'll probably call when he does. He's as involved in this as we are – he's taken the dead doctor's Tesla. *Well, she's not using it, is she? She would want it to go to a good home, I'm sure.* Callous as ever, Tony. Good to know he hasn't changed.

I can see her, picking her way across the field in the early morning light. I bet the dew plays havoc with her suede heels. Turns out Helen has been staying with Sarah-from-across-the-way. Dorrie is thrilled with this knowledge. Feels vindicated, I think. She comes to stand beside me, hands me a cup of tea. We stand and watch as she gets closer and closer to us.

This is the last arrow in my quiver. And I'm about to throw it straight at her head. Hopefully it will stab her right through the eye. Who knows? Maybe it will even get her in the neck.

"This came this morning, love." Dorrie hands me a postcard, never taking her eyes off the approaching figure. It has a picture of the pyramids on it, a single word on the back:

safe x

I don't know where Nia managed to get a postcard with a picture of Egypt on it from her new home on a remote Greek island, but I like her commitment to the subterfuge. She was far too excited about this whole situation. I worry about that girl. But it does reassure me that her and Billy probably would make a good couple. Both mental.

Her parents exceeded my expectations. They weren't just disappointed when they found out who Nadia's real father was, they disowned their only daughter, their only child. They wouldn't even let her use the pool. I liked them much better when they were dead.

You really shouldn't have given me all that money, Helen. Untraceable payment cards were your first mistake. Makes it difficult to get it back, doesn't it? Now that I've broken your rules. Especially now they're halfway across the world, underneath the mattress of a yoga teacher.

Go on, Helen. Try and hurt them now.

You can't threaten our Nadia when you can't find her.

"Ladies." She nods at each of us in turn, slightly out of breath from her journey across the field. It's the first time I've seen her anything less than composed. I'm enjoying it. A lot.

"Helen." Dorrie nods back. "Please."

We both stand away from the door, invite her in.

She makes a point of looking at the brown painted wall on her way past.

"I don't quite know what you think you will achieve with this little meeting, Clementine."

I sit down across from her. That irritating smile is still in place, but it isn't quite as wide as it once was. I cross my legs, settle back into my chair, warm my hands on my teacup.

"Of course, you know my next stop is the police station. To tell them about the callous murder of poor Angus Thompson, a loyal member of my devoted volunteer programme."

I nod. "Oh, yes, I have no doubt you will be heading straight there."

She narrows those unnaturally blue eyes at me.

"Tea, dear?" Dorrie asks brightly, pours her a cup.

She sighs, takes it, sips, and makes a face.

"You will both be joining William in prison. With

all the other murderers and psychopaths. I'm up for promotion, by the way, for my part in the exposure of the scandal."

"Well done you."

We stare at each other over the coffee table.

"Oh, love, you couldn't grab those biscuits for me, could you? Just on the tray there."

Helen pulls the tray out by its small handles, grimaces, and practically throws the biscuits at Dorrie. "Ugh, that tray is sticky."

"Ah, sorry, yes – I'm always dropping things. Old age, you see. Kept breaking the little handle-y things, had to tape them up, stop the bits of plastic from cutting my hands—"

"Why am I here?" She cuts Dorrie off.

"I thought we could all read the article together. But I guess you've already seen it," I say.

"The part which struck me most was this bit." Dorrie begins to read from the paper: "*Helen doesn't eat or drink anything* Entirely Natural. *I think that tells you everything you need to know.* I can't believe you've never sampled your invention, my dear. You've never even tried a little bit? Just to see what it tastes like. A bite of a biscuit, a sip of a drink, perhaps?"

Helen laughs. It's a disturbing sound, lower than it should be, sounds like it comes deep from within her stomach. An ugly laugh. It doesn't go with the rest of her face.

"Of course not. Obviously, I wouldn't touch the stuff."

"Until today," I say.

"What?"

"Until today." I point at the teacup she holds in her hand.

I think I can pinpoint the moment the penny drops. Did you know that the black tar-like gloop all but dissolves in hot water, Mother? Or hot tea.

She gazes at our cups, filled with the same tea, straight from the teapot. Tiny black flakes float on the surface of the liquid.

"But you, you—"

"It's already too late for me," I say.

"And I'm seventy-eight, dear."

Helen starts to stuff her fingers into her mouth, making herself gag. Pink lipstick spreads from her mouth onto her chin, her nose, her cheeks. She starts spewing dark liquid across Mother's favourite rug.

I sit and watch her, and I smile.

She looks back up at us in horror. "You will pay for this."

"Oh, I'm sure we will." Dorrie is smiling too.

Helen makes a kind of snarling noise and stalks from the house – composure very much not intact.

I grin at Dorrie.

"Did she touch it?" she asks.

"Oh, yes." I smile, pulling the biscuit tray onto my lap. "Yes, she did."

Do you know how easy it is to plant someone's fingerprints, Helen? Really easy. I looked it up online. Not on my phone, obviously, I'm not completely stupid. I used Tony's. All you need is something sticky, like tape. Then you can take a print and transfer it to whatever surface you like. Such as the handles of a pair of shears.

Dorrie has never dropped her biscuit tray. She didn't need to tape up the handles. We just put that tape on there this morning. And now it's covered in Helen's fingerprints.

Sure, they won't be perfect, but the police are always talking about partial prints nowadays.

It took a long time to dig the shears up from under the veg patch. I've still got soil in my hair, black tar under my fingernails. It's going to take even longer for us to carefully unwrap the tape from the tray's handles, to carefully transfer her fingerprints onto the filthy shears, to carefully plant what I'm sure they'll start calling 'the murder weapon' somewhere significant in Sarah-across-the-way's shed, where the police will be sure to find it. Oh, Helen, it's going to be so hard to act surprised when they dig up his body from the garden, where *you* so callously hid him.

His blood is still on the blades, you see. Fortunate that none of us ever actually touched the handles.

It might be easy to discredit a letter, written by the father of a family containing a disgraced scientist, a drug addict and a lonely spinster. Especially when that man deliberately killed himself and his wife in a fit of desperation. Bit harder to argue with forensic evidence, though. Fingerprints. DNA. Oh, I'm sure you'll try, but I'm willing to take my chances.

You underestimated me, Helen. And I think you *over*estimated yourself, your own importance to *Entirely Natural*. They were more than willing to pass the blame on to Billy. What makes you think you're any different? No, I think at the first sign of danger, they'll toss you straight under the bus.

I can't wait.

We watch her stagger up the front path as we sip the last of our tea.

And oh, Mother, it tastes so incredibly sweet.